ARSENIC
AND
OLD PUZZLES

ARSENIC AND OLD PUZZLES

PARNELL HALL

If you purchased this book without a cover you should be aware that this book is stolen property. It was reported as "unsold and destroyed" to the publisher, and neither the author nor the publisher has received any payment for this "stripped book."

Arsenic and Old Puzzles

A Worldwide Mystery/February 2016

First published by Thomas Dunne Books, an imprint of St. Martin's Press.

ISBN-13: 978-0-373-26978-5

Copyright © 2013 by Parnell Hall

All rights reserved. No part of this book may be used or reproduced in any form by any means, electronic or mechanical, including photocopying, recording or by any information storage and retrieval system, without permission in writing from the publisher. For information, contact Harlequin Enterprises Limited, 225 Duncan Mill Road, Don Mills, Ontario, Canada M3B 3K9.

This is a work of fiction. Names, characters, places and incidents are either the product of the author's imagination or are used fictitiously, and any resemblance to actual persons, living or dead, business establishments, events or locales is entirely coincidental.

® and TM are trademarks of the publisher. Trademarks indicated with ® are registered in the United States Patent and Trademark Office, the Canadian Intellectual Property Office and in other countries.

TORONTO • NEW YORK • LONDON
AMSTERDAM • PARIS • SYDNEY • HAMBURG
STOCKHOLM • ATHENS • TOKYO • MILAN
MADRID • WARSAW • BUDAPEST • AUCKLAND

For Cary Grant,
a wonderful Mortimer

Recycling programs
for this product may
not exist in your area.

Arsenic and Old Puzzles

A Worldwide Mystery/February 2016

First published by Thomas Dunne Books for Minotaur Books, an imprint of St. Martin's Publishing Group.

ISBN-13: 978-0-373-26978-5

Copyright © 2013 by Parnell Hall

Printed in U.S.A.

Acknowledgments

I would like to thank Joseph Kesselring, who wrote the stage play, Julius J. and Philip G. Epstein, who wrote the screenplay, Frank Capra, who directed the movie, and Cary Grant and the rest of the marvelous cast of *Arsenic and Old Lace*, for inspiring me to write this book. If you have never seen this merry band of poisoners, rent the DVD at once.

I would also like to thank my accomplices, *New York Times* crossword editor Will Shortz, for creating the sudoku, noted constructor Fred Piscop, for creating the crossword puzzles, and American Crossword Puzzle Tournament champion Ellen Ripstein, for editing them.

ONE

"So when's she going to walk?" Cora said.

Sherry Carter shot an amused glance at Aaron Grant. Jennifer Carter Grant was crawling back and forth from Mommy to Daddy on a beach blanket on the front lawn. Cora Felton was sitting on a lawn chair. Not sitting on the ground was one of the privileges accorded a great-aunt, and Cora was taking full advantage.

"She's nine months old," Sherry said.

"What's your point?"

"Babies walk around a year," Aaron said.

"A whole year? That must tire them out." Cora cocked her head. "I don't see why she couldn't start walking. I mean, look at the size of her. You'd never know she was premature."

"That's not the type of thing she needs to grow up hearing all the time," Sherry said.

"You're going to withhold it from her?" Cora said. "My God, the kid will grow up with a complex. She'll have a therapist before she's five."

"Did you ever have a therapist?" Sherry said.

"That's a rather personal question. Particularly in front of a young man. Just because he married into the family doesn't mean he gets to share our household secrets."

"Secrets?" Aaron said. "You mean you did have a therapist?"

"You tell me," Cora said. "Do you think I had a therapist?"

Aaron's mouth fell open. That was a loaded question. Any answer would be wrong.

"Stop teasing Aaron," Sherry said. "Let the poor guy have some Daddy time."

"Oh, you want the wicked stepaunt to go away?"

"You're not a stepaunt. You're a great-aunt."

"The best," Cora said. "Seriously, what are you going to tell the kid when she asks what that scar on your stomach is?"

"You can't even see it," Aaron said. "The doctor was right. It's a bikini cut, and you can't even tell."

Sherry wasn't wearing a bikini, she was wearing shorts and a halter top, but the result was the same. The horizontal scar was below the panty line.

Sherry smiled. "Are you torturing me because you're bored? Can't stand it when things are quiet?"

Aaron grinned. "I think that's it. She's an action junkie. Hasn't had a murder in months, and she's climbing the walls."

"I am not," Cora said. "If I never see another murder case, it will be too damn soon."

Jennifer reached the edge of the blanket and let out an excited whoop. Daddy headed her off.

"Killjoy," Cora said.

"There's germs in the grass."

Cora mentioned another place germs might hang out.

"Cora!" Sherry said. "You are *not* going to talk that way around the baby."

"What, she's going to be offended? She doesn't look offended. Hey, Jennifer. Are you offended with Auntie?"

Jennifer didn't answer.

"When's she going to talk, anyway?"

"She's nine months old," Sherry repeated.

"Well, not full sentences, but a good 'Cora,' would be nice."

Aaron picked Jennifer up, put her back in the middle of the blanket. "I think she's wet."

Sherry dug in the diaper bag. "Care to change the baby, Auntie Cora?"

"Certainly not. I'm the aunt, not the nanny. My job is to look proud and brag at PTA meetings."

"Oh, my God," Sherry said. "It's not enough you want her walking. You've already got her in school."

"Well, you have to plan ahead," Cora said. "If you're not careful, next thing you know she's bringing home some irresponsible bum."

Sherry shook her head. "I'm changing her diaper and you've got her dating already."

"And as for you, Mommy, I thought having a kid wasn't going to change anything?"

"It hasn't."

"Oh, no? I've had to send in the last five Puzzle Lady columns myself. And I'm no good at it. I keep screwing up. An editor called and asked what's wrong. I told her I had to send the stuff myself because my secretary had a baby."

"You're lucky I don't make you write them," Sherry said.

Cora grimaced. While she was the famous Puzzle Lady, whose smiling face graced the nationally syndicated crossword column, in point of fact Cora couldn't solve a crossword puzzle if you gave her the answers. Sherry Carter actually constructed the puzzles. Cora Felton merely lent her name to the project.

Aaron's cell phone rang. He flipped it open. "Hello?... Yes, she's right here."

Sherry reached for the phone.

Aaron shook his head. "No, her." He held it out to Cora.

Cora took the phone. "Hello?"

"Cora? Chief Harper."

"Oh, hi, Chief. What's up?"

"I'm out at the Guilford sisters' bed-and-breakfast. Do you know it?"

"Can't say that I do."

"Fifty-one Elmwood Circle. About a half mile north of town."

"What about it?"

"Wanna take a ride out there?"

"How come?"

"Someone died."

TWO

ELMWOOD CIRCLE WAS actually a square block, or perhaps just one side of the block. Cora wasn't about to drive around to find out. Not with "fifty-one" so clearly marked on the mailbox. And Chief Harper out in front, leaning on his car.

"Okay, Chief, what have you got?"

"Dead tourist. Checked in for the weekend, keeled over during afternoon tea. The Guilford sisters aren't much for breakfast, but they do set an excellent tea."

"This is a natural death?"

"Oh, absolutely. According to Edith he was seventy-six. When a person gets to be that age——" Chief Harper broke off. "Not that seventy-six is that old——" He broke off again. Flushed furiously. "Not to imply…"

"Thanks for clearing that up, Chief," Cora said dryly. "I was afraid you thought I was seventy-six." When Harper floundered helplessly, she changed the subject to let him off the hook. "So, what do you want with me?"

"There's a puzzle on the body."

"Of course there is," Cora said. "There's always a puzzle on the body. I'd be shocked if there wasn't. What kind of puzzle is it?"

"A number puzzle."

"Sudoku or KenKen?"

"Which is which?"

"Come on, Chief. You've had both kinds. You must

not be taking this seriously if you haven't even bothered to sort it out."

"I called you, didn't I?"

"Of course you did. So no one could ask you why you didn't."

Chief Harper took a folded piece of paper out of his pocket, handed it to her.

"Thanks a lot," Cora said.

			8			3		
	3	5		6			4	
		9	5					2
7	5				9		6	1
						4		
							8	
4	1		6				7	
	9	3	7				2	
				4	6			

Two elderly women came bustling in from the kitchen. They wore lacy blouses and wool skirts, looked more suited for the English countryside than a New England town. Cora had seen them around town, but wasn't acquainted. She couldn't even tell which was which.

"Oh," the plumper of the two said. "It's the Puzzle Lady. The chief said he was calling you, but I didn't think you'd come. I mean, it's not like there was a crime."

"Goodness, no," the thinner sister said. "What a shock. One minute he's sitting at our table, the next minute he's lying at our feet."

"He spilled on our carpet," the plumper sister said indignantly. "I'm sorry he's dead, but really."

"And he's still there," the thinner sister said.

"I'm sorry," Harper said. "Dr. Nathan is hung up in surgery, and the EMS unit is on the other side of town."

"There's only one?" Cora said, incredulously.

"It's Sunday," Chief Harper said, defensively.

"So the gentleman is still here?"

"In the middle of our parlor floor!"

"Could I see?"

The dead tourist was slumped over, half on, half off the table. The wineglass lay on its side in front of him. He had apparently knocked it over when he fell.

So. The sisters' famous afternoon tea featured wine. Cora wondered if that was why it was so popular.

"Is this how you found him, Chief?"

"That's right."

"No one moved him?"

"The sisters actually tried to sit him up, but he kept slumping over. That's when they called for help."

"But the doctor was busy and the ambulance was tied up?"

The chief gave her a look. "You going to keep harping on that? I know you got a newspaper reporter in the family, but it's not the type of thing I'd like to read in the press."

"Well, I'm not going to advertise the fact, but if asked, I'm not going to lie."

"That's not exactly a ringing endorsement," Harper said.

"You don't suspect foul play?"

"Not in the least."

"And yet you called me in."

"Because of the puzzle."

"And while you were waiting for the doctor, you figured what the hell. Why not drag a seventy-six-year-old woman away from an afternoon with her great-niece?"

"I think you've paid me back for that remark. Could we move on to this corpse?"

"Love to. Would you like me to examine the body?"

"Probably better wait for the doc."

Cora nodded. "Sure, sure. Important case like this. Come on, Chief. There's no reason to suspect this guy died from anything other than natural causes."

"He had a puzzle in his pocket."

"They're not usually lethal. At least the ones in my books. Even the hard ones are called diabolical, not deadly. So what was he doing in town?"

"I don't know."

"How come?"

"According to the sisters, he keeled over before they could find out."

"That must have been disappointing."

"You're not taking this seriously, Cora."

"Of course I'm not taking it seriously. Here's a man we don't know, who happens to be dead. There's not a lot I can do."

The plumper sister stuck her head in the room.

"Yes, Charlotte?" Harper said.

Cora smiled, happy to have the sisters sorted out. The plump one was Charlotte. The thin one was Edith. As her weight was probably closer to the plump one's than the thin one's, Cora was happy to drop that designation.

"Oh," Charlotte said, "he's still here."

"Of course he's still here. We're waiting for the doctor."

"It was such a shock. One minute we're drinking wine, the next minute he's dead." Charlotte didn't act like it was a shock. She cocked her head, birdlike, and peered up at the chief. "Have you figured it out yet?"

"Figured what out?"

"Well, it's a murder, isn't it? You wouldn't be here if it wasn't."

"It's not a murder," Harper said.

"Then why did you call her in?"

"She's the Puzzle Lady. He had a puzzle in his pocket."

Charlotte smiled. "He probably liked to do them. Widowers often have a hobby."

"Widowers?"

"Yes, he was a widower," the thinner sister said, pushing her way into the room. "We managed to find that out. He was much more willing to talk about what he'd done than what he was doing. Some men are like that."

There was something very spinsterish about the way she said *men*. Cora chided herself for the thought, but she couldn't help thinking it. Having been married five or six times herself, give or take an annulment or two, Cora was sometimes less than tolerant.

"Did you learn anything else about him?" Cora said.

"No," Edith said. "And it was rather annoying. He had an irritating habit of smiling, nodding, and not answering the question."

"I was married to a man like that," Cora said. "He was delightfully vague. It was one of the reasons I divorced him."

"You divorced him for being vague?"

"He's lucky I didn't shoot him. There was also a pole dancer involved."

The front doorbell sent the sisters into a titter, deciding which of them should go answer it. By the third ring,

Cora was ready to jump in and decide for them. Still arguing, they fluttered their way out the door.

"Well, that solves your mystery," Cora said. "This poor man probably dropped dead in self-defense."

Barney Nathan strode in. The good doctor had clearly foregone amenities, as the sisters were spinning in his wake trying to keep up.

Dr. Nathan saw Cora and grimaced. "Oh. Don't tell me."

"It's nice to see you, too," Cora said. "The guy had a sudoku in his pocket, so the chief called me."

"Why?"

Cora smiled. "The same reason you're here to pronounce him dead. So we can say we did. It's not like it's necessary or anything. I could pronounce him dead. And you could probably do the damn sudoku."

"In your dreams." Barney Nathan plopped his medical bag down on a chair, strode around the table, bent down to examine the corpse. After a moment or two he stood up. "All right, he's dead." He picked up his medical bag.

"That's all you're going to do?" Cora said.

"What do you want me to do, bring him back to life?"

Cora knelt down by the body. She looked up at the doctor. "Aren't you interested in what killed him?"

"Not really. He died of natural causes."

"Are you sure about that?"

"I suppose you'd like an autopsy," Barney said sarcastically.

Cora turned to the Guilford sisters. "Ladies. If you would be so good as to boil some water."

Edith's eyes widened. "The doctor needs boiling water to examine the body?"

"No, but I think he'd like some tea."

"Certainly," Edith said. "Charlotte, would you boil some water?"

"I don't need any tea," Barney protested.

"Yes, you do," Cora said. "If the two of you could just whip up something."

Jabbering at each other, the sisters retreated to the kitchen.

"What's the big idea?" Barney said irritably.

"I didn't want to contradict you in front of them."

"Contradict me?" Barney said, incredulously. "You're going to contradict me?"

Cora smiled. "It's not your fault, Doc. You're not a mystery buff. Or you might have noticed."

"Noticed what?"

"The smell of bitter almonds."

Barney Nathan's mouth fell open. "Do you mean...?"

Cora shrugged. "Well, my guess would be cyanide."

THREE

THE FIRST THING Cora noticed was that the sisters were ill at ease. That bothered her. Cora didn't want the sisters to be guilty. Not that she knew them, or anything, but if they were guilty, the case would be over.

"Just a few questions," Chief Harper said.

"Oh dear," Charlotte said. "I have such a problem with questions."

"Why is that?"

"They need answers. I'm not good with answers. I get all flustered."

"She does," Edith said. "You really can't get anywhere asking Charlotte questions. You're better off hinting at the point. For instance, if you wanted to know what movie she saw last week, you wouldn't ask her. You'd just start talking about movies, and she'd chime in with, 'Oh, I just saw such-and-such.'"

"Really?" Chief Harper said with a forced grin. Cora could practically see the poor man trying to frame the right sequence of statements that would prompt Charlotte to volunteer the information that would crack the case.

Not that she was about to. Talking about her getting nervous about answering was only making her nervous about answering. Cora wondered if Edith had done it deliberately. Particularly since she seemed to be having troubles of her own.

"You're the one who checked him in?" Chief Harper asked her.

"Yes. Because Charlotte had gone to the store. Otherwise, Charlotte would have done it. Charlotte does the check-ins, and I do the checkouts. She wasn't here. That's the only reason I checked him in."

"I understand."

"You sound as if you suspect foul play," Charlotte said.

"Of course he suspects foul play. Otherwise he'd be gone."

"I assure you this is just routine, Miss Guilford."

"Which Miss Guilford?" Charlotte said. "Are you talking to her or to me?"

"I'm talking to both of you." Harper took a breath. "There's a chance there's something irregular about the gentleman's death. But, believe me, no one suspects you."

"Who do you suspect?" Edith said.

"I don't suspect anyone."

"Then not suspecting us isn't reassuring. We were with the man when he died. We served him the tea." Her eyes widened. "Was something wrong with the tea?"

"The tea is excellent," Harper said. Even as he issued that assurance, he looked suspiciously at his teacup.

Cora stifled a grin. Now the Guilford sisters had the chief imagining assassins.

"When did he check in?"

"Yesterday afternoon."

"How did he get here?"

"He took a bus."

"There's no bus to Bakerhaven."

"He said he took a bus to Danbury and came in a cab."

"Which would be very expensive," Charlotte said.

"You doubt his story?" Cora said.

Charlotte's mouth fell open. "What do you mean, doubt his story? You mean, do I think he was lying?"

Cora shrugged. "I don't know. Is that what you meant?"

"No one's doubting anyone's story," Chief Harper said. "The man could have taken a cab from Danbury. It would be expensive, but maybe he had money. We don't know because we don't know who he is."

"I suppose that's my fault," Edith said. "But he paid cash. When I asked his name, he smiled and said, 'Tom.' Then he counted out the money. And he gave it to me and he smiled and he kept talking and I forgot to ask him what his last name was."

"It's not like you asked him and he refused to answer?"

"Well, I asked him, and he said, 'Tom.'"

"Just the one time?"

"You think I should have asked him twice?"

"No, I'm just asking what you did."

"Well, that's what happened. And he said he was exhausted and he went up to bed."

"You showed him the room?"

"Of course I showed him the room. You can't just let the guests pick a room."

"And he just had the one suitcase?"

"That's right."

"No briefcase? No other bag?"

"No. Just the one."

"Did we do something wrong?" Charlotte put in.

"No. But you're witnesses, in case there is anything irregular about his death."

"What did the doctor say?"

"I'm not prepared to discuss what the doctor said. He has to make his examination. I have to make mine."

"Of course. Ask us anything you like. Charlotte, pay attention now. We have to help the policeman. What would you like to know, Chief?"

Cora's eyes twinkled. She wondered if the poor man, put on the spot, could think of a single question.

Turned out he could.

"Do you ladies keep weed killer in the house?"

"Weed killer?" Charlotte said. "Certainly not. We do organic gardening with no pesticides. Would you like to see the garden?"

"Not right now."

"On your way out, then," Edith said. "Do you like tomatoes? They're just ripe. We could give you a few."

"And you, too," Charlotte added to Cora Felton. "For your cooking."

Cora, who couldn't recall the last thing she'd cooked that didn't come in a microwavable pouch, smiled and nodded.

"So you say you have no poisons in the house," Harper said.

"I didn't say that. Charlotte, did you say that? I didn't hear you say that. I know we got distracted by tomatoes, but I'm sure Charlotte wouldn't say that."

"You mean you do have poison in the house?"

"We do not have weed killer," Edith said. "I would like to make that perfectly clear. We don't believe in it."

"But you do have poison?"

"Well…" Edith lowered her voice confidentially, smiled, and nodded. "We have a problem with woodchucks."

FOUR

BECKY BALDWIN WAS the prettiest lawyer in Bakerhaven. Granted, she was the only lawyer in Bakerhaven; still, she was probably the prettiest lawyer in all of Connecticut. A willowy blonde in her twenties with the face of an angel, Becky was not the first lawyer one would choose if one were in a scrape.

One would be wrong. Becky was an exceptional lawyer, who deserved a wider practice. In Cora's opinion, her looks held her back. Cora figured that Becky would have a sensational law practice, if she were only ugly. As it was, her one-room law office was down a side street over the pizza parlor.

Becky was sitting at her desk when Cora came in.

"What you up to?" Cora said.

"Bookkeeping. I can't afford a bookkeeper, so I do it myself. Did you know if your income doesn't exceed your expenses, it's hard to make a profit?"

"I know it's definitely time to remarry." Cora slumped into a chair, pulled out a cigarette.

"Can't smoke in here," Becky said.

"I'm bringing you business. You know, that income-producing stuff."

Cora lit the cigarette, took a drag.

"If you don't have a job for me, I'm going to put that cigarette where the sun don't shine."

"Oh, tough talk. This happens to be a genuine job.

You'd do well to take it seriously. Even as we speak, your clients are being deprived of their constitutional rights."

"My clients?"

"The Guilford sisters. Edith and Charlotte Guilford."

"What did they do?"

"Absolutely nothing. As a lawyer, you should know that. But Chief Harper suspects them of poisoning one of the boarders of their bed-and-breakfast."

"You're kidding."

"I was just there. The sisters were serving afternoon tea. The guy keeled over from what Harper suspects was a whacking dose of poison."

"What makes Chief Harper suspect that?"

"Actually, it's the doctor that suspects it."

"Barney Nathan suspects something?"

"Well, I gave him a hint. He's doing the autopsy now."

"Who's the corpse?"

"Tom."

"Tom?"

"He didn't have any identification on him. He checked in as Tom."

"How do you check in as Tom?"

"He paid cash."

"He didn't have a wallet on him?"

"Not when he was killed."

"He checked in last night?"

"That's right."

"What did he do today?"

"Don't know. Chief Harper skipped right to the tea. When the sisters admitted having poison, I thought you'd like to join the party."

Becky frowned. "Did you see this Tom?"

"Yeah."

"What was he like?"

"Elderly gentleman, conservatively dressed. Well, seventy-six, which Chief Harper thinks is elderly, and hopes won't offend me."

"What?"

"Am I really that old, Becky, that people have to worry about hurting my feelings?"

"You're young, you're vibrant, you have a gun in your purse," Becky said irritably. "Could we stick with the potential homicide? What else do you know about him?"

"He was a widower."

Becky raised her eyebrows.

Cora flushed angrily. "I was *not* considering him matrimonial material. I never saw him alive. That was the one detail the sisters managed to get out of him."

"What were you doing there?"

"Harper called me."

"How come?"

"Tom had a sudoku in his pocket."

"Uh-oh. Did you solve it?"

"No. I snuck out to get you." Cora shook her head. "I'm beginning to regret it."

FIVE

THE YOUNG MAN who met them at the door smiled at
Becky, which won him no points with Cora.

"I'm sorry, but it's not a good time just now. My aunts
are a little busy."

Cora, for whom being ignored by a good-looking
young man was just one more kick in the age bracket,
said, "Yeah, well, a dead man will do that. And who are
you?"

Well-bred to a fault, the young man immediately
began to apologize for *her* rudeness. "I'm sorry. I'm Alan
Guilford." He ducked his head boyishly, and his brown
curly hair fell in his face. "I'm afraid there's been an unfortunate incident."

"Yeah," Cora said. "We saw the police chief's car outside. Becky's a big girl, didn't figure he was here collecting for the policemen's ball. She's a lawyer, by the way,
in case you couldn't tell. Some people can't."

Alan blinked. "I don't understand."

Becky smiled. "You must not be from around here.
I'm Becky Baldwin. This is Cora Felton."

His eyes widened. "The Puzzle Lady. I'm sorry. I
should have recognized you."

For Becky it was an education. Cora went from snide
to flirty in the blink of an eye.

"Well, that's so nice of you, young man. Alan, did you
say? And the sisters are your aunts?"

"That's right."

"Ah," Cora said. She actually took him by the hand. "Then this may come as a bit of a shock. It seems the gentleman who died may have ingested poison."

Alan looked astonished.

"Yes, I know," Cora said. "Absolutely ridiculous, but that's why the police are here, and that's why I thought they might need an attorney."

"My aunts? That's ridiculous. They wouldn't harm a fly."

"You know it and I know it. But just let the media get hold of it and look what happens. Poison is a woman's weapon. You mention poison and little old ladies come to mind. Which is why it's foolish to take chances. If your aunts can afford it, they'd be wise to retain counsel."

"They can afford it, all right, but is it really necessary? They're such sweet old dears, I would hate to upset them."

"No one wants to upset them, but I would strongly advise you to let Becky listen in on the questions. In case something should arise, she'd be there to handle it."

"Well, if you think the policeman wouldn't object."

"Object? Nonsense. He'd love it."

Alan ushered them into the living room. Chief Harper didn't look delighted to see them, but he didn't look unhappy, either. Apparently the questioning was not going well.

"Ah," he said. "You've brought in reinforcements."

"I'm sure you know Becky Baldwin," Cora said, "Bakerhaven's attorney-at-law. She's often brought in in the case of an untimely death to help the police sort out the facts of the case."

"There's a way to express it," Harper said dryly.

"Why?" Edith said. "Do you need an attorney, Chief Harper?"

"No, I do not need an attorney. Cora thought you

might. Apparently, she didn't know how adept you are at answering questions."

"Whatever do you mean?" Charlotte said.

"Come in and sit down," Edith said. "Would you like some tea? Alan, you never got your tea. Why don't you pour some for these ladies. We have the most lovely tea biscuits, but the chief won't let us have them."

"Unfortunately, they're in there," Harper said.

Officer Dan Finley came in from the parlor carrying a camera. "Got 'em, Chief. And I put the ribbon up. Anything else you need?"

"Not at the moment, Dan. And did you notice Cora Felton and Becky Baldwin are here?"

Though probably the same age as Alan Guilford, Dan had a boyish quality that made the other man seem positively mature. "Hi, guys. What's up?"

"Has it come to that?" Cora said. "You're processing a crime scene and you ask what's up?"

"Sorry," Dan said. "Didn't mean to be insensitive, but apparently the ladies didn't know the gentleman in question. Isn't that right, ladies?"

"This interrogation is awfully informal," Becky said.

"It's not an interrogation," Harper said. "I'm just asking some routine questions, trying to get the situation straightened out. No doubt this will all turn out to be a misunderstanding."

"Amazing how many suspects have been marched off to jail after just such a pronouncement," Cora said. "What did you learn while I was gone to make you sure this was nothing?"

Alan had come back from the kitchen with three steaming teas. He served Cora first, which would have pleased her if the phrase *age before beauty* hadn't gone through her head.

He took his time serving Becky Baldwin, and seemed to smile more than Cora felt was necessary for a simple cup of tea.

Chief Harper waited until the teacups had been distributed before answering Cora's question. "I've learned nothing. Which is remarkable, considering the amount of time it's taken me to learn nothing. The Guilford sisters live alone in the house, they have four guest rooms, which are unoccupied at the moment, with the exception of the gentleman's overnight bag."

"And what are we to do with that?" Charlotte said. "We can't keep it. Occasionally we hang on to someone's bags until they pick them up, but he's not going to do that."

"No, he's not. At any rate, the house is empty. And was last night when the gentleman checked in."

"Only because I'd gone to the store," Charlotte said.

"I understand. Otherwise, you'd have checked him in."

"Yes, and I would have gotten his name."

Edith's mouth fell open. "Well, I never!"

"Not that I'm blaming you. You're not used to checking people in. That's my job."

"The point is," Chief Harper persisted, "you two live here alone."

"Well, we don't need anyone else," Edith said. "It's not like we have a cook or a maid. We share the responsibility."

"I'm sure you do. And who made breakfast this morning?"

"We both did."

"Uh-huh," Harper said, without enthusiasm. "And who made what?"

"She made the eggs. I made the coffee," Edith volunteered.

"And the bacon. Don't forget the bacon," Charlotte said.

"The bacon's not a problem. It's the toast."

"What's the toast?" Chief Harper said.

"Charlotte puts butter on the toast."

"Doesn't everyone put butter on the toast?" Cora said.

"Not these days," Edith said. "Not with cholesterol. If it turns out that poor man died of a heart attack because of high cholesterol…"

"Oh, for goodness' sake," Charlotte said. "He did not die from buttered toast."

"Well, you slather it on. If you let him butter his own toast, he wouldn't use so much."

"It wouldn't melt. You have to butter it when it's hot or the butter doesn't melt. No one wants to eat butter that's standing in lumps."

"And what time was breakfast?"

"Nine o'clock," Edith said. "I said eight o'clock, but he said nine. Since he was the one eating it, we made it nine."

"What did he do after breakfast?"

"He went out," Charlotte said. "We didn't see him until tea. Could he have eaten something somewhere else?"

"It's possible," Chief Harper said. He turned to Alan. "And when did you get here?"

"Just now. I drove up from New York."

"You came up from New York this afternoon?"

"That's right."

"Was this the first time you've been here?"

"I've been here many times."

"I mean today. The first time you arrived today."

"Sure. My suitcase is in the car."

"So you never saw the dead man? He was gone before you got here?"

"The ambulance was just pulling out. I assume that was him."

"Well, that's disappointing," Harper said. "That makes you rather worthless as a witness."

"Oh, I'm sure he has other attributes," Cora said.

To Chief Harper's amazement, she actually batted her eyes.

Disconcerted, Chief Harper plowed ahead. "And what are you doing here? Just visiting your aunts?"

"No. Not that I'm not happy to see them, but I actually came to see Arlene."

"Arlene?" Cora said sharply. "Who's Arlene?"

The door flew open and a beautiful young brunette burst in and threw herself into Alan's arms.

SIX

AMAZING HOW ONE's estimations plummet. With the introduction of a girlfriend, Alan Guilford went from being an attractive young man to an undesirable intruder and most likely a murder suspect.

The lady in question had several strikes against her. For one thing she was with Alan. For another thing she was young. And not just young, but remarkably young, absurdly young, perhaps even younger than Becky Baldwin. She had dark brown hair, cut short, and falling in excruciatingly casual curls around a baby face with a button nose and flashing blue eyes. Her smile lit up the room, though she directed it mainly toward Alan. She favored the others with the sort of regard a queen might lavish on her subjects. Cora assessed her charitably as a promiscuous gold digger, uncharitably as a crack whore.

Chief Harper was making his own estimation. "You are this young man's girlfriend?"

"Is that what he's telling you? That's rather disappointing, dear. I thought I was your fiancée?"

"Fiancée?" Cora said. "You're engaged to be married?"

"Absolutely."

"When's the date?"

"We haven't set the date yet."

"Ah. So perhaps the word *fiancée* is a bit premature. Perhaps Alan was right to say girlfriend."

"Oh, for goodness' sake," Arlene said. "I know words

are your specialty, but give me a break. It doesn't matter what you call the relationship. Frankly, it's wonderful. I've been in love with Alan ever since I met him."

"When was that?"

"I don't see how this is relevant to the investigation," Chief Harper said.

"Shhh!" Cora, Becky, Edith, and Charlotte said.

Chief Harper blinked.

Arlene smiled, and went on as if there had been no interruption. "I met him this summer when he was up visiting his aunts. I live next door. Big old place, drafty but nice. Moved in last spring. Hadn't been back since I was a child. Next thing I know, there he was."

"No, the next thing I know, there she was. Love at first sight."

"Well, that's perfectly delightful," Harper said. "If I have any more questions, I'll know where to find you. And you, young lady. Could I have your address and phone number?"

Arlene fumbled in her purse. "Let me see. Here's a pencil. I know I have something to write on here somewhere. Oh. That reminds me." She pulled out a folded sheet of paper. "I found this on the way in."

"Found what?"

"Sticking out from under the doormat."

"That's silly," Charlotte said. "No one leaves notes under the doormat."

"It's not a note."

"Well, what is it?"

"I suppose it's meant for you."

Arlene handed it to Cora.

Cora unfolded the paper.

It was a crossword puzzle.

ACROSS

1 Curtain fabric
6 Our last mustachioed president
10 Like bachelor parties
14 Place to play
15 Aloha State port
16 Twist the arm of
17 Yo-yo trick
19 Diamond of music
20 Sloppy digs
21 Basic principle
22 Serene spots
23 Chicago exchange, for short
24 Tiny bits

26 "I did it!"
29 Perform a daring act
33 Magnum ____
34 An Ivy Leaguer
35 "Roots," for one
36 Tick off
37 Think tank nuggets
39 Pizazz
40 Whoppers
42 Quirky habit
43 Artist Magritte
44 Do a farm chore
48 Town sign abbr.
49 "Want ____ with that?"

50 Ship captain's hazard
52 Contribute
54 ____-garde
56 Blond shade
59 Oodles
60 Dispatch a household pest
62 Trim down
63 Regretful hero of 1776
64 Did galley work
65 Sets, as a price
66 Took a gander at
67 Little Eva's creator

DOWN

1 Musical tools
2 Suffix with pluto
3 Count (on)
4 Tattooist's supply
5 Photo finish
6 From that point
7 Staffer
8 Naval formation
9 ____ up (dress finely)
10 Fountain treats
11 Forest scenes, e.g.
12 Opposed to, in dialect
13 Salon supplies

18 Mint or sage
22 Ordinal ending
23 Kettle and Barker
25 Porter's regretful Miss
26 Breaks one's back
27 Month with a prank holiday
28 Prince Andrew, since 1986
30 Bloodletter's need, once
31 One taking a cut
32 Repaired quickly, perhaps
37 Spillane's "____ Jury"
38 Becomes extinct
41 Mischief makers
43 Sports "zebra"
45 Oscar statuette, mostly
46 Mounted the soapbox
47 Polite chap
51 Cultural values
52 Hemingway nickname
53 Word for Yorick
55 Low-lying area
56 Early Jesse Jackson 'do
57 Bumped off
58 Fictional alter ego
60 Nautical pronoun
61 "Mangia!"

SEVEN

"IF THIS IS someone's idea of a joke, I don't find it very funny." Cora bristled with indignation, glared at Arlene.

"Hey, hey," Alan said. He moved himself between the two women.

"It's no joke," Arlene said indignantly. "I found it on the doorstep. I don't know why you're making such a big deal about it."

"That's because no one's going to ask you what it means," Cora said.

"Of course not. I don't do crossword puzzles. Not that I couldn't. I just never have. But I suppose I could. I'm a moderately intelligent woman."

"Stop it," Alan said. He had a huge smile on his face. "You're always running yourself down. The point is, if it's a puzzle, it must be for her."

"There's no must about it," Cora said. "Why, just because it's my job? Becky's a lawyer. If it were a subpoena, would you say it must be for her?"

"It's a little different," Harper said, "since there's already a sudoku."

"There's a sudoku?" Charlotte said.

That set off a whole flurry of conversation. Eventually Chief Harper got it quieted down and explained the situation.

"There you are," Arlene said. "There's a sudoku and a crossword puzzle. Clearly you're supposed to solve them and tell us what they mean."

Cora might have been able to tell what the crossword puzzle meant, but she couldn't begin to solve it. She stuck her chin in the air and said, "Phooey. I'm certainly not solving any crossword puzzles. I'm sitting here having my tea." She turned to Chief Harper. "If you want help with the puzzle, you bring in Harvey Beerbaum."

"Why in the world would you want me to do that?"

Cora took a breath, stalling. Inspiration seized her. She pointed at Arlene. "For just the reason she said. I'm the Puzzle Lady, so it must be for me. And that's how people figure. It's time to change their way of thinking. If you leave a crossword puzzle, it gets taken to me? No. If you leave a crossword puzzle, it gets taken to Harvey Beerbaum. If you make that clear, maybe people will stop sending me cryptic messages in crosswords."

Cora handed the puzzle to the chief. "Take it to Harvey. I don't want to see it. As a matter of fact, I think I'm through with this case. Ladies, thank you for the tea. Alan, it was so nice to meet you. Arlene." Cora nodded without enthusiasm. "Becky, I'm sure you want to stick around and make sure everything's kosher. Can you catch a ride?"

"You're really going?"

"As fast as my legs can carry me."

With that she was out the door.

EIGHT

HARVEY BEERBAUM—PLUMP, precise, and fastidious—lived in the closest thing Bakerhaven had to a gingerbread house. A glorified A-frame, neatly decorated with crossword-puzzle memorabilia, from trophies to puzzles to photos to name tags from the national tournament. As bad as Cora was at solving crossword puzzles, Harvey was good. Chief Harper had employed him in the past when Cora had begged off.

Harvey paused in the middle of solving the puzzle to ask, "Are you sure you wouldn't like some tea?"

Chief Harper took a breath. Everyone was giving him tea today. "The puzzle, Harvey, if you don't mind."

"Certainly."

Harvey's pencil flew over the puzzle. A minute and a half later he handed it back to the chief.

"You're done?"

"I haven't checked my work. In a tournament, I'd have gone over it, as long as it made no difference in the time. You get the same score for five minutes thirteen seconds left as you do for five minutes and four. At four fifty-nine, you lose points. See?"

Chief Harper didn't see at all, but he didn't care. "The puzzle, Harvey."

"Ah, you want the theme answer," he said, referring to the long answer imbedded in the puzzle. "I'm not sure it's going to help you much. Do you think it has something to do with the murder?"

"It's very unlikely."

"And yet you bring it to me."

"Cora suggested I bring it to you."

"Yes, she would."

"What do you mean by that?"

Harvey kicked himself for almost blowing it. He knew Cora couldn't solve crossword puzzles, he just didn't know she couldn't construct them, either. "Cora always sics you on me when she thinks it doesn't mean anything."

"That's not true. You've solved puzzles for me that were very important."

"You didn't tell me what they meant."

That wasn't exactly true. Chief Harper hadn't *known* what they meant. Cora had figured out what they meant after Harvey had failed to do so.

"The problem with puzzles is they don't always mean anything," Harper said.

"Who's this fellow who died?"

"No one seems to know."

"That's very sad."

"Yes, it is," Harper said.

It was also very strange. Usually someone knew something about someone. This man came to town without so much as making a ripple, and died without leaving a trace. He hadn't had a car. It wasn't like he could have gotten into town. What had he been doing?

Harper could interview the neighbors. Unfortunately the nearest neighbor was Arlene, whom he'd already interviewed. It occurred to the chief he'd better talk to Cora.

NINE

CORA WAS RELAXING in the living room. Ever since Jennifer was born, Sherry, Aaron, and the baby were living upstairs in the new addition. There was a bedroom for Cora, she just hadn't moved into it. Originally, she had been graciously given the master suite, but when the baby was premature, Cora had moved Sherry and Aaron into it so they could have the baby with them. Now that Jennifer was old enough to be in her own room, Cora saw no reason to displace them. Cora was perfectly happy in the old house, which was peaceful and quiet most of the day, except when Sherry, who preferred the old kitchen, was cooking, or when they were all eating together in front of the TV. Otherwise the house was quiet, especially since she had persuaded Sherry to turn the extra bedroom in the new addition into an office and do all her crossword puzzle work upstairs. Except for a crying baby, there was nothing Cora was happier to be rid of. She just had to get her own computer so she could go online after Sherry moved hers upstairs. Cora never worked on the computer, but she had become addicted to spending time on eBay, and YouTube, and chat rooms, and sites with soap-opera plot summaries and the like. One thing about Cora's new computer, of which she was rather proud, was that it served no practical purpose whatsoever.

Cora was lounging on the couch with her feet up on the coffee table and a cigarette dangling from her lip, which she could get away with once dinner was over and the kids had retreated to the new addition.

The doorbell rang.

That was annoying. The doorbell shouldn't be ringing. Cora hoped it wasn't Sherry's ex-husband. Or any of hers, for that matter.

It was Chief Harper. He didn't look happy.

"Hi, Chief. What's up?"

"You got any coffee left from dinner?"

"What makes you think we have coffee with dinner?"

"Your niece is a good cook, doesn't skimp on the accessories."

"I think there is. It's been sitting around, though."

"It doesn't matter. I need a jolt."

Harper followed Cora into the kitchen.

There was a half inch of coffee in the bottom of the Pyrex pot.

"Stone cold," Cora said. "I could add milk, zap it in the microwave."

"That would be fine."

Cora poured a cup, put it in the microwave for forty-five seconds.

"Won't that overheat it?" Harper said.

"I never know. You didn't come for the coffee. What brings you here?"

"Barney Nathan called. Guy died of poison."

"I thought you figured that."

"Yeah, but it wasn't cyanide. At least, not just cyanide. There were other poisons involved."

"Which ones?"

"We sent the stomach contents out to Danbury. They're already working on the wine."

"The wine from the glass?"

"Yeah. And the carafe."

"If there was poison in the carafe, wouldn't the sisters be dead?"

"They would be if they drank it. They claim they didn't. Even if there isn't, there's enough in the hollow of the overturned glass for them to get a good toxicology report."

"When will you get that?"

"By tomorrow."

"Why are you here now?"

"Harvey solved the puzzle. I thought you'd like to see."

"Chief, I can't begin to tell you how uninterested I am in that puzzle. I'll give you fifty to one it's got nothing to do with the murder."

He nodded. "That was Harvey's opinion, too."

"Fifty to one?"

Harper smiled. "I don't believe he gave actual odds. He did express his skepticism."

"What did he think the puzzle meant?"

"He had no idea."

"And you thought I would. That's flattering, Chief."

"Yeah, right. I got a mysterious, unidentified dead man who's got no reason to be dead. Which leaves me with nothing to investigate except the stupid crossword puzzle."

"Stupid?"

"That's a figure of speech. There's nothing stupid about it as far as I can tell. Harvey says it's a perfectly ordinary puzzle."

"I'm sure it is. Any reference to numbers? Or rows, or columns, or corners? Or addition, or subtraction, or multiplication, or division? Anything at all that might tie words and numbers together?"

"That's what I was hoping you could tell me."

"I can't, Chief. Even without looking at it I know I can't."

"Did you solve the sudoku?"

"Of course I solved the sudoku." Cora picked up her purse from the kitchen table, pulled out a sheet of paper, passed it over.

2	4	7	8	9	1	3	5	6
1	3	5	2	6	7	8	4	9
8	6	9	5	4	3	7	1	2
7	5	4	3	8	9	2	6	1
3	8	6	1	2	5	4	9	7
9	2	1	4	7	6	5	8	3
4	1	8	6	3	2	9	7	5
6	9	3	7	5	8	1	2	4
5	7	2	9	1	4	6	3	8

"There you are, Chief. What do you think it means?"

"I have no idea."

"Neither do I," Cora said. "Now, I'm going to look at your crossword puzzle for you, and then I'm going to tell you exactly the same thing. And then you're going to go away and wait for your toxicology report and hope it sheds a little more light on this than a stupid puzzle."

Cora took the puzzle from Chief Harper, looked it over.

S	C	R	I	M		T	A	F	T		S	T	A	G
A	R	E	N	A		H	I	L	O		U	R	G	E
W	A	L	K	T	H	E	D	O	G		N	E	I	L
S	T	Y		T	E	N	E	T		E	D	E	N	S
		M	E	R	C		I	O	T	A	S			
T	A	D	A		B	E	L	L	T	H	E	C	A	T
O	P	U	S		E	L	I		S	A	G	A		
I	R	K		I	D	E	A	S			P	E	P	
L	I	E	S		T	I	C		R	E	N	E		
S	L	O	P	T	H	E	H	O	G		E	S	T	D
	F	R	I	E	S		R	E	E	F				
P	A	Y	I	N		A	V	A	N	T		A	S	H
A	L	O	T		S	W	A	T	T	H	E	F	L	Y
P	A	R	E		H	A	L	E		O	A	R	E	D
A	S	K	S		E	Y	E	D		S	T	O	W	E

"Hmm. Not even an idiotic poem. Just four vaguely related phrases. Walk the dog. Bell the cat. Slop the hog. Swat the fly. If you really want a stretch, the fly's going to wind up dead, and so did Tom."

"Tom wasn't swatted, he was poisoned."

"I don't think you poison a fly. Unless you spray DDT or something, and hasn't that been banned? I don't really see a connection between a fly and a dead boarder. Why would a killer leave the puzzle?"

"Aha," Harper said. He pointed his finger at her. "See? You tell me you can't find a connection. You tell me it means nothing. But what do you really think? *Why did the killer leave it?* You accepted that as a given. The killer left it. You merely wonder why."

"I was speaking casually."

"Of course you were. Without any torturous logic or any value judgments. And speaking casually, what do you say? The killer left the puzzle."

Cora put up her hand. "Okay, Chief, I give up. Your infallible logic has backed me into a corner and forced me into an admission. I infer the killer left the puzzle. Why? Because I'm an ignorant fool without the brain power to think anything else. The killer left the puzzle, but I haven't a clue why or what it could possibly mean. So go home, get some sleep, and wait for the toxicology report, because that's going to tell you something and this isn't."

"You're talking a lot, Cora. That's what criminals do when they're nervous. Is there something you're hiding?"

"I'm hiding my irritation. Any moment I'm going to come flying across the kitchen and strangle you."

"I'd rather you didn't," Harper said. "But just so we're clear on this, the puzzle means nothing to you. I know you already said it doesn't, but maybe it could mean something in some other way. Other than the solution, I mean. For instance, is this one of your puzzles?"

"Oh, for goodness' sake."

"Why is that so far-fetched?"

"You're not suggesting a killer wants to give me my own puzzle?"

"Well, it could have a special meaning. Maybe the meaning was contained in the fact that it *was* your puzzle."

"Chief, trust me on this. I did not create this puzzle."

Harper put up his hands. "Okay, okay, you win. But do me a favor. Hang on to it, will you? Maybe something will occur to you."

"Something will occur to me all right, Chief, but I

don't think it will help you." She walked Chief Harper to the front door. "Let me know when you get the toxicology report."

Cora went back to the TV. She'd missed most of the program, but with the DVR she could simply rewind and watch it again.

People on the TV were racing around backward at great speed when Sherry came in.

"Who was that?" Sherry said.

"Chief Harper."

"What did he want?"

"The guy in the Guilford house was definitely poisoned. And he'd like me to interpret a crossword puzzle."

"Did you do it?"

"Nothing to interpret. It's an ordinary puzzle, nothing to do with anything. What you doing down here?"

"Jennifer's asleep. Aaron's reading a book. Mommy's off duty."

"That's nice."

"You have no idea." Sherry sniffed. "You been smoking in here again?"

"You're never down here."

"I'm down here enough. Lemme see the puzzle."

"Why do you want to see that?"

"I'm curious."

"You deal with puzzles all day long. Why do you care?"

"Someone got killed."

"It's not connected."

"How do you know? Maybe there's some secret message imbedded in the puzzle the killer thought only the Puzzle Lady would be able to figure out. Not knowing she's a total sham."

"If you're so smart, why don't you point it out?"

Sherry stuck out her hand. "Gimme."

Cora passed over the crossword puzzle.

Sherry looked it over. "Oh. This is pretty easy to solve. The answers are filled in."

"I know. It doesn't help."

"It helps me. I don't have to do any work. What's the theme? Oh. Actions and animals. Bell the cat. Walk the dog."

"You wanna tell me what that's got to do with the murder?"

"It certainly seems a stretch."

"Yeah, well, Chief Harper's not going to be happy until I give him something. I suppose I could make something up."

"Cora."

"Just kidding. But the guy won't leave me alone. Even if there's no hidden message, he insists it must be one of my puzzles."

Sherry held up the puzzle, took another look. "It *is* one of your puzzles."

TEN

CORA WAS FURIOUS. "What do you mean it's one of my puzzles?"

"Well, actually, it's one of mine. Which means, as far as the chief's concerned, it's one of yours."

"How can that be one of your puzzles? It's not from the newspaper. It's a computer printout."

"That's how the puzzles start, Cora. It's not like they begin in the newspaper. I compose them on the computer, print them out."

"Are you saying someone has access to our computer?"

"No. Just to one of our puzzles. That's not surprising. It's not like they're secret. It's a nationally syndicated column."

"That computer printout isn't."

"What are you getting so excited about?"

"I just got through swearing to God to Chief Harper this wasn't one of my puzzles."

"Of course not. It's one of mine."

"Sherry, this is a serious situation. I told the chief this wasn't my puzzle. It's not like I just glanced at it. I read the damn thing over and didn't recognize it. Which makes me look like either a dotty old woman or a fraud."

"I'd go with fraud."

"Did I warn you I was not in a good mood?"

"Hadn't noticed."

Cora exhaled. "Oh, God save me from the contented

young mother whose baby is blissfully asleep. What conceivable reason can I give Chief Harper for not recognizing my own work?"

"For one thing, it's old."

"Old?"

"Yeah. Four or five years, at least. I can't even remember doing this. I think it's one I knocked off in a hurry when Dennis was bothering me."

"Oh, no," Cora said. "You're not going to play the abusive ex-husband card. You're happily divorced, happily remarried, have a new baby. No one's saying, 'Oh, poor Sherry,' anymore and dropping a conversation. Tell me about the puzzle."

"There's nothing to tell. It's a puzzle I wrote for the column a few years ago. It has no significance whatsoever."

"Hey, hey, that's my column you're talking about. So, tell me something. How did someone get ahold of your computer files from five years ago?"

"I doubt if they did."

"You just said it's a computer printout."

"All that means is someone typed the puzzle into the computer. Anyone with Crossword Compiler could do it. Your column's syndicated to over two hundred papers. Some of them have archives online. Where you can print out old puzzles."

"Do they go that far back?"

"I don't know. It's never been an issue. But if you care, it's something you could research."

Cora shuddered. "What an ugly word."

"Online research? That's what you do all day."

"Yeah, if it's shopping or dating. But puzzles? My point is, I'm not going to do it. It doesn't matter which paper it was in. If it's your puzzle, it's your puzzle. It would have been in one of them, right?"

"Right."

"So anyone could have copied it. Why, I can't begin to imagine. But they could."

Aaron came strolling into the living room.

"Aaron!" Sherry said. "Where's the baby?"

Aaron pulled a speaker out of his pocket. "Baby monitor. Wonderful device. If she burps, I'm on it."

"Even so."

"Was that Chief Harper driving out?" Aaron said.

"You're not going to the paper now," Sherry said.

"Never said I was. Was that the chief?"

"That was him," Cora said.

"What's up?"

"He brought me a crossword puzzle. Duly solved by Harvey Beerbaum. Turns out it's one of Sherry's old puzzles, which is sort of embarrassing since I told him I'd never seen it before."

"What does it mean?"

"Absolutely nothing."

"Is that what you think, too?" Aaron asked Sherry.

"That's the general consensus."

"That's depressing. What did the chief have to say? Anything I can write?"

"Not now, you can't," Sherry said. "Hasn't the paper gone to press?"

"We could get out an extra."

"Not for this," Cora said. "The doctor confirmed the victim died of poison. The only question is which poison. There were traces of more than one."

"Oh, that's interesting."

"Yeah," Sherry said. "You should write it. There's

nothing more exciting than a columnist speculating on an outcome with no facts."

Aaron put up his hands. "Whoa! I got the monitor in my pocket and I'm not going anywhere. I just want to know what's up."

"The wine and the stomach contents went to Danbury for quantitative analysis. Should get it tomorrow."

"Harper going to call you when he does?"

"You want me to tip you off?"

"It crossed my mind."

"I'll see what I can do."

"Is this the puzzle?" Aaron said, picking it up.

"That's it," Sherry said. "Cora and I can't make anything out of it."

"Maybe you're too close to it," Aaron said. "Maybe you need the point of view of a total outsider."

Aaron studied the puzzle. Cora could practically see his mind going. As a brilliant journalist, he was used to figuring things out. But only in terms of a story. Not in terms of word games, though he often played them with Sherry. In the puzzle business, Aaron was strictly an also-ran.

"All right, hotshot," Cora said. "Put us to shame. What's it mean to you?"

Aaron looked up from the puzzle. "Not a damn thing."

ELEVEN

THE PHONE RANG at three A.M. The phone in Cora's bedroom. Not the phone in the kitchen, which rang everywhere else in the house. But the private line, installed just for her. Chief Harper had that number, which was to be used only for emergencies. At three A.M. it pretty much had to be an emergency.

It was.

"Cora?"

"Yeah?"

"There's been a break-in at the Guilford house."

"Anyone hurt?"

"No, but the sisters aren't happy. Seem to feel it's my fault."

"Anything taken?"

"I can't tell."

"You're out there now?"

"Yeah."

"Want me to come over?"

"Could you? I'm not good at dealing with women in their nightclothes."

"You mean I have to dress first?"

"Wish you would."

"See you there."

Cora pulled on her Wicked Witch of the West dress, a tattered smock that went on quickly and hid a multitude of sins. Not that there were any sins lately—Cora's love life had been depressingly dull.

Was she getting old?

Cora snuck out of the house, nodded in satisfaction that Sherry and Aaron's light was still out. She got in the car, started the motor, let it idle, didn't gun it. She inched the car gently toward the top of the drive, coasted down. She neared the bottom before she snapped on her headlights.

Cora was worried about finding the Guilford house in the dark. She needn't have been. The bed-and-breakfast was all lit up. Even down the side street it shone like a beacon in the night. Cora pulled in behind Chief Harper's cruiser, went up and rang the doorbell.

Harper answered the door.

"The sisters are in the living room. If you could deal with them, I'd be grateful."

Cora found Edith and Charlotte huddled together, talking animatedly in whispers. They were decked out in layers of silk, cotton, and lace, some of which might have been nightgowns and some of which might have been robes, though Cora had no real clue which was which. She could tell the sisters apart, however. The one in curlers and a hairnet was Edith. The one with cold cream on her face was Charlotte.

"Ladies," Cora said. "How awful to have a break-in. Are you all right?"

"We're fine," Edith said. "It's just very upsetting."

Cora wouldn't have known it. The woman's eyes sparkled. Clearly, now that the police were on the scene, she and her sister found it very exciting.

"Of course it is. So how did the intruder get in?"

"Oh, oh, let me show you."

The living room of the Guilford house was spacious, anchored at one end by the mantel of a working fireplace, and at the other end by an old-fashioned window seat.

Edith marched over to the window seat. "He came right through here."

"Was the window locked?"

"It is *now*," Edith said, raising her eyes at her sister.

"I locked the window," Charlotte said.

"So you say."

"So I say because so I did. I remember it specifically."

"You could remember it from the night before."

"No, it was last night. I know, because I was thinking that poor man is dead, and we should lock up."

"And how do you lock the window?" Cora said.

"With the latch. Right here."

Charlotte pointed out the lock. It was the typical window latch, a circular piece of metal on the top of the lower window that twisted into a metal slot on the bottom of the top window.

"It's locked now."

"Yes," Edith said. "I locked it when I found it open."

"You woke up and found the window open?"

"That's right."

"Your bedroom is upstairs?"

"Of course."

"What made you come down and check the window?"

"I heard someone moving around."

"You came down by yourself. That's very brave."

Edith smiled patronizingly. "No one's going to hurt me. Not in my own house."

Chief Harper shot Cora a glance, as if to say, see what I'm dealing with?

"Are you sure nothing's missing?" Cora said.

"There doesn't appear to be." Edith glanced around the room. "Not that there's anything much to take."

"Did you look?"

"Where?"

"Did you open drawers? Did you look in the window seat?"

"There's nothing in the window seat."

"How do you know?"

"We never keep anything in the window seat."

"Why?"

"Because we forget that it's there. Like Charlotte's sewing kit. We left it in the window seat, forgot it was there. We looked for it all over, couldn't find it. We haven't kept anything in there since."

"Uh-huh." Cora raised the lid of the window seat, looked in. She lowered it, turned to Chief Harper, who was peeking in the door. "Chief. I think I solved your break-in."

"Oh?"

"I don't want to jump to conclusions, but I'm willing to bet it's the drunk passed out in the window seat who did it."

"What!?"

Harper strode over, raised the lid. "Oh, my God."

The man in the window seat was about sixty years of age, with a scraggly white beard, liberally stained with red wine and tobacco. He wore tattered blue jeans and a Van Halen T-shirt that was probably last washed when Van Halen was still performing. His arms were folded over his chest, and his hands were clamped firmly around a bottle of what appeared to be the vilest rotgut known to man. If he'd paid a dollar for it, he'd been taken. Indeed, Cora figured, he'd been overcharged even if it was a gift.

"You know him?" Cora said.

"Sure. That's Ned Crumley, the town drunk. He's a frequent flyer down at the station. We have him sleeping it off in lockup every other week."

"Well, it looks like he tied one on this time," Cora said. "I'm amazed he got the window open."

Edith and Charlotte bustled over. "What is that man doing in our window seat?" Edith said indignantly.

"At the moment, not much," Cora said. "He's passed out."

"No, I mean, why is he here? That man has no right to sleep in our window seat."

"I'll be sure to point that out to him," Chief Harper said dryly. "Well, as Cora said, it would appear that the break-in is solved. As soon as we get the gentleman out of your way, you can lock up and go back to sleep."

"You going to carry him?" Cora said.

"Not if I can help it. Let's see if we can wake him up and get him walking."

Chief Harper extracted the wine bottle from between the drunk's fingers, handed it to Cora. "Ned must have been really plastered. It's not like him to pass out with booze still in the bottle."

Harper reached down, shook him by the shoulders. "Come on, Ned. Let's get up."

Ned didn't move.

"Come on, buddy. You can sleep anywhere you want, but not here."

Ned's head rolled sideways, hung down.

Harper's face froze. "What the hell?"

"Oh, no," Cora said. "Don't tell me."

"Tell you what?" Charlotte said. "What's wrong?"

Edith's eyes widened. "Oh, no! Is he dead?"

"He's dead, all right," Harper said. "And that's not all."

Harper whipped out a handkerchief and used it to carefully hold up the crumpled paper that had been in Ned's coat pocket.

It was a sudoku.

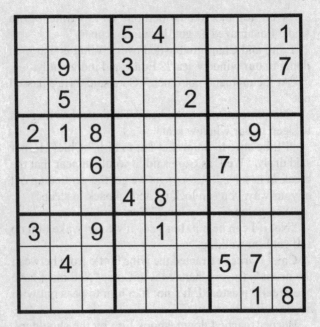

TWELVE

SAM BROGAN WASN'T HAPPY. The cranky officer was seldom happy, but being awakened at four in the morning on a night he wasn't supposed to be on duty didn't sit well. Sam had strung the crime scene ribbon as if it were a garrote with which he wished he could strangle someone. But having to fingerprint Cora Felton was the last straw.

"This is stupid," he said, rolling her fingers in the ink pad.

"You think I like it?" Cora said.

"If you don't like it, you shouldn't have touched the bottle."

"Chief Harper handed me the bottle."

"Harper handed you the bottle?"

"That's right."

"Then I gotta do *his* fingerprints."

"You don't have them on file?"

"The chief hasn't been booked that often. I try to arrest as many people as I can, but when you keep arresting your chief you get a bad reputation."

"All right, you gotta fingerprint the chief. You gonna grouch at him?"

"No. Your fingerprints are your fault. The chief may not know any better, but you should."

"Can I quote you on that, Sam? The chief doesn't know any better than to contaminate crime scenes?"

"You quote me on that and I'll deny it. It's not what I said and you know it."

Sam rolled the last finger onto the fingerprint card.

"You want a mug shot, too?"

"I want a nap. I want to go home and go to bed." Sam stroked his moustache. It didn't stand out so much with his five A.M. stubble. He closed the ink pad, stowed the fingerprint card in a plastic envelope. He held up the bottle of wine. "I don't know how he could drink this stuff."

"Evidently he couldn't. You mind if I wash my hands now? I hate to leave such visible prints at a crime scene."

"Knock yourself out."

Cora went to the kitchen sink, washed her hands with dish soap, scrubbed away the worst of the ink. The remaining faint traces would take days to wear off. She dried her hands on a paper towel, tossed it in the trash, and followed Sam Brogan out into the hall.

Barney Nathan came in the front door. It had taken the doctor a little while to respond to the call. He was wearing slacks and a white shirt, open at the neck.

Cora blinked. "Oh, my God. Hell must have frozen over. Barney Nathan, without a red bow tie. Sam, get the crime scene camera. Snap off a few shots so I can prove I wasn't dreaming."

Barney stopped in midstride, wheeled on Cora. "Do you really give a damn what I wear?"

He turned, stomped into the living room.

"Well," Cora said. "Look who got up on the wrong side of the bed."

"Four in the morning either side is the wrong side," Sam said.

"You gonna photograph the body once it's out of the window seat?"

"No, but I should photograph the seat."

"Why?"

"So no one can say I didn't," Sam grumbled, and stomped off after the doctor.

Cora followed Sam into the living room.

Barney Nathan was stooped indecorously over the window seat. He stood up, said, "He's dead," and brushed off the knees of his pants.

"Any idea when?" Harper said.

The doctor shot a glance at Cora. "Very recent," he said.

"The sisters were awakened by the sound of someone breaking in around three A.M. Anything inconsistent with that was him and he crawled into the window seat and died?"

"It's a stupid thing to do," Barney said.

"I meant medically."

"I know what you meant. He could have done that."

"What about the cause of death?"

"What about it?"

"You think he was poisoned?"

"I won't know till I do the autopsy."

"Any smell of almonds?"

Barney Nathan stiffened. He turned back, bent over the body, stood up. "Yes, there is."

"So it could be the same guy."

"Or girl," Cora said.

The Guilford sisters, relegated to the parlor, were losing their patience. After all, it was their house, and something exciting was going on.

Edith stuck her head in the door. "Excuse me, Chief, but the guests are awake, and we don't know what to tell them."

"The guests?" Chief Harper said.

"Yes," Charlotte said. "A nice young couple checked in yesterday. And a widower who might become a lodger.

But no one's going to want to stay in a place where people keep dropping dead."

"Now, that's a fine way to describe it," Edith said. "I hope you don't talk that way in front of the guests."

"Of course not. Chief Harper's family." Charlotte smiled. "We do think kindly of you, even if you do keep bringing murders."

That seemed a rather unfair assessment of the chief's actions.

"Where are the guests?" Harper said.

"In the foyer. We told them they couldn't come in and they're not happy."

"And you'd like them to be not happy at me instead of at you. Well, I suppose it's only fair."

"I'll give you moral support, Chief."

Harper followed the sisters out in the foyer with Cora tagging along.

The couple, who appeared to be in their thirties, wore pajamas and robes. Cora wondered if they were married.

The widower was a frail thing, somewhere on the north side of sixty. He was, to Cora's amusement, dressed in a suit and tie. She wondered whether he slept in it, or simply put it on to come downstairs. She wasn't sure which was more pathetic.

"Sorry to disturb your sleep," Harper said. "You people are guests here?"

The woman was indignant. "Yes. What's going on? All this commotion, and *they* won't let us go see."

"I'm the one who won't let you see. There's been a break-in, and the perpetrator is dead."

"They killed him!" the widower said.

"I strongly doubt it. The intruder was a drunk who crawled into the window seat and died. It's a suspicious death, so we have to treat it as a crime scene, but, trust me, no one suspects your hosts of having helped the man along."

The widower gasped at the suggestion.

"Well, I don't know how you expect us to sleep with this going on. We should check out and go to a motel."

"No, you shouldn't," Chief Harper said. "This is a potential crime scene. You don't leave a crime scene until you've been cleared by the police."

The woman was belligerent. "Why not?"

"If it turns out this is a crime scene, we'll have to take your statements."

"Why?" the man said. "We didn't see anything."

"Wait a minute," the woman said. "We have to make a formal statement, give our names? Why do we have to do that?"

"I don't think you do," Harper said. "Unless you want to check out. If you're checking out now, I'll need to see some identification and take down your permanent address. If you're hanging around, I'll talk to you if I need you."

The woman immediately reversed field. "No, no. That won't be necessary. We're staying here."

The EMS team went by with a gurney. The dead man was covered with a sheet; still it had a chilling effect.

"All right," Harper said. "The show's over. So, why don't you go back to your rooms. There's nothing more to see."

Harper waited while the guests, chastened, slunk back upstairs.

"All right, ladies," Harper said. "Assuming Ned hadn't crawled into the window seat and died, what would he have found to steal?"

"Nothing," Edith said.

"There's the brass candlesticks," Charlotte said.

"Oh, who cares about the brass candlesticks."

"Well, I like them, and they've been in the family."

"Been in the family. Now there's an expression. They belonged to Uncle Edward, who was as nutty as a jaybird."

"Are the candlesticks valuable?" Harper said.

"Not in the least," Edith said. "They appear to have sentimental value for Charlotte, but you couldn't get a dime for them."

"What about the grandfather clock?" Charlotte said.

"A little hard to carry, even for someone sober," Chief Harper observed.

"Yes, of course. That's not what he means, Charlotte. He means, do we have any money or jewelry?"

"Do you?"

"Certainly not," Charlotte said.

Harper could have assumed that. The bed-and-breakfast, though neat and tidy, had not been painted in years, and probably could use a new roof. The sisters, by reputation, were frugal to a fault, with the exception of the afternoon tea.

"There's no money in the house?"

"Of course not," Edith said. "It's in the bank."

"You have money in the bank?"

"Doesn't everyone? We have a checking account and a savings account."

"And a safety deposit box," Charlotte added.

"You have a safety deposit box?" Harper said.

"For the jewelry," Edith explained. "We certainly don't keep jewelry around the house. Anyone could break in. Not that we blame the police department. But you see."

"You have expensive jewelry?"

"Just a little costume jewelry. For dress up. But we feel safer if it's not in the house."

"Does anyone know you have a safety deposit box?"

"Well, you do now. I'd prefer you didn't tell. Then people will think we're rich."

"What about your nephew. Does he know?"

"Of course. But he's family."

"I see."

Cora followed Chief Harper back to the living room.

"Well, that seemed promising for a while," Harper said.

"Yes. Very promising. I thought you were onto something. A drunk climbs through the sisters' window, hoping to poison them and steal the key to their safety deposit box. Unlucky for him, he can't resist sipping the poisoned rotgut and winds up in the window seat."

"Sarcasm? At four in the morning? Isn't that a little harsh?"

"Murder is a little harsh. If Ned turns out to be poisoned, it would appear you have a serial killer who targets elderly men associated with the Guilford house. If I were that lodger, I'd make a statement right now and check out just as fast as I could call a cab."

"There's no cabs in Bakerhaven."

"Then I'd walk. Seriously, Chief, do you have the faintest idea what's going on here?"

"Do you?"

"Not at all. But then, I'm not the chief of police. Did Barney Nathan really miss the smell of almonds?"

"No, he got it."

"After a little prompting. And his tie wasn't tied. What's that all about?"

"It's four in the morning, Cora."

"And did you hear the way he snapped at me? No, I guess it was Sam who was with me then. Anyway, he was downright rude."

"Well, if you're going to accuse a man of incompetence…"

"I never said he was incompetent. I said he was careless and made a lot of mistakes."

"That's sure to win his heart."

"Yeah." Cora took a look around. "Well, it would appear my work here is done."

"What?"

"Well, I solved your break-in. What more do you want?"

"There is the sudoku."

"Which I will be perfectly happy to solve. But I don't know what you expect it to tell you."

Sam Brogan came in carrying a plastic evidence bag. "You're not going to like this, Chief."

"That's not surprising. I haven't liked anything so far."

"I found this in the bush outside. Just a piece of garbage. I nearly threw it away."

"You *handled* it?" Cora said.

"Just an old newspaper. Old, faded, discolored junk. Just the type of thing you keep from cluttering up your crime scene."

"So?" Harper said.

"So, I turned it over, and, here, take a look."

Sam held up the evidence bag with the newspaper.

It was open to the crossword puzzle.

THIRTEEN

"You couldn't have just thrown it away," Cora muttered, disgustedly.

"Of course not. It's evidence."

"Evidence of what?"

"How should I know?" Sam said. "I'm just the dumb cop who finds the clues. You're the Puzzle Lady who figures them out."

"A puzzle in a newspaper," Cora said. "How can it possibly mean anything? I mean, look at this." She pointed to the top of the page. "This is the Hartford paper from September 17th, 2005."

"Yes, it is," Chief Harper said. "You will notice this happens to be one of your crossword puzzles."

There was no denying that. Cora's smiling face adorned the column.

"So what?" Cora said. "You wanna tell me what a crossword puzzle of mine from 2005 has to do with a drunk who got poisoned now."

"I have no idea. We'll know more after you solve the puzzle."

"I'm not solving the puzzle."

"Why not?"

"For one thing, it's already been solved. See those pencil marks? It's been solved and then erased."

"Why would anyone do that?"

"I have no idea, but they did."

Harper peered at the puzzle. "Yeah, there's pencil

marks left. But not enough to read. You'll still have to solve it."

"Come on, Chief, it's bagged as evidence. You're going to want to process it, find Sam Brogan's fingerprints."

Sam muttered a choice comment under his breath.

"What was that, Sam? I didn't quite catch it."

"Sam, take this down to the station, run off a copy. I want to know what it says."

"You'll have to wait, Chief," Cora said. "Harvey Beerbaum isn't up this early."

"No, but you are."

"Yes, I am. But I'm not solving any crossword puzzles. Particularly, not this one."

"Why not?"

"Harvey solved the first one. Why? Because it wasn't important. If you don't let him solve the second one, everyone's going to think it's important."

"Who cares what people think?"

"You do if it's the Channel Eight news team. The last thing in the world you want is Rick Reed blowing the case out of proportion."

"No one even has to know there is a crossword puzzle."

"Oh. Bad move, Chief. To start withholding things from the public and the press. The word *cover-up* rears its ugly head."

"Cover-up of what? It's a stupid old newspaper."

"Exactly. Unless you make a big thing out of it. After breakfast, run it to Harvey Beerbaum. Point out how it's an old puzzle from the paper. Ask him if he remembers solving it before."

"Why should he?"

"I don't know. Some of these puzzle people, they have photographic memories."

"These puzzle people? You exclude yourself from the category?"

"I exclude myself from the crazies who let it be an obsession. I don't remember this puzzle, but Harvey Beerbaum might. Not that it matters. All that matters is that you treat it as if it weren't important, and exclude it as a potential clue. I hate to say it because he's such a sweet old fuddy-duddy, but being able to say you gave it to Harvey will go a long way toward convincing people you didn't think it was important."

Before Chief Harper had a chance to argue, Sam Brogan came back in the door grinning from ear to ear.

"Got him, Chief!" he announced.

Sam was wrestling with a young man who was struggling mightily to get free. He was hampered by the fact that Sam had already clamped handcuffs on his wrists.

Cora's mouth fell open.

It was the Guilford sisters' nephew, Alan.

FOURTEEN

"Found him sneaking around in the bushes, Chief," Sam said. "I asked him to stop, he tried to run."

"Oh, big brave cop," Alan said. "Like you outran me. I tripped and fell."

"What were you doing prowling around the house?"

"Prowling? Who said I was prowling? I was on my way home."

"At four in the morning? What were you doing up at four in the morning?"

"None of your business."

"Now, see here. This is a murder case."

"Murder?"

"If I could step in here, Chief," Cora said. "Sam, could you go see if you could arrest anybody else?"

"Oh, are you running the police force?" Harper said.

"Just trying to speed things along. Sam, why don't you unlock this young man. I'm sure the chief and I will be safe."

"Chief?"

"This is the Guilford sisters' nephew, Sam. I don't believe he's a flight risk."

Sam grudgingly took off the handcuffs and left.

"Now, dear boy," Cora said to Alan. "If you would allow me to expedite. Chief, you will recall Alan is engaged to Arlene, who lives next door. Alan has doubtless escaped staying with his aunts by pleading a motel room somewhere. Whether he has one, or whether it is merely an invention to appease his aunts, in either case he was at Arlene's now, and what Sam Brogan took for guilt was merely his embarrassment at having the fact he was staying over with the young lady in question found out. The thing I don't know is whether he was apprehended attempting to sneak back to his motel in case the police searched Arlene's house, or whether he was merely trying to see what was going on. Which is it, young man?"

Alan was wearing slacks and a white shirt open at the neck. His face twisted into a boyish grin. "You're quite amazing," he said.

Cora shuddered. "Please. *Amazing* is one of those words you use to describe a bad date. 'She was amazing.' 'She had personality.' All the other synonyms for I-wouldn't-touch-her-with-a-ten-foot-pole. I'm not that old, young man."

"No, no, of course not," Alan said. "Arlene is amazing, too."

"Yes, I'm sure she is," Cora said dryly. "Well, Chief, you wanna interrogate this prisoner a little before deciding Sam's cracked the case?"

Harper sighed. "You see anything?"

Alan shook his head. "No. Arlene woke up, saw the lights. Woke me up to see what was going on. I couldn't see anything out the window so she suggested I go outside."

"Well done," Cora said. "The young hero ventures forth for his lady fair, gets nabbed as a Peeping Tom for spying on his own aunts. Ain't love grand?"

FIFTEEN

CORA WAS UNHAPPY driving home. And it wasn't just that it was four thirty in the morning. Or that she'd been confronted with yet another crossword puzzle that didn't mean anything, but which she had to sidestep solving. Or a sudoku that she could solve, but which she damn well knew would be meaningless.

Something about the case was bothering her. Was it because a harmless old drunk got killed? Or was it because a harmless old man got killed? Because the word *harmless* could be applied to both victims.

Or could it? How did she know they were harmless? The drunk had lived here for years and never hurt anybody, at least as far as she knew; she could check with Chief Harper on that. The old man, on the other hand, was a stranger. So was it fair to assume he was harmless? He might well have been a serial killer himself. Perhaps some ruthless bluebeard who set wealthy women's hearts afluttering, and married them and murdered them to get their cash. Somehow, Cora doubted it. The old man hadn't set *her* heart afluttering. Granted, he was dead, but even so. He certainly didn't look like a catch.

He might have been some armed robber on the lam, lying low at a bed-and-breakfast. Perhaps even hiding out from his partner, with whom he had failed to divide the loot. The accomplice had shown up, poisoned him, and then stolen the money back.

And his wallet. And his gun. And any trace of his existence. And then stuck around to poison an old drunk just for the hell of it. No, because the drunk had seen him do it. The drunk had seen him climbing out of the window. So he poisons him and throws him in the window seat? Not likely. Cudgels him over the head, Cora could buy, but poisons him?

The way Cora saw it, these murders were either related or they weren't. It made no sense that they were related. On the other hand, it made no sense that they were not.

If they were related, which was the main murder? It would probably be the old man, partly because he died first, and partly because he was a stranger. Nothing was known about him, so his history was wide open. As were the motives for his murder. Whereas no one seemed to profit from the old drunk's death. Unless you counted Dan Finley and Sam Brogan, who wouldn't have to lock him up anymore.

Cora turned into the driveway, drove up to the house. The lights were out in the addition. Sherry, Aaron, and the baby were asleep. The only light was the faint glow from the back hallway seeping out through the living room window.

Cora went up the walk. Slipped quietly inside, taking care not to let the screen door bang.

Someone was in the house!

Cora could tell at once. She didn't see anything, she didn't hear anything, but she knew. She fumbled in her purse, reached for her gun. Found it, pulled it out. She stood in the doorway while her eyes became accustomed to the dark. There was no one lurking in the shadows of the living room. But was that a faint sound from down the back hall?

Cora tiptoed through the living room, peered down the hall. The light wasn't just coming from her bedroom. The light in the study was on. Someone was going through her things. Why, she couldn't begin to imagine, but she meant to find out.

Cora tiptoed down the hall, peered around the door.

Sherry was sitting at the computer. She looked up, saw Cora holding the gun.

"Don't shoot. I'm unarmed."

"Sherry. What are you doing down here?"

"I couldn't sleep. I didn't want to wake the baby."

"But you didn't mind waking me."

"You weren't here."

"You didn't know that."

"Why are we arguing? You weren't here, I was using the office."

"What for?"

"Catching up on my work."

Cora looked, saw Sherry was constructing a crossword puzzle.

"Hey. I don't have Crossword Compiler."

"Yeah, I ordered it."

"You ordered a program for my computer?"

"Cora, I helped you buy this computer. You got gigabytes up the wazoo. The program's not a problem. You won't even know it's there." Sherry frowned. "Where were you, anyway?"

"Oh."

"What do you mean, oh?"

Cora told her about the murder.

"There was a sudoku on the body?"

"Yes."

"That's ridiculous."

"And you haven't heard the worst of it. Sam Brogan found a newspaper with a crossword puzzle."

"With a clue to the murder?"

"I doubt it. It's from 2005."

"Where did that come from?"

"Somebody's trash."

"Then how can it mean anything?"

"It can't. But the chief wanted me to solve it."

"What did you do?"

"Pawned him off on Harvey Beerbaum."

"Poor Harvey."

"He loves it. It's not like the chief's going to wake him up to do it. It's not important; he'll ask him tomorrow." Cora pursed her lips. "I'm wondering."

"What?"

"Two thousand and five. The other puzzle's pretty old. Could it be from 2005?"

"Could be. That would be kind of creepy."

"The whole thing's kind of creepy. You got a killer littering crime scenes with vintage crossword puzzles that don't mean a damn thing."

"How do you know they don't mean a damn thing?"

"The first one didn't. The second one should be just the same."

"How do you know?"

"Because no one plots a murder based on a crossword puzzle in 2005 and holds on to it all this time waiting to carry it out."

"What did the crossword puzzle say?"

"I don't know. Chief Harper's taking it to Harvey Beerbaum to solve."

"Will he show it to you then?"

"I suppose so. I could ask for it, but I don't want to make him think it's important."

"Why not? It's all right if it isn't."

"Yeah, but what if it is?"

"You just got through telling me it can't be. What is the date of the puzzle?"

"Why?"

"You remember the date?"

"September seventeenth."

Sherry began typing into the computer.

"What are you doing?"

"Google search."

"What for?"

"Newspapers with puzzle archives."

"You think there is one?"

"The first puzzle was a computer printout. It had to come from somewhere." Sherry pointed to the screen. "Here we go. The *Richmond Daily* has archived everything since 1998. We plug in September 17, 2005." She pressed Enter. "Voilà."

Cora looked over Sherry's shoulder. "That's the puzzle?"

"That's right. Now I click on Printable Version, and there we go."

The printer spat out a copy of the puzzle. Sherry handed it to Cora. "Here you go."

ACROSS

1 Flat topper
4 Letter starter
8 Saturday-night hire, perhaps
14 Work of Sappho
15 1-Across material
16 Capital that replaced Istanbul
17 Start of a message
19 Like a ski run
20 Lizards popular as pets
21 First baseman in a comic routine
22 Run-throughs
23 More of the message
29 Davis of film
31 Send, so to speak
32 Lavender, for one
35 Set the pace
37 Old PC screens
38 Ill temper
39 Humble in position
41 Does a bakery job
42 Keister
43 "-ite" compound, often
44 Tribal leader
46 Lint-collecting body part
48 Forest clearing
50 Still more of the message
52 Sunlit areas
57 Trinity member

58 Putting out
60 With freedom of tempo
64 End of the message
65 Did penance
66 To____ (just right)
67 Suffix with Brooklyn
68 Upper crust
69 Does fairway work
70 Patch up

DOWN

1 Namely
2 Almanac tidbit
3 Beanery handouts
4 Name in frozen dinners
5 Caucuses state
6 Insults, playfully
7 Like Reynard
8 "Peter and the Wolf" bird
9 Head over heels
10 Clay-Liston result, briefly
11 Dance like Hines
12 Poetic preposition
13 Half a diam.
18 Body art, slangily
21 Big hunk of cheese
24 Gusher

25 Heston title role
26 Marx Brothers' specialty
27 Out-and-out
28 Capone adversary
30 D-Day invasion town
32 Tuscany city
33 Chain sound
34 Like King novels
36 Did some batiking
38 Beeb watcher
40 Transplant need, maybe
45 Pet store array
47 Parade day
49 A lot like
51 Abounding in trees
53 Payback time for Wimpy:
　　Abbr.
54 Goes up
55 Lavatory sign
56 Veep who resigned
59 Hobo fare
60 Sleazy periodical
61 Beehive State Indian
62 ____ mot
63 Aardvark's tidbit
64 "How Dry ____"

Cora took a look. "So, you wanna solve it?"

"Not really, but you're not going to let me alone until I do. Even though it means absolutely nothing."

"We don't know it means absolutely nothing."

"Yes, we do. We figured it out by deductive reasoning."

"Would you just solve the damn thing."

There were footsteps in the hall, and Aaron came in, carrying Jennifer on his shoulder. He looked half asleep. "What are you girls doing?"

"Sherry was doing a Google search, and now we're going to do a crossword puzzle. What's new with you?"

"The baby woke up. She wants to nurse, and I'm not equipped."

"Sorry, Cora. Duty calls." Sherry took Jennifer from Aaron.

"Where you going?" Cora said.

"Nurse her and put her back to bed."

"What about the puzzle?"

"Harvey Beerbaum's going to do it."

Sherry and Jennifer went out the door.

"What's that all about?" Aaron said.

Cora filled Aaron in on the murder.

"Hmm. Town drunk. Not worth getting out an extra. Unless it turns out to be poison."

"You won't know in time to do you any good. Dan Finley will leak it to Rick Reed. By the time you get out an extra, it will be all over the tube."

"I could write it now," Aaron said.

"What?"

"Assume it's poison, and write it now. We could have it on the street before Rick even aimed a microphone."

"Could you really do that?"

Aaron made a face. "Nah. It's not like we have news-boys screaming on street corners. The *Gazette* gets delivered. It's only sold in half a dozen stores. Half of those are convenience stores that are really out of town. And none of the stores on Main Street even have a rack outside."

"Whoa, back up!" Cora said. "It's the mother who's supposed to have postpartum depression. You're not competing with television. You're a successful young journalist. People read your stories, not because you're the first on the scene, but because you put an intelligent spin on what Rick Reed has already mangled." She put up her hand. "That being said, if I can get you a scoop, I will. In the meantime, it's five in the morning. So, unless you'd like to take a whack at this crossword puzzle…"

"I'll leave that to Sherry."

"Then I'm going to bed."

SIXTEEN

CORA WOKE UP at a quarter to ten. She knew it was a quarter to ten because the digital clock said so, and there was no arguing with cold, hard numbers. A clock face you could misread, particularly if the minute hand and the hour weren't that different in length, but the numbers didn't lie. Unless some of the lines were burned out, like in that digital watch Cora used to have that made the four look frighteningly like half a swastika. But the clock on her dresser was in depressingly good repair.

Cora got up, padded in the direction of the bathroom. Stopped short at the sight of a piece of paper shoved under her bedroom door. She picked it up. It was the solved puzzle.

Cora sat on the bed, read the puzzle over.

After careful examination, she was delighted to be able to report that it didn't mean a damn thing.

Cora got dressed and drove into town. She seldom made breakfast for herself. Not when Mrs. Cushman's Bake Shop provided such tempting treats. This morning, Cora had an apricot scone and a latte. Mrs. Cushman made the latte. The scone, like all her baked goods, she trucked in from the Silver Moon Bakery in Manhattan.

Chief Harper came in behind her, ordered a large black coffee and a blueberry muffin.

"Just getting up, Chief?" Cora said.

"Are you kidding? It's my second time today."

"Your second blueberry muffin?"

"Let's not count calories. It's unfriendly to count calories."

"Any progress on the case?"

Harper glanced around the bakery. It was still crowded, even at ten in the morning. "Let's not talk here."

Cora followed the chief down the street to the police station, which was only a tempting half block from the bakery, increasing the allure. Cora wondered which came first. Had the cops seen the bakery and decided to open the station? Or had Mrs. Cushman figured it couldn't hurt to open a bakery near the cops?

The Bakerhaven Police Station, like most other houses in town, was a white frame building with black shutters. Harper went up the front steps, held the door for Cora.

Dan Finley was at his desk. He looked bleary-eyed. Cora wondered how early Chief Harper had called him in.

"Anything happen?" Harper said.

"In the five minutes you were gone? Not a thing."

"Great."

Harper led Cora into his office, closed the door. He sat down, put his coffee and muffin on the desk.

Cora flopped into a chair, sipped her latte. "What's up, Chief? You identify the corpse?"

"Ned Crumley."

"Glad you can joke about it."

"Well, what else can I do? I got two men killed for no apparent reason under the most bizarre circumstances. Unless the Guilford sisters poisoned them, I don't see how it was done. If they did, I have to congratulate them for committing the most stupid and obvious murder in the history of law enforcement. Sit the man down and feed him poison, call the cops when he dies. It's hardly the perfect crime."

"On the other hand, Chief, they've got you convinced they didn't do it."

Harper opened his mouth, closed it again. "Damned if they haven't. Could they be that diabolically clever?"

Cora put up her hands. "Whoa. I was kidding. Don't go off the deep end."

"See, even you ridicule the suggestion. We have an absolutely senseless crime that doesn't adhere to any pattern. We have an unidentified corpse who materialized in town without using any mode of transportation. We have a serial killer unlike anything I've ever seen before. This is an absolutely unique sort of crime."

"Yes, and no."

"What do you mean by that?"

"I don't know. I can't put my finger on it. Driving home last night I had the funniest feeling. Granted, it was four thirty in the morning and I hadn't had any sleep. Still, I couldn't help feeling there was something very familiar about it."

"What?"

"I have no idea. It's like nothing else I've ever encountered. I wish my brain was working right. It's been tough ever since I turned—"

Cora broke off. Her face flushed.

"Turned what?" Harper said.

"Turned into my driveway and went home," Cora improvised. "I felt like something was wrong, but I was too tired to figure it out."

Harper let it go, as if that was what Cora had meant to say. He knew damn well she was talking about her last birthday. He wondered which one it was.

"You get the report back from the lab?" Cora said.

"No. Now I'm waiting on two of 'em. We should get the results on the first murder soon, but they're taking their own sweet time. Luckily, nobody gives a damn."

"I beg your pardon?"

"Well, it isn't a very sensational murder, is it? An old man and an old drunk poisoned for no reason. Rick Reed hasn't even bitten. You can bet Dan Finley's tipped him off, but he doesn't think it's worth the bother. And that, I have to admit, is the saving grace. No one's pushing me to solve this crime. Not that they won't, but right now expectations are low."

"You invited me over here to tell me nothing?" Cora said.

"I invited you over here to eat your scone. So I won't have to admit in public I got nothing. Well, I got one thing."

Harper took a paper off his desk, passed it over. "Here's the puzzle. Harvey solved it."

"Seen it, Chief. It doesn't mean a thing."

"Huh? You went over to Harvey's?"

"No, Sherry copied the puzzle off the Internet."

"How the hell did she do that?"

"I had the date from the paper. She plugged it in, found a puzzle archive. She's clever that way. I studied the solution to the puzzle, and it is my pleasure to tell you it doesn't mean a damn thing."

"You don't think so?"

"I certainly don't."

"I suppose you're right. Of course, if it had said cyanide…"

"Yes, that certainly would have made a difference," Cora said sarcastically. "Or if it had named the killer. A neat trick, to have known who did it way back in 2005."

"Yeah. I was hoping there'd be some tie-in with the sudoku. But Harvey couldn't find one."

"Harvey solved the sudoku?"

"Not as fast as you could, but he solved it."

Harper handed her a copy.

7	2	3	5	4	8	9	6	1
8	9	4	3	6	1	2	5	7
6	5	1	9	7	2	8	3	4
2	1	8	6	5	7	4	9	3
4	3	6	1	2	9	7	8	5
9	7	5	4	8	3	1	2	6
3	8	9	7	1	5	6	4	2
1	4	2	8	3	6	5	7	9
5	6	7	2	9	4	3	1	8

"Well, that's fine work, Chief. Harvey may not have been as fast, but I guarantee you he got the same numbers I would have."

"Does it suggest anything to you?"

"Nothing you could print in a family newspaper."

"Ha, ha," Harper said. "Well, hang on to it. And the crossword, too. Maybe something will dawn on you later."

"That's fine, Chief, but I guarantee you it won't."

Cora folded the papers, and stuck them into her floppy, drawstring purse.

SEVENTEEN

CORA LEFT THE police station, went down the side street to Becky Baldwin's. She found the young attorney hunched over her desk.

"What you doin'?"

"Believe it or not, I'm paying my bills. They don't tell you in law school. That's over half of what the job consists of, and no one pays you to do it."

"You up to date on the second murder?"

"I know there was one."

"At the Guilford house."

"So they say."

"Who's they?"

"Confidential sources."

"Give me a break."

"Dan Finley. Who also tipped off Rick Reed. Who couldn't care less."

"Oh?"

"Said there wasn't anything sexy about it."

"In other words, you don't have a client yet."

"I beg your pardon?"

"Well, you're sexy. If you had a client, Rick Reed could interview you."

"Ha, ha."

"I wasn't kidding. Without you, there's no story. All they've got is Police Have No Leads. Throw in a defendant, they got an angle."

"Just because someone is a client doesn't make them a defendant."

"It does to Rick Reed. The Guilford sisters don't want to hire you?"

"You were there. You heard them."

"That was when there was only one crime. They got two murders, maybe they'll think twice."

"They didn't."

"You called them?"

"I would be remiss in my duty as an attorney if I failed to point out the nuances of the situation."

"Nice sidestep! And they still weren't biting?"

"Not a bit."

"What about the nephew? You know, that handsome young man you were so upset to find out had a fiancée."

"I was nothing of the kind."

"You looked like someone stole a prize out of your Happy Meal. It's understandable. Your childhood sweetheart gets married, has a kid. The next eligible young dreamboat you meet immediately tosses a fiancée in your face."

"I think you were more disappointed than I was."

"That goes without saying. But I don't try to hide it. I wear my six-plus marriages on my sleeve like a badge of honor."

"Six?"

"Plus."

"Do I want to know what that means?"

"There's a gray area. What actually constitutes a marriage? Like in *The Threepenny Opera,* when Macheath— that's 'Mack the Knife' of Bobby Darin fame, though God knows that's before your time, too—marries Polly Peachum during a drunken revel in a ceremony performed by the Reverend Kimble, who may or may not have an official standing with the law or the church. And the marriage wouldn't be legal anyway, since Macheath has already gone through numerous ceremonies of the kind. See what I mean?"

"God save me."

"Eligible bachelor or not, you might want to consider him as a client."

"Why?"

"He was apprehended prowling around his aunts' house last night. He said he was staying over at his girl-friend's, heard the police activity, and wanted to see what was going on without alerting his aunts to the fact he was sleeping over. Afraid he might shock their sensi-bilities. Though it takes quite a lot to shock a sensibil-ity these days."

"And you find his story suspect?"

"I find his story pretty much what he had to say. I mean, you're an attorney. Could you think of another plausible reason for his being there?"

"Just because it's the most logical doesn't mean it isn't true."

"It doesn't mean it is, either. Anyway, he's the nephew."

"So?"

"So the aunts must have a bit of money. They own that big house. They must have some cash put away, because the B and B business isn't exactly booming."

"My law business isn't booming, and I don't have any cash put away."

"Don't digress. The point is, if the aunts have money, the nephew could inherit."

Becky shook her head. "Couldn't happen."

"Why not?"

"The aunts don't have any money, except for the house, and I don't think it's valued at much. Look how close the neighbors are. They're on a very small plot of land. The house is old, and in rather poor repair. I imagine the cost just to bring the plumbing and wiring up to code would seriously cut into anything they might recognize from a sale. They have a small income from the money inherited from their parents, and that's it. Besides, there's another nephew."

"What?"

Becky smiled. "See how much you can uncover when you're not trying to twist all the facts to support one of your own cockeyed theories. Alan has an older brother. Skipped out, lives on the West Coast, hasn't been heard from in years. Assuming he's still alive, he's next in line to inherit."

"Even so, what if loving nephew Alan slipped his aunts a whacking dose of poison?"

"Yeah, but they didn't die. A lodger and the town drunk did."

"Sure. Because they happened to drink the poison. Which was out of the nephew's control. It's easy enough to poison a bottle of wine. It's hard to make sure who actually drinks it."

"In the first place, we don't know that the wine was poisoned."

"That's only because the boys in Danbury are late with their analysis. The poison is sure to be in the wine."

"Why?"

"Because it couldn't be in anything else. How else was he going to ingest it? Unless the guy happened to have a hypodermic mark on him. And I don't think even Barney Mac-Bumble-Fingers would miss that. What's wrong with him, by the way?"

"Who?"

"Barney Nathan. He showed up at the crime scene last night and almost snapped my head off."

"Is that really so surprising?"

"No, I'm sure I had it coming. Only I hadn't even stepped on his toes, yet. He jumped on me the minute he came in the door."

"I'm sure you said something to provoke it."

"I just mentioned he didn't have his bow tie on. And what's with that? I've never seen him without a bow tie."

"Oh." Becky nodded. "He's having marital problems."

"You're kidding."

"No. His wife's leaving him."

Cora's mouth fell open. "How do you know that?"

"Actually, he asked me out."

"He did what?!"

"Well, it's your fault. You had me make a play for him so you could get into the morgue. And now he thinks I like him."

"Did you go out with him?"

"I made some excuse. I'm trying to let him down gently."

"That never works."

"I know."

"You gotta look him in the eye and say, 'Dude, you haven't got a prayer.'"

"That's cruel."

"No, that's swift and painless. The cruel thing is stringing him along."

"I have a problem telling men I don't like them."

"There's a name for girls like that."

"It's not funny, Cora. I got enough problems trying to live off my law practice without dealing with unwanted advances."

"A few free dinners would help that along."

"I thought we had a name for girls like that."

"What, thrifty? So, Dr. Barney Nathan's back on the market. That's interesting."

"Don't tell me you're interested."

Cora shrugged. "It's been a lean year." She heaved herself to her feet. "Well, I think I'll go see what Chief Harper thinks of my nephew-did-it theory."

"You were just trying it out on me?" Becky said.

"Just seeing if you'd like him as a client. I gather you wouldn't mind."

"Not at all. But no one suspects him of anything."

Cora grinned. "Not yet."

EIGHTEEN

"GOOD NEWS, CHIEF."

"What's that?"

"The nephew's not nearly as good a suspect as you thought."

"I didn't think he was a suspect."

"Really?" Cora looked at him skeptically. "You didn't think he tried to poison his aunts and got the other guys by mistake?"

"No. Where'd you get that crazy idea?"

"I didn't. And for good reason. There's no money to inherit. And even if there was, there are closer living relatives. Do you know Alan has an older brother?"

"No, because I don't suspect him."

"Well, he does. And the aunts are not wealthy. The house is theirs, but it's in poor repair, and can't be worth that much money. Surely not enough to kill for."

"What are you talking about?"

"The idea that someone would bump off the Guilford sisters to get their hands on the house. I can't believe that nice young man would do that."

"I can't, either. In fact, it never crossed my mind."

"Really? How narrow *is* your scope on this, Chief? Is your whole investigation geared on identifying the corpse?"

"Not at all. The Guilford sisters had poison. I'm having it analyzed now."

"And if it matches the poison used to kill the lodger, you'll arrest them for the crime?"

"Of course not."

"Oh? Who *will* you arrest?"

"Oh, for Pete's sake!"

"No, I understand your feelings. Who but the Guilford sisters would have access to the poison? Except their nephew, of course. He could come and go, would know where the key was kept. I'm assuming the poison was locked up."

"It was in a potting shed."

"Was the shed locked?"

"Yes, it was."

"And who would have access to the key but a close relative? By the way, do you know what Alan's relationship to the Guilford sisters is?"

"He's their nephew."

"Yes, but who was his father?"

"I have no idea."

"Didn't think so. Anyway, Alan Guilford isn't *nearly* as good a suspect as he looks, since he doesn't stand to come into any money. Of course, he may not know that. He may look at the big house and think his aunts are loaded. He's really just a big kid.

"Of course, he wants to get married. That's always an interesting complication. I wonder if that affects the situation in any way. If it pleases the aunts. If it offends the aunts. If there's some provision in the aunts' will that upon their death he comes into some money, unless he's married, in which event the money goes to charity."

"Who in the world would write a provision like that?"

"Some unscrupulous lawyer. I know you can't imagine such a thing since the only lawyer around here is Becky Baldwin, who's straight as an arrow, but there are some pretty devious people in the world. Suppose someone wanted to get their hands on the aunts' money, and manipulated them into a situation where upon their death the bulk of their money would go to a charity that this unscrupulous person controlled?"

Harper blinked. "Run that by me again."

"It's perfectly easy. You want to get your hands on the aunts' money. You're drawing up their will. You write a provision whereby under certain circumstances the money will go to a dummy corporation, which is actually you."

"That seems incredibly convoluted."

"It's a simple situation. Alan comes into the money. Unless he's married. In which case the money goes to X. Lawyer controls X. Everything's fine until Alan decides to get married. Then the aunts have to go."

"That's ridiculous," Harper said.

"Why?"

"You said so yourself. Alan gets the money unless he's married. He's getting married. The lawyer's not going to bump the old ladies off now. He doesn't inherit. He's got to wait until Alan gets married, *then* bump the old ladies off."

"You're right, Chief. If the sisters die before Alan gets married, practically everybody loses out."

Harper frowned thoughtfully. "Except Alan."

NINETEEN

CHIEF HARPER OFFERED Alan Guilford a chair. "Thank you for stopping in."

"Glad to do it. I just don't know why. I already told you everything I know."

"There's a few loose ends I have to tie up. Very confusing crimes, aren't they? Two men poisoned, no apparent motive."

"It's definitely poison?"

"Oh, it's poison, all right. We're still on the fence about which one. It could be cyanide. It could be weed killer. Would it surprise you to learn your sweet aunts used to poison woodchucks?"

"Yes, it would."

"You didn't know they kept poison on the grounds?"

"I certainly did not."

"So if someone saw you going into the toolshed, it would not be to get the poison?"

Alan frowned. "Someone saw me going into the toolshed?"

"If someone did."

"You're saying someone did?"

"I'm saying if."

"Then I don't understand the question."

"Would that statement necessarily be erroneous?"

"Yes. I couldn't have done it. I wasn't there."

"See?" Harper said. "That wasn't so hard, now, was it?"

"It would have been a lot easier if you just asked me if I went in the toolshed."

"Did you go in the toolshed?"

"No."

Harper smiled. "See, that's a rather unsatisfactory exchange. For a police officer, I mean. Ask the question, get a one-word answer. Hard to judge anything from that. Whereas the other way, we had a whole conversation about the toolshed."

"With exactly the same result," Alan pointed out.

"True. But I got to watch your responses, size up your character. It wasn't wasted."

"Are you serious?"

"No. Some cop said that on television. It sounded better."

Alan threw up his hands. "Is everyone in this town mad? It's that Puzzle Lady, isn't it? Her zaniness rubs off on everybody. Did you really drag me down here just to joke about my aunts keeping poison in the toolshed?"

"No. I wanted to ask you about your relationship with them."

"It's friendly. I don't see them much. I'm hardly ever here."

"I meant your family relationship. How are you related? Are you their nearest relative? That sort of thing."

"Oh. Why?"

Harper took a breath. "If your aunts were to die, would their money come to you?"

Alan's eyes widened. "Oh. That's how you're thinking. Do I need a lawyer?"

"You have the right to an attorney."

"Yeah, yeah, I know the drill. You mean if someone were trying to kill my aunts, would I be a likely suspect?"

"Would you?"

"No. The idea is absurd."

"Let me put it another way. Are you their principal heir?"

"I have a brother. I'm not sure where he is. We're not close. He's older, if that makes any difference. I'm not even sure if he's still alive."

"What about your parents?"

"My father lost all his money on Wall Street, blew his brains out. My mother died a year later. Just wasted away. I dropped out of college. Never finished."

Harper nodded. "Are you familiar with the extent of your aunts' estate?"

"I think they own the house. I don't know. I don't think they're making much money."

"Do they approve of Arlene?"

"I think so. They're so sweet, it's hard to tell."

"Have they offered to pay for the ceremony? Hinted at a wedding gift to help you kids along?"

"You're way off base."

"Oh?"

"I have a job. Arlene has money. We're not hurting. We don't have to depend on the generosity of my aunts."

"Particularly if they weren't going to give you anything anyway," Harper observed. "You didn't sleep over at your aunts' house last night."

"You know that."

"When is the last time you did?"

"I don't remember."

"Try."

"I really can't recall."

"But you could if you wanted to?"

"What do you mean?"

"You have the run of the house?"

Alan said nothing.

"Do you have a key to the door?"

Alan frowned.

"I don't think I like this."

TWENTY

BECKY BALDWIN LOOKED up from her desk. "Why Mr. Guilford. What brings you here?"

The young man shrugged ruefully and grimaced, as if confessing to something embarrassing. "I think I need a lawyer."

Becky nodded judiciously. "When will you know for sure?"

Alan smiled. "I just had a long talk with Chief Harper."

Becky raised her eyebrows. "Oh?"

"It was not of my own volition. The chief seemed to feel he could get a line on the murders by investigating my family history."

"Really? Where would he get such an idea?"

"It's that Puzzle Lady person. That Cora Felton. She seems to think she has an insight into crime. Like some storybook detective who sits back and says enigmatic things and has people running around chasing extraneous facts and then at the end of the book makes it all make sense."

"You read a lot of detective fiction?"

"Enough. That nosey Miss Marple character, for instance. A lot like Cora Felton. Always one-up on the police."

"You think Cora Felton's one-up on the police?"

"I think she *thinks* she's one-up on the police. Anyway, Chief Harper's asking me all these questions about my marriage, which is really none of his business, particularly since the date isn't set yet. And you know women. Arlene's a little nervous about the fact the date isn't set, even though she's the one who balks at setting it. And if she's having a hard time naming a date for me, it's going to be ten times worse when it's a police officer asking for it. Anyway, he got all pushy, and I said, 'Do I need a lawyer?' and he said, 'You have the right to an attorney,' yada, yada, so I told him I wanted to consult you."

"And what does your fiancée think about that?"

"Why?"

"She didn't appear too smitten with me out at your aunts' house."

"She wasn't seeing you as an attorney."

"No kidding. And just what does Arlene do?"

"Why?"

"It's a typical lawyer question. We attorneys always ask it of prospective clients with significant others who hate us."

Alan smiled. "Wow. That was a mouthful. Are you this good in court?"

"Better. I usually know what I'm fighting. Look, you come in here, want me to defend you from some unspecified charge of which you have not been accused. Fine, I need the money. But if you want me to do it, I need to know what I'm dealing with. If Chief Harper's looking at you, he's going to look at your fiancée, particularly since she lives next door. I'm not trying to pry into your personal life, but what's she like?"

"Arlene's an actress. You know what that means in New York City. A waitress. Her parents died and left her a little money, so she doesn't have to do that anymore. They also left her the house. Which is how I got to know her. Which is funny. We're both from New York City, but we met here."

"What do you do, Mr. Guilford?"

"I freelance."

"At what?"

"Whatever I can get. Computer work. Proofreading. Stuff like that."

"You have an apartment in New York?"

"If you can call it that. I have a studio apartment the size of a broom closet. Don't tell the aunts, but I'm giving it up."

"Arlene's got room?"

"Oh, sure. It's a two-bedroom."

"She inherit the apartment?"

"No, it's a rental. There was a roommate, but she moved out. She was looking for another roommate, then she came into money and didn't have to."

"You're moving in?"

"When we go back to New York. We've actually been here for a while."

"You're staying at Arlene's house, but you don't want your aunts to know?"

"I'm old enough to have a girlfriend, and my aunts are old enough to disapprove. They're just so straight-laced. In that old house, and the way they dress. It's like they're straight out of an Agatha Christie novel. All prim and proper, with a body in the library. Poisoned. No trace of blood. A genteel sort of crime."

"Just a casual mystery reader?"

"I do like Agatha Christie."

Alan gave Becky the rundown of the family situation that he'd given Chief Harper. She didn't let on she knew most of it.

"So," Becky said. "You can't remember the last time you stayed in your aunts' house?"

"No, I can't. It was probably a few months ago. That's the best I can do."

"You have a key to the front door."

"I don't have a key to the garden shed."

"You'd know where it was kept. Look, Mr. Guilford—"

"Alan."

"I have trouble calling men who are engaged to be married by their first name."

"Even when there's no date set? As your friend Cora said, with no date set you don't have to think of it as an engagement."

Becky smiled. "You should have been a lawyer."

TWENTY-ONE

CORA STUCK HER head in the door of Becky's office. "Hear you got a client."

"Where did you hear that?"

"Actually, I saw him leave. I'm assuming he hired you. If he just tried to hit on you, I would say it spoke poorly of his engagement."

"There's some question about that, too."

"Oh?"

"He pointed out the date wasn't set. Don't worry, he gave you full credit for the idea."

"He *was* trying to hit on you?"

"He was flirting. Men flirt."

"But he hired you?"

"Yes, he did. I assume I have you to thank for that."

"Why, whatever do you mean?"

"It seems Chief Harper picked him up and grilled him as a suspect. I suppose you wouldn't know anything about that?"

"I have very little influence with the police. I'm sure Harper wouldn't arrest anyone on my say-so."

"No, of course not. Anyway, I got a client, so I owe you one. Unless he turns out to be guilty."

"Why, don't guilty clients pay?"

"Yeah, they do. It just doesn't look good on your record."

"It does if you get them off."

"That's just cynical."

"Oh, yeah? Look at Johnnie Cochran."

"He's dead."

"Well, aside from that. Anyway, I wouldn't sweat it. The chance of Alan being involved in this is practically negligible."

"I'm sure that's how you presented it to Chief Harper."

"I don't make the facts, I just report them. What the chief does is out of my hands. Anyway, aren't retainers nonrefundable?"

"Damn right they are."

"Then what have you got to worry about?"

Cora went down to the police station where Dan Finley was manning the desk.

"Hey, Dan, what's up?"

"Not much. Still waiting on the lab report. I called over there, but they're on lunch hour. Did you want to see the chief?"

"Is he in?"

"He went over to the Guilford house, to talk to the sisters. Don't think it was anything special. Just got antsy waiting for the lab."

"I know how he feels. If he comes in, give me a call."

Cora came out the front door and nearly bumped into Arlene on her way in.

Arlene was furious. "You! At the police station. I might have known."

Cora shrugged. "Why? Are you a psychic?"

"What the hell do you think you're doing?"

"I give up," Cora said. "What do I think I'm doing?"

"You accused my boyfriend of murder."

"Oh, that."

"You admit it?"

"*Accused* is such an ugly word. I don't believe I've accused anyone of anything."

"You told Chief Harper he's a suspect."

"That's not an accusation, just a statement of fact. He *is* a suspect. So are you, for that matter. If I tell Chief Harper, are you going to say I accused you?"

"Very funny. Now he's hired that Becky Baldwin. He thinks he needs protection."

"Oh. There's a Freudian slip. Nice double entendre."

"What?"

"Not very quick on your feet, are you? Most angry women aren't."

"Why are you meddling in my affairs?"

"Your affairs? I thought you said I accused Alan."

"I'm his fiancée."

"There seems to be some question about that."

"I beg your pardon?"

"Oh, don't worry. It's a matter of semantics."

"What?"

"It means words are involved. Granted, not your strong suit. Which would be youth and beauty. Of which you are not bad, by the way. Almost in Becky Baldwin's league. Of course, she's a lawyer, and you're not. Which is understandable. You probably had trouble with the bar exam."

"Oh, aren't you the laugh riot," Arlene said scathingly. "I guess that's what happens to women when they lose their sex appeal. They develop 'personality.'"

"That's better. Now you sound halfway intelligent. I bet with a little work you could have a personality, too."

Arlene offered a brief, pungent opinion of Cora's suggestion.

"Tell me," Cora said. "What do you see in Alan? Clearly, it's not the Guilford estate. You already have money. And he has none. Is he really such a catch?"

"You're rude and impertinent. And you're meddling. In matters that don't concern you. There have been a couple of accidental deaths, no big deal, but you've got to be the great and wonderful Puzzle Lady and drum up some conspiracy plot with Alan in the center of it just to make yourself seem important. And you're all wet."

"Is that right?"

"Yeah, that's right. Alan couldn't have poisoned those people. He was with me."

Arlene pushed by her in the front door.

Cora watched her go.

So. Alan was with Arlene at the time of the murder. Which made no sense, since there *was* no time of the murder. Not if the wine was poisoned. The killer could have poisoned it at any time. But Arlene had been eager to make that point.

And now Arlene was complaining about her to the cops. Chief Harper wasn't there, but Dan Finley would get an earful.

Cora didn't care.

She had bigger fish to fry.

TWENTY-TWO

DR. BARNEY NATHAN came out of his office into the waiting room and stopped dead.

Cora Felton sat on the couch.

"What are you doing here?"

Cora shrugged. "I'm sick."

"I'm not your doctor."

"How do you know?"

"Excuse me?"

"You could very well be my doctor. I just never happen to be sick."

"That's ridiculous."

"Actually, it is. My doctor is in the city. I've been with him for years. I see no reason to give him up. That's why I've never come to you."

"I thought it was because you didn't trust my work."

"Now, now, Barney. Just because I go after you in court doesn't mean I don't respect your work. If you make a mistake, I'm going to point it out. It's no reflection of you. It's a reflection on the state of medicine. The practice of which you know medically. If I disagree, that is usually based on *non*medical factors. Almost always, as I have no medical training. Anyway, I'm sick, you're here, I'm not driving to New York for a cold remedy. Come on, Doc, check me out."

Before Barney Nathan could object, she pushed by him through the door.

Cora had never been in the doctor's office before. It

was cozier than she'd expected, with an oak desk, cedar file cabinets, and wooden bookshelves bowed with massive medical tomes. The chairs for the doctor and patient, large and upholstered, gave the feeling of a den. An oak sideboard, closed, had an ice bucket on top. It hadn't occurred to her, but she wondered if the good doctor occasionally favored a nip.

"Say. Nice digs. This is where you sit the patient down, talk them out of being sick. Or deliver some momentous pronouncement—I'm sorry, ma'am, you have Monterey Fishman's disease."

"There's no such thing."

"Yeah, but the patient doesn't know that, and by the time they find out you've already Xeroxed their BlueCross BlueShield card and copied down their American Express card number."

Dr. Nathan was not amused. "Miss Felton, if you're not really sick, I'm rather busy."

"Really? I was the only patient in the waiting room."

"It's my lunch break. I was trying to close up the office."

"Don't worry, I'll be brief." Cora marched to a door on the side wall. "Is this the examining room?" She flung it open. "No, that's the bathroom. Must be this one. Ah! There we go."

It was a small examining room: stark, sterile, lit by fluorescent bulbs. A sink and cabinets along one wall. An examining table covered with paper on the other.

"Well," Cora said, "shall I get undressed?"

"That won't be necessary."

"Oh, come on. Don't be a killjoy. One of the joys of going to the doctor is you can take your clothes off in front of another man and it doesn't count as cheating."

Cora hopped up on the examining table. "I have a cold. I think it's settled down in my chest."

Dr. Nathan put on a stethoscope.

Cora unbuttoned the top two buttons of her blouse, pulled it open wider than could possibly be necessary. "Here, Doc. I hope it isn't cold."

Dr. Nathan ignored the open shirt, felt her forehead with the back of his hand. "Cool as a cucumber."

"I never understood that expression. Just how cold are cucumbers, anyway. If you ask me—"

Dr. Nathan stuck a digital thermometer in her mouth.

Cora clamped her lips around it, favored him with an I-wasn't-finished look.

"Let's get your blood pressure here."

He wrapped a cuff around her arm, took the bulb and pumped it up, released it and let the air out.

"Your blood pressure is a little high. For you, that's probably your normal state."

The digital thermometer beeped.

"Ninety-eight point six."

"For me that's high," Cora said.

"Your heart rate's a little accelerated."

"My pulse is always high at the doctor's. I'm afraid you might find something wrong."

"Let's check those lungs." He slipped the stethoscope under her shirt.

"Why, Doctor. We barely met."

"Breathe in, please."

Cora did so.

"And out."

She exhaled.

He listened to the other side, then lowered the stethoscope. "You smoke, don't you?"

"Why? What do you hear?"

"Nothing. Your lungs are fine."

"Then why did you say that?"

"Just an observation. You're lucky to have good lungs. You shouldn't abuse them." He looked at her closely. "There's nothing wrong with you. Why are you here? As far as the case goes, I'm sure Chief Harper told you everything I know. There's no reason for you to be here unless you're working on some angle to trip me up on the stand."

"That wasn't my intention."

"Oh, no? Becky Baldwin's got a client, doesn't she? The nephew. I don't know what you're trying to prove, but cut me a break, I'm not in the mood."

"Yeah, I know," Cora said.

"I beg your pardon?"

"I understand you're going through some hard times. Been there, done that. I know it's hell. I've been there four of five times, so I know how you feel. The first one's always the hardest. This is your first one, isn't it? I'm sorry, I don't mean to be personal, but you're not yourself lately, and I had to know why.

"First time I didn't handle it well. Drank too much. Chased after men. Your basic, self-destructive behavior. Anyway, you start feeling self-destructive, give me a call; I'll try to talk you down."

"I don't need your help."

"Of course not." Cora buttoned up her blouse. "I'm just saying, if you do, you know who to call."

TWENTY-THREE

CORA GOT IN her car and drove home. She went in the front door, was surprised to hear sounds coming from the living room. Her hand ventured into her drawstring purse, gripped the butt of her gun. She crept to the door of the living room, peered in.

Sherry was playing with Jennifer on the living room floor.

Sherry looked up, smiled. "Hi, Auntie Cora."

"I thought you were a burglar." Cora set her purse on the coffee table, flopped down on the couch.

"Say hi to Jennifer."

"I'll say hi to Jennifer. I don't need any prompting. Hi, Jennifer. You having fun on the carpet?"

"It's a little dirty. You might want to run the vacuum cleaner."

"I certainly would have if I'd known you were going to be hanging out on the floor. What are you doing at this end of the house?"

"Jennifer has to get used to it. I don't want my daughter growing up thinking this is the secret, forbidden place where wicked Aunt Cora lives."

"Great," Cora said. "You want to post a daily schedule so I'll know which room to clean?"

"It won't do much good when she's a toddler. She'll be everywhere."

"How soon can I look forward to that?"

"Don't be a killjoy. I thought you were impatient for her to walk."

"I was impatient for her to walk out there. In the grass. Which doesn't have to be vacuumed."

"No, but the leaves could use a raking."

"That sounds like a job for Daddy. If I were you, I'd ask him."

"He's at the paper. Writing about the murders. He's trying to find an angle that doesn't make you and Chief Harper look like total incompetents."

"He can write about the chief all he wants. It's got nothing to do with me."

"Except for the puzzles."

"The puzzles don't mean anything. They're just a red herring to keep the chief from finding the real killer."

"The real killer. You know who you sound like?"

"Rita Hayworth." Cora picked up her purse, pulled out a pack of cigarettes.

Sherry waggled her finger. "Uh-uh. You can't smoke around the baby."

Cora's eyes widened. "Oh. My. God. So *that's* your evil plan. That's why you're so keen on bringing the baby into this part of the house. So I won't be able to smoke."

"Well, you wouldn't want to set a bad example."

"I don't believe it. You had this kid to get me to stop smoking?"

"No. It's just one of the fringe benefits."

Cora shoved her cigarettes back in her purse.

On the coffee table were the folded pieces of paper Cora had dug out with her cigarettes.

Sherry picked them up. "What's this?"

"The sudoku. And the crossword. Chief Harper made a copy for me. I told him I'd already seen it, but he gave it to me anyway."

"Did you look it over?"

"I don't have to. It's the one you solved last night. Off the Internet. We know it doesn't mean anything."

Sherry unfolded the crossword, studied the puzzle. "This isn't the puzzle I solved last night."

"What?"

"It's a different puzzle."

"Hey, let me see that."

"You watch Jennifer. I'll check it out."

Sherry hopped up, ran out of the room.

"Hey!" Cora said. "What, taking care of a baby is supposed to make me nervous? Like there's something so tough about it. Well, Jennifer, you and Auntie Cora are going to get along just fine."

Jennifer burst into tears.

"Oh, for goodness' sake."

Cora hopped down off the couch, waggled a toy cat in Jennifer's direction. "Look at the kitty. Isn't she nice? Nice kitty, nice kitty."

Jennifer was having none of it.

"Not a cat lover, huh?"

There came a scrabbling at the side door.

"Oh, come on," Cora said. "How did Buddy get locked in the end?"

Cora knew immediately how the toy poodle had gotten locked in the end. Sherry had put him out there so the baby could play on the floor. On hearing Cora's singsong baby voice, he'd gone nuts, and was desperate to get in.

Cora picked up Jennifer, threw her over one shoulder, and struggled to her feet. She stumbled through the foyer to the breezeway that led to the addition, and managed to open the door before the little poodle tore it down.

Buddy came through like a rocket, circled the living

room, slammed to a stop in front of Cora, and sat, expecting a treat.

Jennifer giggled.

"That's better. Wanna give the puppy a treat? Let's give the puppy a treat. Except we don't have any treats, they're in the kitchen, here we go to the kitchen, umpty dumpty bumpty dumpty da di into the kitchen."

Jennifer began bawling again at being taken away from the dog. The fact that Buddy came along failed to mollify her.

Cora went into the kitchen, grabbed a handful of biscuits out of the box. Tried to figure out how to hand Buddy just one without dropping the baby. It would have been easy with three hands.

"Jennifer. Want to give the puppy a biscuit?"

Jennifer took the biscuit and put it in her mouth.

"No!" Cora yelled, pulling the baby's hand away.

The biscuit, however, remained in the mouth.

Cora threw the biscuits on the table, stuck her finger in Jennifer's mouth.

"What in the *world* are you doing?" Sherry demanded, from the doorway.

"She's got a biscuit in her mouth."

"You gave her a *dog* biscuit?"

"Not to eat."

Sherry took the baby, reached a little finger in, flicked the biscuit out. "What in the world were you thinking?"

"Hey, I was trying to deal with a baby and a dog. It's not easy. You couldn't do it. You locked the dog out."

"If you want to be a babysitter, you're going to need more practice."

"Who said I wanted to be a babysitter?"

"Every aunt wants to be a babysitter. It's what aunts are for."

"Good to know."

Cora followed Sherry back into the living room.

"The problem with the dog is, when she's on the floor he's on her level. Buddy's a nice dog, but he doesn't know any better not to jump on her and knock her down." Sherry sat on the couch, held Jennifer on her lap. "So if he's going to be in here, the baby's gotta be on the couch. Unless you're letting him up on the couch now."

"Of course not," Cora said. She remained standing, hoped Buddy wouldn't jump up. He'd taken to lying next to her.

"I found Harvey's puzzle." Sherry held out a sheet of paper. "Here. I printed you a copy."

ACROSS

1 Cake with a kick
5 Coffeehouse reading
9 Sacked out
14 Ltrs. near "0"
15 Up to it
16 "What hath God wrought?" sender
17 "North by ____"
19 Spectrum producer
20 Some auto-sticker listings
21 Org. with a noted journal
23 Uniform features: Abbr.
24 Stock unit
26 Sleep like ____
28 You can't take it with you
31 Church figure
35 Performed superbly
36 Explorer Tasman
37 "Puppy Love" singer
38 Pit yield
39 "____ and Old Lace"
42 Eight pts.
43 ____ out (barely made)
45 "The auld sod"
46 45 degrees, say
48 A bit
50 Brunch fare
51 He directed Marlon
52 Country's K.T.
54 June, to the Beaver
56 Lockout org. of 2011
58 Nicaraguan rebels
62 Hitting
64 Movie star, and clue to four answers in this puzzle
66 Jobs in computers
67 Ashtabula's waters
68 Ratio words
69 More steamed
70 Dirty Harry's law org.
71 Shot from the apron, perhaps

DOWN

1 Singer-turned-congressman Sonny
2 Each, slangily
3 A Bobbsey twin
4 Apt anagram for "Sinatra"
5 "Dances With Wolves" tribe
6 Needing a seatbelt extender, say
7 Raised rails
8 Intro to physics?
9 Classic Chevy
10 Scand. land
11 "____ Baby"
12 Flying "A" competitor of old
13 Many govs.
18 Chinese restaurant freebie
22 Bruno _____ (designer shoe brand)
25 Clemente in Cooperstown
27 ____ first-name basis
28 ____ Park, Colo.
29 Parade hat
30 "An Affair ____"
32 Coty or Clair
33 Pursue a puck
34 Whoppers
36 Home to many Georgians
40 Drying-out place
41 Compassionate
44 One of the orig. 13
47 Suffix with helio- or ethno-
49 Time for plowing, maybe
50 Was too sweet
53 Rx, for short
54 Physics measurement
55 "Beetle Bailey" pooch

57 Part of a dead man's hand
59 Diaper problem
60 Prefix with trust

61 Boarding place
63 Forum greeting
65 Comics bark

"What are you talking about?"

"That's the one Harvey solved. The one in the newspaper. The one that appeared in the Hartford paper on September seventeenth."

"I thought you already found it."

Sherry shook her head. "No. That's where I made a mistake. It's a syndicated column. But it's an evening paper. It doesn't print the puzzle that comes out on the morning of the seventeenth. It prints the puzzle that comes out on the morning of the eighteenth. Of course most people *get* the paper on the morning of the eighteenth, but it's still dated the seventeenth."

"You're saying the puzzle you found online isn't the puzzle Harvey solved?"

"No. This is the puzzle Harvey solved. And it's kind of interesting. Here, take a look."

Cora looked up from the puzzle. "It's not solved."

"Oh. Sorry. Here's the solution."

Sherry passed it over.

```
 B  A  B  A  ▮  P  O  E  M  ▮  I  N  B  E  D
 O  P  E  N  ▮  A  B  L  E  ▮  M  O  R  S  E
 N  O  R  T  H  W  E  S  T  ▮  P  R  I  S  M
 O  P  T  I  O  N  S  ▮  A  M  A  ▮  N  O  S
 ▮  S  T  E  E  R  ▮  A  L  O  G  ▮
 E  S  T  A  T  E  ▮  O  R  G  A  N  I  S  T
 S  H  O  N  E  ▮  A  B  E  L  ▮  A  N  K  A
 T  A  R  ▮  A  R  S  E  N  I  C  ▮  G  A  L
 E  K  E  D  ▮  E  I  R  E  ▮  A  C  U  T  E
 S  O  M  E  W  H  A  T  ▮  C  R  E  P  E  S
 ▮  E  L  I  A  ▮  O  S  L  I  N  ▮
 M  O  M  ▮  N  B  A  ▮  C  O  N  T  R  A  S
 A  T  B  A  T  ▮  C  A  R  Y  G  R  A  N  T
 S  T  E  V  E  ▮  E  R  I  E  ▮  I  S  T  O
 S  O  R  E  R  ▮  S  F  P  D  ▮  C  H  I  P
```

"Let's see. What are the theme entries. 'BRING-ING UP.' 'TO REMEMBER.' 'NORTHWEST.' 'CARY GRANT.' Oh! They're Cary Grant movies. *Bringing up Baby. An Affair to Remember. North by Northwest.* Right?"

"Right. And the one that matters—"

"Don't tell me. I can do it. *Bringing up Baby.* That's you. Though you'll be happy to know I don't really sus-pect you. *An Affair to Remember.* That's Becky Baldwin and Alan Guilford."

Sherry blinked. "What?!"

"Yeah, I sort of maneuvered Alan into retaining her to defend him from murder."

"You what?"

"Well, Becky needs the money, and he is the most likely suspect."

"Why?"

"All right, he isn't the most likely suspect. But I managed to get Chief Harper to at least consider him."

"Why in the world would you do that?"

"I kind of wanted him to hire Becky."

"You're going around again. Why did you want him to hire Becky?"

"Oh. His girlfriend pissed me off."

"What?"

"I'm not sure he should marry her. He really ought to think it over."

"You're trying to break up his marriage?"

"He's not married. It's an engagement. They haven't even set the date. He seems a nice sort. There's no reason he should get stuck with the wrong girl."

"You're pimping Becky Baldwin?"

"Oh. It's all right when *you* use words like that in front of the baby. Jennifer, just pretend you didn't hear that. Your aunt Cora is not a procurer. But you gotta feel sorry for Becky. I mean, here you are with a kid, happily married to her high school sweetheart. It's time the girl got a break."

"I'm surprised you're not snapping him up yourself."

"Who do you think I am, Demi Moore?"

Sherry took a breath. "Aren't you interested in the puzzle? You're ignoring the main clue."

"I am? Let's see. *North by Northwest*. That's our direction from New York. No. We're northeast."

"Oh, for goodness' sake. I mean the one in the middle."

"The one in the middle? What do you mean, the one in the middle?"

"The theme answer in the middle of the puzzle."

Cora looked. "'Arsenic'? Oh, for goodness' sake. *That's* why Chief Harper said *if* it was cyanide."

"He said what?"

"I was telling him the puzzle didn't mean anything, and he said if the answer was cyanide maybe it would. I had no idea what he was talking about because I hadn't seen this puzzle, but he meant if it was cyanide instead of arsenic. Then his remark makes sense." Cora frowned. "Damn it, he's right. Arsenic doesn't fit. Cyanide would. So the puzzle really doesn't mean anything. All right, what's the clue?"

Cora picked up the questions, read, "'_____ and Old Lace.'"

Her eyes widened and her mouth fell open.

The phone rang.

Cora nearly jumped a mile, and uttered an ejaculation not entirely appropriate for a preschooler.

"Cora!"

Cora raced into the kitchen, snatched the phone off the wall. "Yes!"

"Hey, don't bite my head off," Chief Harper said. "I got the report back from the lab."

"Was it cyanide?"

"There was cyanide, but it wasn't the only poison."

"What else was there?"

"There was also arsenic and strychnine. In significantly greater quantities."

"Let me guess. Two parts arsenic to one part strychnine to just a pinch of cyanide."

"Yes. How did you know?"

"Tell me, did they analyze the wine?"

"Of course they analyzed the wine. The poison was in the wine."

"No, not the poison. I mean the wine itself. Did they analyze the wine?"

"Why?"

"Bet you it's elderberry," Cora said, and hung up.

TWENTY-FOUR

CHIEF HARPER WAS on the phone when Cora came in. He hung up and said, "I've been trying to reach you."

"Here I am."

"What made you think it was elderberry wine?"

"Was it?"

"You know it was."

"I do now."

"What made you think it was?"

"*Arsenic and Old Lace.*"

"Huh?"

"It was in the damn puzzle Harvey solved. I never saw it because Sherry got the dates wrong."

"What?"

"Sherry went on the Internet, found an archive that had that date's puzzle, and printed it out. Only it was the wrong date, so it was the wrong puzzle, so I never knew until I looked at the one you gave me. That's why I didn't understand when you said it might mean something if it had said cyanide. You never said *instead of arsenic.*"

"I don't get it. Just because there's more arsenic than cyanide, now you think the puzzle means something?"

"No, because it's two parts arsenic to one part strychnine to a pinch of cyanide."

"What the hell are you talking about?"

"*Arsenic and Old Lace.* It's a Cary Grant movie in the puzzle. And it's *featured* in the puzzle. Arsenic is dead center. Didn't you see the movie?"

"No."

"You never saw *Arsenic and Old Lace*?"

"Hey, don't make a federal case of it. I never went to the movies much when I was young."

"Well, you wouldn't have gone to this one. It came out before you were born. At least, I hope it did. My God, are we that old?"

"Cora."

"*Arsenic and Old Lace* is a movie based on a stage play, which is set in a rooming house run by two little old ladies who have a habit of poisoning their guests. They prey on little old men, preferably widowers."

"You mean…?"

"Exactly. Cary Grant plays the nephew, who's about to get married—any of this starting to sound familiar?—until he suddenly finds out his sweet little old aunts have been blithely poisoning people. He confronts them with it, but they not only show no remorse, they're proud of what they've done, and they describe their recipe: two parts arsenic, one part strychnine, and a pinch of cyanide."

"My God!"

"And they put it in elderberry wine because they find it disguises the taste."

"Are you telling me the aunts are copying the movie?"

"Don't be silly. Why would they want to do that?"

"Then what *are* you saying?"

"Life is copying art. I don't know why. I don't know who. But it is."

"Cary Grant is a good guy?"

"Cary Grant is *always* a good guy."

"So Alan Guilford is innocent."

"Oh, for goodness' sake, Chief. Let's not confuse the

picture with reality. It's not like you could rent the movie and figure out who did it. There's just certain similarities."

"Who did it in the movie?"

"I told you. The aunts did it. They poisoned thirteen people."

"Thirteen?"

"They poisoned everybody. Except Mr. Spenalzo."

"Who's Mr. Spenalzo?"

"The body in the window seat."

"There was a body in the window seat?"

"Of course there was. That's why the killer got the drunk to climb in and take poison."

"Mr. Spenalzo?"

"Yes."

"But the aunts didn't kill the body in the window seat?"

"No. Well, actually they killed the other body in the window seat."

"There's *another* body in the window seat?"

"It's a comedy, Chief. People keep going in and out, swapping bodies. So every time Cary Grant looks in the window seat there's another body."

"Every time?"

"Well, actually it's only twice. But that's enough to get his attention."

"Wait a minute. Wait a minute. Who killed the body in the window seat?"

"Which body?"

"The one the aunts didn't."

"Cary Grant's crazy brother."

"He has a crazy brother?"

"Yes. Who looks like Boris Karloff."

Chief Harper's mind was melting. "Why does he look like Boris Karloff?"

"In the play he *was* Boris Karloff. Which probably helped. In the movie he's Raymond Massey, but they made him up to look like Boris Karloff."

"Why?"

"Oh. Because he's a criminal and the cops are after him so Peter Lorre keeps giving him a new face."

"Peter Lorre?"

"Yeah. Jonathan's partner. He's a plastic surgeon."

"Who's Jonathan?"

"Boris Karloff."

Chief Harper blinked. "And how does any of this make any sense?"

"It doesn't. That's what's great about it."

"You'll pardon me if I don't share your enthusiasm. We have two real-life murders here. How in the world are they connected to a movie made fifty years ago?"

"It's nearly seventy, Chief, but who's counting."

Harper rubbed his head. "Hang on a minute. This crazy Boris Karloff brother. Is he the older or the younger?"

"Older. Why?"

"Well, Alan's got an older brother."

"Great. Get him in here, see if he looks like Boris Karloff."

"That's not what I meant."

"Yeah, but now that I mention it, you can't get the idea out of your head, right?"

"Damn it." Harper took a breath. "Tell me, did this movie have a crossword puzzle in it?"

"No. It didn't have a sudoku, either. Of course, seventy years ago there weren't any."

"And nobody killed the town drunk?"

"Well, I can't speak for Spenalzo. He might have been known to hoist a few."

"Can you point out any other discrepancies between our murders and the movie?"

"Sure. The aunts' other crazy nephew doesn't live with them, blow his bugle and shout, "Charge!" as he runs up the stairs."

"He does in the movie?"

"Yeah. He thinks he's Teddy Roosevelt. You really ought to see this movie, Chief."

"I can hardly wait. What else?"

"You mean different? The girl. Arlene. In the movie, the girl Cary Grant's engaged to lives with her father, who's a minister. Arlene's an orphan, lives alone, and Alan spent the night."

Dan Finley stuck his head in the door. "Excuse me, Chief. Henry Firth's on the phone."

"What's Ratface want?" Cora said.

Dan tried to stifle a grin, but couldn't help snickering. "Sorry, Chief." To Cora he explained, "I promised the chief not to be amused when you degrade the county prosecutor."

"I imagine that would be hard," Cora said.

"What's he want?" Harper said.

"He wants to know how come we suddenly got three poisons in the case, and why you're telling the guys at the lab what type of wine they're testing."

"I suppose that's my fault," Cora said.

Dan was shocked. "You added poison to the wine?"

"No. I told them it was elderberry."

"How did you know that?"

"It's from the movie, *Arsenic and Old Lace*. The crime's just like the movie."

"Oh, my God, you're right!" Dan said. "You mean the aunts are guilty?"

"You've seen the movie?" Harper said.

"Everyone's seen the movie."

"I haven't seen the movie."

"Better bone up, Chief," Cora said, "if you're going to talk to Ratface."

TWENTY-FIVE

THE COUNTY PROSECUTOR Henry Firth was somewhat conflicted. Cora Felton's courtroom antics had often made him look foolish. On the other hand, his rather impressive conviction record was largely due to those antics. Not to mention the fact that Cora had often saved him embarrassment by steering him in the right direction when he was prosecuting the wrong person. Not that she couldn't have slipped him a nod and a wink *outside* the courtroom, rather than show him up in public, and often on TV. In short, if Cora Felton had not existed, Henry Firth would not have created her. He would have been quite content to go about his merry way, prosecuting the cases as he saw fit. And in the long run, he was sure, that reputation for figuring out the tough cases that Cora Felton now had, would be his. Not that he was jealous, or bitter, or resentful. Nonetheless, Chief Harper's association with Cora Felton had put a strain on their relationship. Often he had found himself second-guessing the chief, and wondering if the opinion the officer was expressing was actually his own.

In this case, he was certain. "This is Cora's doing, isn't it?" Before Chief Harper could reply, Firth said, "Of course it is. Asking the crime lab if the poison was in a certain type of wine. I bet you don't even know the different types of wine."

"I can tell the whites from the reds."

"I'm impressed. You want to tell me how Cora Felton knows what type of wine we're dealing with?"

"You're not going to like it."

"I hate it already. What gives?"

Chief Harper told the prosecutor about *Arsenic and Old Lace*. Not having seen the movie, his description was suspect at best, but Henry Firth, who hadn't seen it, either, knew no better.

"In the movie, the poison was in the wine?"

"So I understand."

"And Cora assumes a connection?"

"That's right."

"Only—and forgive me if I'm wrong—but the wine being…what was the type?"

"Elderberry."

"Right. The wine being elderberry—was a supposition on her part. It wasn't the wine being elderberry that made her think this was like the movie. She thought this was like the movie, and therefore asked if it was that type of wine."

"That's right."

"So what made her think that?"

"You're not going to like this."

"You keep saying that. And you keep being right. Just give me the bad news."

"It was in a crossword puzzle."

"Of course." Henry Firth shook his head. "And where did she get this crossword puzzle? Was it in the pocket of the corpse?"

"No."

"Well, where was it?"

"It was found in the bushes right where the sister's nephew, Alan, was apprehended sneaking around the grounds on the night of the murder."

"Apprehended?" Henry Firth raised his eyebrows. "I was not aware anyone had been arrested for this crime. Since I would be prosecuting such a person, I would be apt to be informed."

"Sorry, sir. Sam Brogan found him prowling around in the bushes at four in the morning and brought him inside. He had a reasonable story, so he wasn't arrested."

"And Sam found a crossword puzzle in the bushes?"

"That's right."

"Was it a computer printout?"

"No. It was a Puzzle Lady puzzle in a newspaper."

Henry Firth's eyes narrowed. "Worse and worse. Cora Felton predicted the type of wine based on something she read in the crossword puzzle that she wrote herself?"

"I admit that sounds bad."

"How the hell did she know to put the crime in the crossword puzzle? I'm assuming this happened before the murders."

"Well, actually…"

"Actually?"

"It wasn't the *Gazette*. It was a Hartford paper from 2005."

Henry Firth stared at him. "A Hartford paper from 2005 predicted the type of wine the poison was in?"

"No, it just named the movie in which it happened."

"And who was the killer in the movie?"

"Two sweet old ladies who run a rooming house."

"Does that mean the aunts are guilty?"

"And another crazy nephew."

"A crazy nephew. And is there a crazy nephew?"

"There's another nephew. I'm not aware of his mental state, but he seems to be out of the picture."

"Wonderful. Tell me, aside from this movie, do you have any significant leads in the case?"

"I'd like to say yes."

Firth groaned. "Great." He pointed his finger at the chief. "I'll tell you one thing. You better make damn sure news of this doesn't leak out."

TWENTY-SIX

"Murder in Bakerhaven!" Rick Reed proclaimed. "In a bizarre twist, the murders in Bakerhaven turn out to be a case of life imitating art!"

Rick paused after that pronouncement, as if for emphasis, but actually because he was unsure if he'd said it right or the other way around. No one on the TV crew was waving at him, so he forged ahead. "That's right, ladies and gentlemen, the murders in Bakerhaven, unusual as they are, could have come straight out of that classic Cary Grant movie, *Arsenic and Old Lace*. In the movie, Cary Grant's aunts run a boardinghouse, and cheerfully poison elderly widowers they feel are lonely. The resemblances to the movie are eerie. In both cases the poison is a mixture of arsenic, strychnine, and cyanide, administered in elderberry wine. The Guilford sisters protest their innocence, and claim while they might have served the elderberry wine, they had no idea where it came from, they just found it in the carafe."

The picture cut to a shot of Charlotte Guilford with a microphone shoved in her face. "We just found it in the carafe."

The camera cut back to Rick, who cocked his head knowingly, as if to say, there you are. "The sisters are here today due to the fact they do not drink."

Rick let that sobering thought lie there a moment, then said, "Police Chief Dale Harper could not be reached for comment, but if you want to know more about the crime, perhaps Cary Grant can help you. The movie, again, is *Arsenic and Old Lace.* I would assume there will be a huge run on Netflix. This is Rick Reed, Channel Eight News."

TWENTY-SEVEN

DAN FINLEY CRADLED the phone receiver to his chest, made a face, and held up his free hand in the universal keep-it-down gesture.

Cora, who'd just come in the police station front door, stopped and mouthed, "What's the matter?"

"He's not in a good mood," Dan whispered.

"Because you tipped off Rick Reed?"

Dan grimaced. "Henry Firth didn't want to let the news out."

"So, he's pissed. For a district attorney, that's part of the job description. They're better pissed."

"That's not all," Dan said.

"Oh?"

"You should hear it from him. Then it won't be my fault for telling you."

Cora went down the hall to Chief Harper's office, stuck her head in the door.

Harper was also on the phone. "Okay, thanks," he said, and slammed it down. He picked up a pencil, made a notation on a pad of paper.

"Hi, Chief. How's it going?" Cora announced cheerfully.

Harper raised one eye from the paper to glare at her.

"That good, eh? What happened?"

He held up one finger. "If this winds up in the paper," he warned.

"It won't come from me. Of course, if they're quoting Rick Reed…"

"Dan Finley will be looking for another job. I've had enough of these news leaks."

"I'm sure you have. You mind telling me what it is I'm not leaking?"

Harper sighed. "The couple took off."

"What couple?"

"The couple from the Guilfords'. The ones I didn't drag in and interrogate. Because they agreed not to check out."

"They checked out?"

"They took off. Didn't tell a soul. Went out for a drive and never came back. I'm checking car rental companies for rentals that came back early."

"You have the license number?"

"No, I *don't* have the license number. I didn't *take* the license plate number. I was dealing with suspicious relatives found in the bushes with crossword puzzles. The couple was unimportant. Until they took off."

"They're unimportant now, Chief. They're married, and not to each other. They're scared to death of having to make a statement and give their names."

"I know that. You think I don't know that? They're not a lead. They're a loose end I have to tie up. So some unscrupulous defense attorney—and God forbid Becky Baldwin should fall into that category—can't trot them out as reasonable doubt and get a killer off. In the event that happens, I don't want to live in the same town as Henry Firth."

"Chief. If you'll pardon me saying so, you're spending a lot of effort protecting your backside when the attack isn't coming from the rear. You rent the video yet?"

"No, I have not had time to rent the video."

"That's a shame. It would tell you what to look out for."

"You mean like suspects skipping out?"

"They're not suspects. They're a red herring. Don't waste your time on them."

"There's no such thing as red herrings, except in fiction."

"The movie *is* fiction."

"Huh?"

"Did you think it was a documentary? Some writer made it up."

"Yeah, but he didn't kill these people. A killer did. A flesh-and-blood killer. And I have to track him down."

"Bad pronoun, Chief."

"What?"

"Assuming the killer's male. Particularly in this case. In the movie, most of the killings are done by the women."

"You want to see a murder done by a man? Keep taunting me about this damn movie."

"I'm not taunting you. I'm just saying, now that it's been on TV and everyone's talking about the movie, it would behoove you to know something about it."

"I got more important things to do."

"Yeah. Tracing two people who've got nothing to do with anything. Look, if you're not going to watch the movie, at least take some advice from someone who has."

"That would be you?"

"Well, I'm right here. You don't even have to pick up the phone."

"Fine. What's your great advice?"

"You probably ought to dig up the cellar."

"What?"

"The Guilford cellar. You ought to dig it up."

"Why?"

"Because that's where the bodies are buried."

TWENTY-EIGHT

CHIEF HARPER WAS giving a good impression of a man who'd been kidnapped. He sat in the front seat of Dan Finley's cruiser, arms folded, mouth clamped in a firm line.

Cora Felton, on the other hand, had the triumphant look of an officer who'd bagged a perp. She sat in the backseat and kept quiet. Having made the sale, she saw no reason to prod the chief, for fear he might change his mind.

Dan Finley had no such restraint. "This is a good idea, Chief. After all, it's been on the news. You wanna check it out before some clown takes it into his head to do it himself."

"And *why* was it on the news?" Chief Harper snapped.

"Water under the bridge," Dan said. "Just because you didn't think to clamp the lid on the story is no reason to beat yourself up."

Harper smoldered in silence. Cora could practically see the steam coming up from his head. She prayed Dan Finley would shut up and drive.

"I don't suppose the missing couple is buried in the basement," Dan said.

Cora would have kicked him if she'd been in the front seat.

Dan pulled into the Guilford driveway, killed the motor.

Chief Harper didn't move. "I feel like a fool."

"You're not a fool," Cora said. "You're the chief of police. There's a subtle difference."

Dan Finley was already on his way up the walk.

Harper got out of the car and trailed along behind.

Cora brought up the rear, as if, left to his own devices, Chief Harper might suddenly make a run for it.

Edith Guilford opened the door. "Why, Chief Harper. And your young officer. And Cora Felton. Do come in, let me make you some tea."

"That won't be necessary," Harper said.

"Nonsense, everyone needs their tea. Charlotte, we have company."

There was no answer.

"Maybe she went out," Dan Finley said. "There's no car in the drive."

"Oh, yes. She was going to the store. Well, come in, come in. I'm a big girl, I can handle the tea myself." Edith led them into the kitchen, looked around. "Now where did Charlotte put that teakettle?"

"It's on the stove," Dan Finley said.

"Oh, so it is." Edith grabbed it, took it to the sink. "I'm so sorry about that couple, but they didn't check out. If Charlotte hadn't gone in to make up the bed, we never would have known."

"That was right before you called?" Chief Harper said.

"Well, not right before. There was some talk about what we should do. I said, 'Chief Harper told those people to stay and if they're gone he should know.'"

"It was today they left, not last night?"

"No, the bed was slept in. Well, at least it was unmade." Edith blushed, perhaps considering why people might use the bed and not spend the night. "You don't think anything's happened to them?"

"Not at all. They probably just didn't want to be questioned."

Edith lit the burner, put the kettle on.

"If you don't mind," Chief Harper said, "while you're making tea, we'd like to check out the cellar."

"The cellar?" Edith said. "For goodness' sake, why would you want to look down there?"

"Don't you watch television?" Dan said.

"Oh, no, we don't have a television. Some of the guests complain, but most of them like it. Makes it easier to get away from it all. Why do you ask?"

"When's the last time you used the cellar?"

"We never use it. It's just a dank, empty cellar. You can't store anything down there because of the moisture. It's not insulated. And there's just a dirt floor."

Dan Finley nudged Chief Harper in the ribs. "Dirt floor."

The chief ignored him, said, "When's the last time you were down there?"

"I really can't remember."

"Within the last two weeks?"

"Oh, no. There's nothing down there I need, so I never go there."

"What about your sister?"

"She doesn't use it, either."

"Perhaps her recollection would be better."

"Perhaps, but I don't know how it will help you. It's surely been years."

"Then you won't mind if we take a look."

"Oh, of course not. As long as you're not going to judge us by what's down there. I can't imagine what you'll find."

"Me, either," Dan said.

Harper gave him a dirty look. "Where's the stairs?"

"Oh. Right through the pantry." Edith pointed through an archway to a small room lined with cupboards.

"There's no door," Dan said.

"It's on the wall to your right."

"You were hoping some cupboard unit pulled open, weren't you?" Cora whispered to Dan.

Harper opened the door. Rough wooden stairs led into the darkness below. "Where's the light switch?"

"Oh, I'm sorry," Edith said. "There's no light switch."

"There's no lights?" Chief Harper said, dryly.

"There's a bare bulb hanging. You have to pull the string."

"From down there?"

"Yes." Edith smiled. "You see why we don't use the cellar. It's really a nasty place."

"I don't suppose you have a flashlight."

"I think I do. I wonder where Charlotte put it."

"Oh, for goodness' sake," Cora said. "Here I come to save the day." She fished a cigarette lighter out of her drawstring purse, and pushed by Chief Harper onto the top step. "Count yourself lucky I haven't stopped smoking."

The flame from the lighter didn't show much. Just the raw wooden planks the stairs were made of. And the rickety-looking handrail jerry-rigged out of two-by-fours.

"Okay," Cora said. "Hold on to the rail but don't lean on it, and watch your step. I don't want a few hundred pounds of policeman crashing down on me."

"Thanks a lot," Harper said.

"I meant the two of you."

Cora held the lighter ahead of her, picked her way carefully down the stairs.

Halfway down it went out.

"Do that again and you'll have to marry me," Cora said.

"Chief!" Dan said. "What did you do?"

"I didn't do anything," Harper said irritably. "She's trying to get my goat."

"You brought a goat down here, Chief?" Cora said. "I'm not sure that's wise."

"Did your lighter just run out of fuel?"

"I don't know. Let's make this simple home test."

Cora spun the dial. Flame shot up for a brief instant, illuminating the ceiling of the basement.

"I think I saw it," Cora said.

"Saw what?"

"The lightbulb. I can't see it anymore, but I know where it is. Okay, cover me, men, I'm going in."

"Will you stop horsing around."

"Oh, come on, Chief. It's a situation that practically calls for horsing around. Anyway, I'm almost at the bottom."

Cora stepped off the last step. "It's a dirt floor, all right, and pretty uneven. I think the lightbulb's right ahead of me."

Cora took a step toward it. The flame went out as she pitched forward with a short, profane yelp.

"My God! What happened?" Harper said.

"I fell in a hole."

"What?"

"Fell in a hole. Fell in a hole. What part of *fell in a hole* don't you understand?"

"You fell in a hole?"

"There you go. Come on, give me a hand, will you?"

"Where are you?"

"Over here."

"You wanna light the lighter?"

"I *dropped* the lighter. Get me out of here. I'll find the light switch."

"There is no light switch," Dan Finley said.

"The cord. Whatever the hell turns on the light."

"I got you," Dan said. "Here, take my hand."

Dan grabbed Cora, pulled her out. "That's not a very deep hole."

"Hey, it's not like I couldn't get out of it myself. I just didn't want to crawl out on my hands and knees in the dark. Okay, the cellar door's there. Assuming there's no more holes, the lightbulb is right about here."

Cora picked her way in the dark, testing each footstep before she put her weight on it. She flailed her arms, batted the string.

"Aha!"

"You got it?"

"No, but I hit it. It was right here somewhere. And… there we go!"

Cora pulled the string.

The lightbulb came on. It was low wattage, probably a sixty, but after the pitch-darkness that had engulfed them, it was like a spotlight.

Cora looked at the hole she'd fallen in.

She gasped.

As Dan said, it wasn't really deep. But by the dirt piled along one side, and the spade stuck into the ground at one end, there was no doubt what it was.

It was a freshly dug grave.

Attached to the shovel was a sudoku.

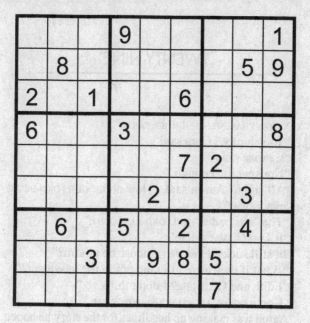

TWENTY-NINE

"GUILFORD BASEMENT MURDER FARM."

"Too clunky," Cora said.

"MURDER FARM."

"Not specific enough."

"All right," Aaron said. "How about GUILFORD HOUSE MURDER FARM?"

"That's as bad as GUILFORD BASEMENT."

"It's one fewer syllable."

"It still sucks. How can a house be a farm?"

"What if they were growing pot in the basement?"

"Edith and Charlotte? I don't think so."

"Come on. GUILFORD HOUSE POT FARM."

Aaron was making up headlines for the story he hoped to write if the police uncovered anything. If they did, Aaron wouldn't know it because Chief Harper had booted Cora out of there right after they found the grave. Which, in Cora's opinion, was somewhat high-handed. After all, she was the one who found it. Granted, by falling in it, but still.

Nonetheless, the lid was on tight. The Chief had booted Cora, called in Sam Brogan, who wasn't happy about it—no surprise there, there was very little Sam *was* happy about—and Chief Harper, Dan Finley, and Sam Brogan were digging up the basement.

Before he kicked her out, Chief Harper had read Cora the riot act, which killed Aaron because he was family, and because he had promised not to go, a promise he made grudgingly in order to get her to open up. Banned from the house till the news broke, Aaron was working on a story in case it did. He had already banged out a draft on his laptop. If bodies were forthcoming, he was good to go.

"You gotta remember you're talking front-page headline," Cora said. "Banner headline. Less is more. A single word could be really effective."

"What single word?"

Cora made a face. "That's the problem. You've already got MURDER. You've already got POISON. You've already got a second killing. A new angle's hard."

"Could I run the sudoku?"

Cora grimaced. "That's tricky. Chief Harper hasn't even seen it yet. The solution, I mean."

"Well, there you are. Can't you drive out there and give it to him?"

"He figured I'd do that. He told me not to."

"He doesn't want to see it?"

"It's not urgent. It doesn't mean anything anyway."

"Are you sure?"

"See for yourself."

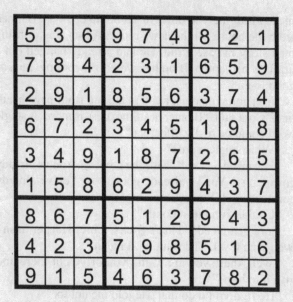

5	3	6	9	7	4	8	2	1
7	8	4	2	3	1	6	5	9
2	9	1	8	5	6	3	7	4
6	7	2	3	4	5	1	9	8
3	4	9	1	8	7	2	6	5
1	5	8	6	2	9	4	3	7
8	6	7	5	1	2	9	4	3
4	2	3	7	9	8	5	1	6
9	1	5	4	6	3	7	8	2

Aaron picked it up, looked it over.

"So what does it mean?" Cora said.

"I have no idea."

"Exactly."

Cora and Aaron were in the living room of the new addition. With modern, stainless steel furniture, more like a company reception area than a living room, it was a space rarely used. Sherry was usually upstairs with the baby, or in the living room of the old house, the latter too often for Cora's liking. Jennifer was a cute kid, of course, but babies could be boring, particularly when they hadn't learned to walk or talk yet.

Sherry came in with the baby, said, "What are you doing here?"

"Daddy's making up gruesome headlines for his newspaper story. If you heard some of them, you'd divorce him."

"You wrote the story already?" Sherry said.

"Two versions," Aaron told her.

"Two?"

"One version if they find a dead body. Another if they find more than one."

"That's pretty ghoulish," Sherry said. She put Jennifer down on the wood floor. The baby immediately took off for the fireplace.

"This room is not childproof," Aaron said.

"I'm watching her," Sherry said. "You think I'm not watching her?"

Buddy, who'd been sleeping under the couch, jumped up and ran to the baby.

Sherry picked Jennifer up.

"Why do you do that?" Cora said. "You'll make her afraid of dogs."

"She's too little to play with one."

"Buddy wouldn't hurt her."

"What if she pulls his tail?"

"She'd have to catch it first."

"If you want her to meet the dog, we have to have a supervised meeting, where we're all paying attention and Daddy isn't writing newspaper headlines."

"Don't be silly," Cora said. "Daddy will *always* be writing newspaper headlines."

Sherry sat on the couch, bounced Jennifer on her knee. Jennifer giggled appreciatively. "How will you know if they found anything?" Sherry said.

"Chief Harper will call me."

"Really? Then why did he boot you out of there?"

"He couldn't let me stay. It wouldn't look good."

"When has he ever cared how things looked?"

"He's keeping it quiet. He doesn't want any publicity if he can help it."

"Then he won't call you."

"He'll call me."

"In time to do Aaron any good? Dan Finley's going to tip off Rick Reed. Who's tipping you off?"

"She's got a point," Aaron said. "If I'm going to be a good boy and not go out there. Suppose they already found a body?"

"There's no body," Cora said. "If there was, it would have been in the grave."

"Yeah, if it's the only grave down there. If we're talking murder farm…"

"You're really stuck on that headline."

"Yeah, but he's right," Sherry said. "If they're finding bodies down there, he needs to know."

"Okay," Cora said. "I'll drive out there. If there's an EMS unit, we'll know it's pay dirt."

"What will you do then?"

"I'll come back and tell you."

"You can't call me?"

"I don't have a phone."

"I'll give you mine."

"The hell you will. I'll lose it, or I won't figure out how to dial it."

"Okay, I'll drive out there."

"I promised Chief Harper I wouldn't say anything. If you do, he'll know I did."

"He won't even know. I'll just drive by."

"With my luck, he'll be outside when you do." Cora heaved herself up from the couch. "There's an easier way."

Cora went into the new kitchen. Like the living room, it was gleaming bright and barely used. Like the old kitchen, it had a phone on the wall.

Cora called information, got the phone number for Dr. Nathan, punched it in.

The receptionist answered. "Dr. Nathan's office."

"Dr. Nathan, please."

"Did you want to make an appointment?"

"No, I just want to talk to him."

"Who's calling, please?"

"Cora Felton."

"Just a moment."

Cora was on hold.

Moments later, Barney Nathan's voice came over the line. "Hello?"

"Barney. Cora. Still in the office?"

"Actually, I'm with a patient. Why?"

"Didn't mean to bother you. Just wanted to know if you were okay."

There was a pause.

"Yeah. I'm with a patient right now."

"Of course. Didn't mean to bother you, Doc." Cora hung up, went back into the living room. "There you go. Barney Nathan's in his office. If they'd found a body, he'd be at the crime scene."

"That's pretty convincing," Sherry said. "See? Nothing's going on."

"I suppose so," Aaron said grudgingly.

"I know so," Sherry said. "Good thinking, Cora."

"Huh?"

"Good deduction. I'm sure you're right."

"Oh," Cora said.

She was sure she was right, too, but her mind was elsewhere.

She was thinking about that pause before he said he was with a patient.

THIRTY

CORA SNAKED HER arm out from under the covers, flailed for the phone, knocked the receiver on the floor. She groped for it, picked it up, snarled, "Hello?"

There was a pause.

She tried again, slightly less hostile. "Hello?"

A rather hesitant voice said, "Cora?"

"Yes?"

"It's Barney Nathan. I'm sorry to call so late."

"It's not late," Cora said. She looked around in the dark for the glow of the digital clock. It was ten to twelve. "Not late at all. What's up, Barney?"

"Ah, nothing. I, eh, I was at the Country Kitchen…"

"You're there now?"

"Yeah."

"Hang on, I'll be right there."

Cora hung up the phone, missed, cursed, picked up the receiver, finished the task. She threw back the covers, swung her legs over the side of the bed.

She was wearing a long, flannel nightgown, perfect for sleeping alone, loose and roomy, but still snug and comfy. She staggered into the bathroom, slapped cold water on her face. Looked in the mirror.

She was a wreck. An old racehorse trotted out too many times with nothing left for the stretch run.

The hell she was, Cora told herself. Even her ex-husband Melvin was still interested. Of course he hadn't seen her staggering out of bed half asleep in her finest flannels.

Cora pulled the nightgown over her head, surveyed herself in the mirror. Not bad. She could afford to take off ten pounds—well, maybe twenty.

Cora brushed her teeth, staggered back into the bedroom.

Okay, what the hell could she wear?

Well, bra and panties would be a start. Okay, how much lace were we talking? Somewhere between spinster and slut. Black? White? Sheer?

Aw, hell, it was almost midnight. She couldn't be all dolled up at midnight. What, was she sitting around in nylons and high heels in case somebody called? What the hell would she have been wearing if she weren't in bed?

In point of fact, she'd be lounging in her Wicked Witch of the West outfit, the tattered stained smock with the cigarette holes in it. Not exactly clothing to be seen in.

But what was?

It occurred to Cora life didn't used to be so hard.

THIRTY-ONE

BARNEY NATHAN WAS sitting at the bar, nursing a drink. Cora had wondered if he would have his bow tie on. He did, so at least he hadn't had that many. No one could sit in a bar long without untying a bow tie.

His back was to the door, and he didn't see her come in. Cora walked up, sat on the stool next to him. "Hi, Barney."

He looked over, gave her a somewhat sheepish grin.

Cora was dressed in a tan sweater and brown skirt, simple, understated, earth mother. Not her usual role, though she wasn't sure what her usual role was anymore.

"Sorry to call so late."

"You already said that, Barney. When you're sitting in a bar alone, it's never that late."

"I'm not drunk."

"I could tell."

There were few people still drinking at that hour. The bartender was attentive.

"Diet Coke," Cora said.

Barney's glass was half full. He shook his head.

"You don't drink?"

"Not anymore."

"Why not?"

"I quit to get married."

"That was a requirement?"

"It wasn't a deal breaker. He wanted me to."

"You stayed sober, even after you got divorced?"

"I never got divorced."

"Oh?"

"I never got married, if you'll recall."

"Oh." Barney flushed, recalling he had performed the autopsy on Cora's prospective husband. "Sorry. Stupid of me."

"Water under the bridge. Anyway, I've stayed clean and sober. Or at least sober. What's your situation? Wife move out?"

"No."

"She gonna?"

"*She's* not."

"So you are. Good thing your office isn't in your home."

"Yeah, lucky."

"Have any kids?"

"No."

"Then it's a piece of cake."

"Really?"

"No, hurts like hell. Every single time. It's your first time, so it hurts more. You blame yourself?"

"No."

"Good. Well, that you don't blame yourself. Not good if she was running around."

Barney sighed heavily. "This was a mistake."

"Sorry, I don't mean to be flip. I'm just not used to sitting in a bar with a man without drinking." Cora picked up her Coke. "You know I almost made work for you?"

"Oh?"

"Found a grave in the basement of the Guilford house."

"What?"

"No body, just a grave. Freshly dug. The cops dug up the basement looking for a body. Couldn't find anything."

"What the hell is going on?"

"I have no idea. None."

"They said on TV it's like that movie. Of course it's Rick Reed, so you don't know what to believe."

"Ain't that the truth. But it is like the movie. Have you seen it?"

"No."

"You're kidding. You haven't seen *Arsenic and Old Lace*? You ought to see it." After a pause, she said, "I've got the DVD."

There was another pause.

"You said some nasty things about me," Barney said.

"Of course I did. But that wasn't personal, it was business. Like in *The Godfather*. If Ratface is trying to prove somebody guilty, and I don't think he did it, of course I'm going to start poking holes in the evidence."

Barney snorted. "Ratface?"

"Huh?"

"You really call him Ratface?"

"Well, just to Chief Harper. Not to his ratty face."

"What do you call me?"

"I don't have a nickname for you, Barney."

"You said I missed a cause of death or two."

"Oh, that."

"But I'm not a bad doctor."

"Not at all. Think about it. There was nothing wrong with your medical findings. Any doctor in the world would have come up with the same thing. Any fault I might find with the result is not based on any medical expertise. I have none. I merely used nonmedical factors of which you had not been informed and which you were not called upon to judge to indicate the possibility of another result. Is that your fault? I don't think so."

"You certainly implied it was."

"Implied, schmied. You gonna throw a pie in a knife

fight?" Cora frowned. "That is a strange metaphor, but you get what I mean." She put her hand on his arm. "Barney. So I called you incompetent. You ought to hear what I called some of my ex-husbands. I called Henry a moron. I called Frank a loser. You wouldn't *believe* the things I called Melvin."

Cora smiled, patted Barney on the cheek. "Hell, *incompetent* is practically a term of endearment."

THIRTY-TWO

CORA WOKE UP to the sound of the doorbell—loud, long, and insistent. She hopped up, pulled on a robe, closed the bedroom door behind her, and hurried through the house.

Chief Harper stood on the stoop. "What the hell is it with everybody, you can't even answer your phone?"

"I turned off my phone."

"What?"

"The ring. I turned off the ring. So I wouldn't be woken up in the middle of the night again."

"Even for a murder?"

"You got one?"

"I got two."

Cora's mouth fell open. "Oh, my God! The old ladies?"

"No. The guests."

"What guests?"

"The ones who disappeared. They didn't skip out, they just got killed."

"Where?"

"Back of the high school. Where the kids go to make out. Couple of seniors found 'em. Probably scare 'em off sex for years."

"I wouldn't count on it. Where were they? In their car?"

Harper shook his head. "No. In the back of the abandoned school bus."

"Abandoned?"

"Broken down; they haven't managed to tow it away. Kids go in there to neck."

"How do you know that?"

"Sam Brogan did."

"Sam Brogan necks in a school bus?"

"He's rousted kids out of it. Busted in on them with a flashlight."

"Now *that's* enough to put them off sex. IDs on the body?"

"No."

"Then how do you know it's them?"

"I've seen them."

"Oh. Right. So you don't know their names?"

"No."

"Why don't you trace the car?"

"It's gone, too. Dan's calling rental agencies."

"I thought you already did that."

"We were looking for a car that got returned early. Now we're looking for one that didn't come back at all."

"That's incredible."

"No kidding." He shook his head. "You live in a house where people are being poisoned, you'd think you'd be careful about what you eat."

"Was it poison?"

"That's what I'd like to know. Barney Nathan's not answering his phone, either. I'm on my way over there now."

"You came here first?"

"You're on the way."

"Why did you come here at all?"

"Oh. Here." He handed over a sudoku. "Found it on the body."

			5		9			
	9			2		4		3
	4			1			8	
4						2	9	
		3					1	6
9				6				
	6					3	5	
	8				2	6		
						8		

"Oh, great, Chief. The murder's practically solved."

"You don't think it means anything?"

"I think it means the killer'd like to tie these murders to the other murders."

"Why?"

"See, that's why I don't like to answer your questions. You always ask another one. Yeah, yeah, I'll solve the sudoku. I solved the other one, by the way. The one you couldn't be bothered to look at."

"I was busy. So what's it mean?"

"Nothing. Just like this one. But I'll solve it for you. Now get out of here and let me get dressed."

Cora peeked out the window until Chief Harper went down the driveway, then hurried back to the bedroom where Barney Nathan was sitting up in bed with the sheet around his neck.

"Get up! Get up! You look ridiculous."

"Who was that?"

"Chief Harper."

"What did he want?"

"You."

"What?!"

"You turned your cell phone off."

"How did he know?"

"He doesn't."

"Why was he looking here?"

"He's not. He's on his way to your house because he couldn't get you on the phone."

"I'm not there."

"Really? Hadn't noticed."

"Cora."

"Get up. Get dressed. I'll take you to your car. Good thing we left it at the Country Kitchen."

Barney hopped out of bed, began pulling on his clothes. "I hate sneaking around."

"Get used to it."

"Huh?"

"You're in the middle of a divorce. Sneaking around is the name of the game. I hate being named correspondent."

"When were you named correspondent?"

"Never, Barney. It's a figure of speech."

Barney tied his shoes. "Oh, my God. Harper's going to my house. What do I do?"

"Pick up a quart of milk at the convenience store, tear ass home, tell Chief Harper you ran out of milk."

"Will he buy that?"

"Of course he will."

"Why?"

"Because you're not married to him." Cora tossed him the red bow tie. "Here. Put this on."

Cora watched Barney knot the tie around his neck. She smiled. "Thank God I took it off before I answered the door."

THIRTY-THREE

THE HIGH SCHOOL was in session, adding an eerie aura to an already macabre scene. The crime scene ribbon was up, and the bus was cordoned off, holding back those students who did not have class that period, or those who were cutting. Cora had a feeling the latter number was large and growing, as the news spread, and students snuck out. There were also faces pressed against the glass of the upstairs windows that were shooed away by teachers and quickly returned.

And for good reason. Aside from the police activity, Rick Reed had set up shop, using the side of the bus outside the crime scene as a backdrop. The Channel 8 News van, a familiar enough sight to residents, was catnip to kids, and they thronged around to hear what Rick had to say.

"More murders!" Rick proclaimed. "Incredibly enough, there have been two more killings, bringing the total up to four." He paused for a moment, an unfortunate choice, as it made it appear as if he was checking his math. "Cora Felton, the Puzzle Lady, has just arrived, which would tend to indicate... Well, I'll let her tell you what it indicates. Miss Felton, what can you tell us about this gruesome double homicide?"

"It's a double homicide and it's gruesome? Well, Rick, that's more information than I've got. Perhaps I should interview you."

Rick chuckled good-naturedly, not to be put off. "You

know that's not true. If you've been called in, there's un-doubtedly a clue worthy of your expertise. Could you let us know what it is?"

"Wow. I'm trying to think of a clue worthy of my ex-pertise. If your facts are right, two people are dead, it's a tragedy, and we shouldn't make light of it. I just got here, so I'm probably even less informed than you. If you don't mind, I'm going to bring myself up-to-date."

Cora escaped from Rick's clutches, slipped behind the back of the bus, and ducked under the crime scene ribbon.

Two EMS crews were waiting by the door. Cora pushed by them, hopped up into the bus.

"You're contaminating a crime scene," Sam Brogan snarled.

"And a good morning to you, too." Cora raised her arms. "Look, Sam, no hands. I haven't touched a thing."

Cora squeezed by him.

The bodies were in the middle of the aisle with their heads toward the back of the bus. Chief Harper was kneeling in front of them, blocking her view. He stood up and turned around.

"Solve that puzzle for me?"

"No."

"No?"

"I'll solve it while I'm waiting. But I'm not sitting in my house playing with a puzzle while you scam-per around the scene of a double murder. It is murder, isn't it? This whacky couple didn't just overdo the auto-asphyxiation?"

Harper made a face. "For God's sake, Cora. What if Rick Reed heard you?"

"He's on the bus? I promise not to give him that quote. So, what's the holdup? Where's the doc?"

"He wasn't home."

"Where is he?"

"His wife wouldn't tell me where he was. Just between you and me, she was downright rude."

"They've been having troubles," Cora said. "At least according to Becky Baldwin."

"Becky? What's she got to do with it?"

"Nothing, I'm sure. Forget I said anything."

"Becky Baldwin?"

"I'm sure it's nothing, Chief. What about the killings? Any sign of a murder weapon?"

"Not that I can tell. Of course, I don't know what we're talking about here. They haven't been shot or stabbed. There's no sign of blood. But I'm thinking blunt trauma to the head. I don't want to move them, but the man looks good for it, if you peer around from the side. See, right on the bald spot. And the woman could be, too, but you can't tell, she's got too much hair."

Harper looked around. Barney Nathan had just come up onto the bus. "There he is. Better late than never, Doc."

Barney's mouth fell open. Cora could practically see him sifting through rejoinders trying to come up with a suitable response.

His mind blown, he fell back on the old standard. "What's *she* doing here?"

"She was home when I called," Harper said. "You weren't."

"I know. I went out for milk."

Cora winced. Barney, clearly unskilled at dissembling, had immediately made a rookie mistake, offering an unnecessary explanation.

"So, what have we got here?" Barney said.

"You tell me."

Barney squeezed past Cora without meeting her eyes, pushed by Chief Harper, and bent over the bodies.

"What's it look like?" Harper said.

"You want me to tell you in front of her?"

"We're all family here, Barney. Of course, Becky Baldwin isn't."

Barney looked up, frowned. "Becky Baldwin?"

"She's representing the nephew. We might wind up charging him with the crime."

"You think he did it?"

"Well, someone did. Anyway, is there anything about the death of these two people that might cause you embarrassment if Becky Baldwin were to grill you about it?"

Barney shrugged. "A lawyer can argue anything. There are indications of blunt trauma to the head that could have been the cause of death. I can pin it down when I get them to the morgue."

"Any chance it was poison?"

"Why?"

"Well, the other ones were. You ever see *Arsenic and Old Lace*?"

Barney had the worst poker face in the world. He looked as if Chief Harper had just bared his innermost secrets. "What?" he croaked.

Harper frowned. "Well it's been all over the television. How the killings were like in the movie. I haven't seen it, have you?"

"Yes, I have. And, no, this doesn't seem to fit in with it at all. As to poison, I couldn't rule it out. But I would say blunt trauma was at least a contributing factor."

"Any idea when it happened?"

"Body's gone through rigor. It's been quite a while."

"They've been gone since yesterday afternoon."

"Sounds about right. Can I get them out of here?"

"Be my guest."

Barney went outside, sent the EMS crews in.

"Jumpy, isn't he?" Harper said.

"Oh? Didn't notice."

"Particularly when I mentioned Becky Baldwin."

"Well, you mentioned her ripping him apart on the stand."

"That's not quite how I phrased it. Even so, it didn't seem like that. And it was Becky who told you he was having trouble with his wife. You don't suppose that's why he wasn't home?"

Cora had a wonderful poker face.

"I have no idea."

THIRTY-FOUR

CORA FLOPPED HERSELF into Becky Baldwin's client's chair. "I don't see how you can sit there so calmly when there's been two more murders."

"What?" Becky said.

"Don't you have a television?"

"Not in my office."

"Too bad. No one should start the day without a hearty dose of Rick Reed. Well, brighten up. There's two more people you can defend Alan Guilford for killing."

"What in the world are you talking about?"

Cora brought Becky up to speed on the two new murders.

"Got a time of death yet?"

"No, but they disappeared yesterday afternoon. Everybody thought they ducked out because they weren't married. We still don't know if they're married or not, but they didn't duck out."

"And no one knows who they are?"

"No, but they shouldn't be too hard to trace. They got a rental car kicking around somewhere. And they're more apt to be local."

"Local?"

"Well, say from the New York area. On the other hand, the geezer could be from anywhere."

"You may not want to call him a geezer."

"Why?"

"In case he turns out to have friends who think he's more important than you portrayed him."

"No one's going to sue me, Becky."

"Why not?"

"I'm not rich."

"You got insurance, don't you?"

"Not for slander."

"Too bad."

"On the other hand, I wonder if it's slander to call the guy a geezer. You call an eighty-year-old guy a geezer, you're fine. You call a fifty-year-old guy a geezer, you get sued. Where do you draw the line?"

"I'd prefer you not to find out."

"Why not? You need the work." Cora fished her cigarettes out of her purse. "By the way, Chief Harper thinks you're sleeping with Barney Nathan."

Becky had opened her mouth to tell Cora she couldn't smoke. She closed it again. Blinked. "What!?"

"That's one of the dangers of being a femme fatale. Your name gets kicked around."

"What the hell are you talking about?"

"Not me. Chief Harper. Not that he's one to be spreading rumors or anything. I was the only one there when he said it."

"Damn it, Cora. What made Chief Harper think I'm having an affair with Barney Nathan?"

"Oh. You're not?"

"Cora."

"Don't blame me. It's Chief Harper who said it." She struck a match, lit her cigarette.

"Why? What put the idea in his head?"

"Actually, it was Barney himself."

"What did he say?"

"Nothing. Chief Harper made a remark about how

Barney could talk in front of me because we're all family. Then he said, except Becky Baldwin."

"Barney said, except Becky Baldwin?"

"No. Chief Harper said it. Barney flushed. Like he'd been caught trying to peek up your skirt."

"Cora!"

"Not to imply he's been peeking up your skirt. I'm just telling you how it looked."

"Could you use another metaphor?"

"Not as apt. Unless you want me to get more graphic."

"That's all you're going on? Chief Harper mentioned my name and Barney Nathan flushed?"

"And Barney wasn't home when Chief Harper went to find him."

"Where was he?"

"He said he went out for milk."

"That's probably what he did. I assure you, he wasn't with me."

"It's not me you have to assure. It's Chief Harper."

"Oh, for goodness' sake."

"You have any idea why Barney reacted like that?"

"I told you. He asked me out on a date."

"That usually doesn't push men over the edge."

"Yeah, well, it's really *your* fault."

Cora raised her eyebrows. "Oh?"

"Telling me not to string him along. I tried that dating-someone-your-own-age crap. He looked like I told him there was no Santa Claus."

"There's no Santa Claus? That's terrible. What will the reindeer do?"

"Trust me, stringing him along would have been a kindness."

"Not in the long run."

"Anyway, that's why he reacted that way. Becky Baldwin, the woman who emasculated him. The bitch who stole his manhood."

"Stole his manhood?"

"That came out wrong."

"You're getting in deeper with the double entendres."

"Stop it. The point is, I don't care. What about the killings?"

"You know as much as I do."

"I only know what you told me."

"Well, I've been very forthcoming."

"You're in an awfully good mood today."

"Two people got killed. That's always a mood lifter."

"Cora."

"What can I tell you? There's murder going on. It makes no sense at all. It seems to be related to a movie, but then it isn't. Because the philandering couple is not part of the movie. Any more than the wandering drunk. Less, actually. Because the drunk fits the pattern of the lonely, elderly man. And apparently these two weren't poisoned, they were bludgeoned."

"What does Barney say?"

"Oh, now it's Barney?"

"Don't start with me."

"I'm not starting with you. I'm just saying when I report back to Chief Harper I need to know which portion of this conversation to quote for him. If he hears you calling the doc Barney it's just going to set him off again."

"Oh, for Christ's sake."

Cora shook her head. "You're new at this game, Becky. You gotta learn not to get your name linked with someone going through a divorce."

"He's not going through a divorce."

Cora's cigarette stopped halfway to her lips. "I thought you said he was."

"I said they were fighting. But they're not even separated yet. That's what I was stalling him with. Until you came along with your know-it-all advice."

"Oh, for goodness' sake. You were thinking about going out with a married man?"

"I was never thinking of going out with him."

"You couldn't have said that from the beginning? 'Don't be silly, Barney, you're married'?"

"I *said* that from the beginning. That's how I was stalling him along."

"Well, you might have said so."

"Why?"

"I wouldn't have given you my know-it-all advice. I thought I was saving you from making a big mistake, not pushing you into one."

"I don't see what's the big deal."

"Well, Chief Harper thought you were involved with a man who was divorcing. Now you're involved with a man who's married. The gossip's going to get worse."

"Why did Chief Harper think Barney was divorcing?"

Cora waved it away. "Who knows where he heard it. Water under the bridge."

THIRTY-FIVE

"CORA?"

"Yes."

"It's Barney."

"Hi, Barney."

"Don't hi Barney me. You nearly gave me a heart attack."

"I do have that effect on men."

"In front of Chief Harper. I was nervous, and you didn't help."

"Oh. Sorry. What was I supposed to do? Act like we're not having an affair? I don't recall reading that manual. What's the first rule? Look people straight in the eye and give 'em your best Obi Wan Kenobi: 'These are not the lovers you're looking for.'?"

"Couldn't you just act normal?"

"Take your pick, Barney. Acting normal means making fun of you. Which I did. Is it my fault if you didn't know how to react?"

"Why are you so hostile?"

"Don't be silly. I'm not hostile. By the way, I understand you're not getting divorced."

"Oh."

"Oh?"

"I never said I was."

"You never said you weren't."

"The question never came up."

"Gee, I wonder why."

"So, you're angry."

"Just a little disappointed. My mother wanted me to fall in love and marry a doctor. Not fall in love with a married doctor."

"Fall in love?"

"I was making a joke. You gotta lighten up, Barney. You wanna be a dashing man of the world, you gotta take things more in stride. You know they ID'd the bodies."

"Harper called."

"You give him the autopsy results?"

"Yeah."

"Well, what are they?"

"I don't think I'm supposed to tell you."

"What?"

"Harper said to keep my mouth shut."

"From the media, Barney. Not from me."

"He meant anyone."

"I've got an idea. Let's call your wife, and ask her what she thinks he meant."

There was a silence on the line.

"Low blow," Barney said.

"Absolutely. Wasn't it beautiful? I just lobbed it in there sidearm when you weren't expecting it."

"You're not serious."

"Do I look suicidal? Barney, parading infidelities in front of people's spouses is not my idea of a good time. You could have medical evidence that identified the killer and I wouldn't go to your wife. You're really no good at this. Acting like you're separated when you're not. It's an amateur move, and always a turnoff. Who's gonna trust you after that? You gotta be up-front with a person. It may not get you where you wanna go, but in the long run it'll work out better. Now, you wanna tell me anything about the autopsy, it's your call."

There was a pause.

"They died right around the time Chief Harper thought they did. About two to three hours after ingesting their last meal. It happened to be breakfast, which makes fixing the time easier. There's no poison involved. They died from a blunt instrument. Narrower than a two-by-four. No wider than the head of a hammer, but it wasn't a circle. It was something long and round. Like a lead pipe."

"Ah," Cora said. "Professor Plum in the conservatory with the lead pipe. Was there a trace of metal or anything to indicate the pipe was lead?"

"It didn't have to be lead, but it had to be heavy. Or swung with considerable force."

"Is that all you got?"

"That's not enough?"

"Unless you got more."

"I don't."

"Then it's enough."

There was a pause.

"You still mad?" Barney said.

"About what?"

"Me not getting a divorce."

"Oh, please."

"So I guess I won't be seeing you again."

"It's not a deal breaker."

THIRTY-SIX

"ALL RIGHT, GET back to me," Chief Harper said, and slammed down the phone.

"Gee, you're in a good mood," Cora said.

"Been better. At least we ID'd the bodies."

"How'd you do that?"

"Found their car. Abandoned by the side of the road, not that far from the high school. Both names were on the rental agreement."

"Oh?"

"Barry Stein and Julia Rose. Both of Manhattan. Both married. Not to each other. Barry leaves behind a wife and kids. Julia just a husband."

"Hmm. You don't think they did it, do you?"

"Who?"

"The wife and husband. Decided to get rid of their cheating spouses."

"That's ridiculous."

"You just say that because you've got a stable marriage. When you've been married as many times as I have, it's the first thing you think about. What would be the best way to off the son of a bitch. Not that I think there's the slightest chance that happened. The way I see it, those two are collateral damage."

"You think they saw something?"

"That's the only thing that makes sense. Because they're not in the movie."

Harper exhaled. "The damn movie. Everybody and his brother's seen the damn movie."

"You still haven't?"

"No."

"If I give you the DVD, will you watch it?"

"Oh, for Christ's sake."

"It would be nice to have you on the same page when we're talking."

"You got the DVD?"

"Doesn't everyone?" Cora reached in her drawstring purse, pulled out a copy.

"You carry it around with you?"

"Well, you never know when you're going to bump into some ignorant cop who needs to be wised up. So, you get the autopsy report yet?"

"Yeah."

"Gonna let me in on it?"

Harper sighed. "Oh, all right."

He told her what she already knew.

She pretended to listen. "Interesting."

"You think so?"

"Absolutely. It confirms the fact those two aren't important. More like an afterthought."

"There was a sudoku with them."

"Sure there was. And I solved it."

Cora pulled out a copy, handed it to the chief.

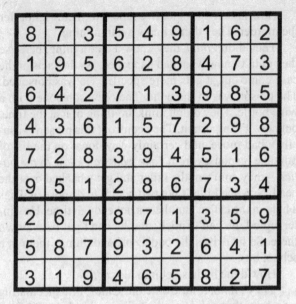

"And the middle square is nine, the four corners are eight, two, three, and seven. And what does that tell you? It tells me the killer put the sudoku on the bodies to try to make it look like they are part of the pattern, when they are in fact not. They were witnesses at best. More than likely, they were unwitting witnesses who didn't know what they saw."

"What did they see?"

"They saw somebody doing something consistent with the movie."

"Like what?"

"I don't know. You'll have to watch it. But that's just the convoluted explanation. The simple, straightforward explanation is they saw the killer committing the crime."

"How is that possible? We talked to them right after the murder. They didn't know a damn thing."

"They didn't *think* they knew a damn thing, because they didn't know what had happened. As the facts of the case come out, it gets more specific. He was poisoned. The poison was in the wine. They saw someone with a wine bottle. They didn't think anything of it at the time, but now it's important. They confront this person—usually a bad move, and certainly way down on the list of possible responses from *Take what you know to the police*—they confront the killer and get whacked over the head. Now the killer's got two bodies to dispose of. Digs a hole in the cellar. But there's not enough time. He's interrupted, he can't finish, and he can't get back down there. So he drives the bodies off and dumps them in a school bus."

"How'd the bodies get into his car?"

"They *climbed* in. Come on, Chief, I'm speculating on a hypothetical. How the hell should I know?" Cora shook her head. "By the way, Becky says Barney Nathan isn't divorcing."

"Becky says that?"

"Straight from the horse's mouth."

"So she *is* involved with Barney."

"Did I say that? I didn't say that, and you didn't hear it from me. But he's not divorcing, she *knows* he's not divorcing, and she claims she never said any different."

"And she doesn't care?"

"She didn't seem concerned."

"Well," Harper said. "That's a bit of a surprise. I wouldn't have figured Becky for that type of girl."

Cora winced. "*Girl* is a poor choice of words in that context, Chief. It's a ticklish enough subject without tossing around sexist terms."

"Has Becky told you anything?"

"About what?"

"Her relationship with Barney."

"Well, there you go. Assuming a relationship. Unless the girl's told me she is, I have to assume she isn't."

"You realize you said *girl*."

"Yeah. But I'm a woman and a wordsmith and I can get away with it."

The phone rang.

Chief Harper looked at it in annoyance. "Oh, hell."

"What?"

"Dan Finley's out."

"So?"

"The main number rings through to my office. I don't like picking up the phone if I don't know who's calling."

"Why don't you get caller ID?"

"Yeah." Harper grabbed the phone. "Hello?"

"Oh, thank goodness I got you! I'm so worried! I don't know what to do!" the caller said.

"Hey, hey, calm down. Who is this?"

"I'm sorry. It didn't occur to me you wouldn't know. I know who I am, so I thought you would know who I am because I'm only thinking from my point of view. It's Edith Guilford. Charlotte's missing! She went shopping and she didn't come home!"

"Oh," Chief Harper said. His interest was rapidly beginning to wane.

Edith could hear it in his voice. "No, you don't understand. It was late, she didn't come back, she didn't call, it was taking too long. I looked in the garage and the car's there!"

"Oh, I'm sure Charlotte's fine, but I'll come over and check it out." Harper hung up the phone. "You get all that?"

"Her sister's missing?"

"Yeah."

"You sure she's fine?"

"No."

THIRTY-SEVEN

ALAN GUILFORD LOOKED CONFUSED. "I don't understand."

"It's perfectly simple," Becky said. "Two of your aunts' guests were found murdered on a bus."

"*That* I understand. I don't understand why it concerns me."

"Don't be silly," Becky said. "If you're a suspect in the other killings, you're a suspect in these. The assumption is the second murders were to cover up the first ones."

"But I had nothing to do with the first ones."

"And yet you hired me as your lawyer."

"Are you saying I shouldn't have hired you?"

"Not at all. Hiring me was a shrewd move, definitely in your best interests. Since you made that move, you would be wise to listen to your attorney."

"Do we have to do this in your office? It seems so formal."

"You wanna go have a drink? What would your fiancée think of that?"

"A business meeting? How could she object?" Alan squirmed uncomfortably. "That's the thing. Business meeting. Are you billing me for this? I don't have much money. I'd have to get it from Arlene. I don't like asking her. We're not married yet."

Becky's estimation of the young man dropped considerably. And it wasn't just that she wasn't getting paid. "I'm not billing you. I thought this might concern you. I'm glad that it doesn't. But the police thought you might be involved with the other murders. If they get it in their heads that you were involved in these, I'd like to be prepared. In case I *do* have to take action, which I certainly hope I do not. But I'm not going to do anything without your knowledge and bill you for it, unless you get in a situation where you've made it clear that that is what you need."

Cora Felton burst in the door. "Oh, good. You're together."

"What do you mean by that?" Becky snapped.

Cora put up her hand. "Whoa! No offense. I was going to tell you to tell him. He's here, so I can tell you both at once."

"Tell us what?" Alan said.

"Your aunt's missing."

"What!"

"Well, not officially missing. It hasn't been twenty-four hours. But she's not there. Chief Harper's on his way over to check it out."

"Which one?" Alan said.

"Charlotte. According to Edith, she went shopping, never came back."

Alan waved it off. "She's scatterbrained. She could have wandered into a clothing store and got lost looking at fabrics."

"Her car's in the garage."

"Well, there must be some simple explanation." He sighed. "I suppose I should run out there."

"You want me to go with you?" Becky said.

"Why?"

"Chief Harper's there. You wouldn't want to make any statements in front of him."

"See?" Alan said. "This is just what you were talking about. Protecting me from something I haven't asked you to. My aunt's missing. I want to find her. Not stand around worrying about what might make me look bad."

"Bravo," Cora said. "Just the right attitude. Be sure to project like that on the stand."

"On the stand!"

"Don't let her rattle you," Becky said. "She's just a troublemaker. Go on. Run out there and make sure everything's okay."

"Yeah, show some concern for your aunt."

Alan gave Cora a look and went out.

"Do you have to make trouble?" Becky said.

"Yeah, that's pretty much what I'm reduced to," Cora said. "We have motiveless crimes that make absolutely no sense. Which seem to be related to a movie except when they're not. Then we have crossword puzzle and/or sudoku clues that mean absolutely nothing. Except when they do. Only they don't, except when it refers to the aforementioned movie, which also means nothing."

"For someone who knows nothing, you're mighty happy."

"Yeah, I'm ignorant and proud of it. No one's expecting me to solve these crimes, which suits me fine. If they start making sense, maybe I'll take a look." Cora cocked her head. "So, how about a latte and a scone? I'm buyin'."

"Oh, big spender. Come into a fortune?"

"I got a royalty statement. Turns out my sudoku books are doing rather well."

"Lattes it is," Becky said. "I'm not sure my figure can stand a scone."

"That's the type of thing skinny girls say that makes you want to strangle them. If I buy you a scone, you're damn well gonna eat it."

"Fine, ruin my career. See if I care."

"I don't think there's a weight limit for lawyers."

Bickering, Cora and Becky made their way down the stairs to the street.

The bake shop was busy. Mrs. Cushman was behind the counter.

"Lattes," Cora said.

"Skim lattes," Becky amended.

"Skim lattes," Cora conceded. "Any scones left?"

"One cranberry and one apricot."

"Sold. Which one you want, Becky?"

"Which one is smaller?"

"Apricot."

"I'll take that."

"Figures."

Cora and Becky stood nibbling on the scones while Mrs. Cushman made the lattes.

Becky picked up her latte and turned from the counter.

A woman with black hair and rather red cheeks walked up to Becky, slapped her across the face.

Heads turned.

Becky's mouth fell open.

The woman turned on her heel and stalked out.

"My God!" Becky said. "Who the hell was that?"

"That's Judy Nathan," Mrs. Cushman said. "The doctor's wife. What's she got against you?"

THIRTY-EIGHT

"MY WIFE THINKS I'm sleeping with Becky Baldwin."

"Really."

"She screamed at me and threw me out of the house."

"Excellent. Now you can get a room at a motel."

Cora and Barney were in Cora's bed. She had picked him up at the Country Kitchen, left his car in the parking lot, snuck him in while Sherry was nursing the baby.

"Why is that excellent?"

"It's easier to meet in a motel. No one's gonna walk in on us there. Leave my car at the Country Kitchen and we can park right in front of the unit because it's yours."

"And when my wife shows up and begs me to come home?"

"I'll hide in the bathroom and lock the door and she'll think it's Becky Baldwin."

"Great. That'll be a big help."

"Calm down, Barney. If you think about it, it actually will. You're new to this, so you don't know all the angles. Your wife's gonna sue you for divorce, right?"

"I guess so. Unless she wants a reconciliation."

"Do *you* want a reconciliation?"

"No."

"You don't sound convinced."

"Well, what do you expect? I've never been divorced before."

"You're in that situation where there are only two possible outcomes. The marriage ends. The marriage continues. In either instance there's a winner and a loser."

"What are you talking about?"

"You're either going to get back together with your wife or you're not. If you are, you want it to be on your terms. You don't wanna go slinking back with your tail between your legs. If you're not, and your wife actually is going to file for divorce, you don't want to be taken to the cleaners. You're a doctor, doctors make money, she'd like to have some. You wanna see she's provided for, but you don't wanna drape her in diamonds while she's out looking for the next sucker."

"Good lord, is that your view on marriage?"

"I've had a lot of views. Some were better than others. Anyway, you're missing the point. Your wife thinks you're having an affair with Becky Baldwin. That's wonderful. Say she goes ahead with the divorce. She files suit and names Becky as correspondent. She can't prove it. Because it's not true. A good attorney would have a field day with that in court. You know who's a good attorney? Becky Baldwin."

"Are you saying I should hire her to prove I'm not having an affair with her?"

"I admit that sounds iffy. But take the premise. If your wife names Becky as correspondent, she can't prove it. But the best part is, she won't be naming me."

"Good for you."

"For you, too, goosey. Me, she can prove. It's a lot harder to prove you're not having an affair with me, since you are. Not impossible, but still. Whereas, Becky Baldwin is a snap."

There was a sudden pounding at the front door. Buddy, who'd been sleeping on the floor, sprang to his feet and began barking hysterically.

Barney Nathan sat bolt upright. "Oh, my God! It's my wife!"

"Don't be silly, Barney. She doesn't know you're here."

"What should I do?"

"Hide under the bed."

Cora jumped up, pulled on her robe, and went to answer the door. The toy poodle trailed along behind. The minute she opened the front door, he plunged through it like an avenging fury.

Chief Harper stood in the doorway. From his expression, he might have come to arrest her. He ignored the little dog, glared at Cora. "Again. You did it again."

"What did I do, Chief?"

"Turned off your phone. Have you figured it out yet? Every time you turn off your phone, everything goes to hell."

"What happened?"

"It's what *hasn't* happened. Charlotte Guilford hasn't come home. I went out there this afternoon, tried to calm her sister down. It wasn't working. Then her nephew showed up, God bless him. I sure hope I don't have to charge him with murder."

"Well, you've gotta charge someone."

"What?"

"Come on, Chief, I'd prefer if he didn't do it, too, but someone killed those people."

"You really think he did it?"

"I have no idea. But I wouldn't wanna rule anyone out."

Harper noticed her robe. "You're in bed early."

"People keep waking me up in the middle of the night. I have to sleep when I can."

"Then I hate to ask you."

"Ask me what?"

"Edith's hysterical. I'm no good with hysterical women. If you could calm her down."

"What about her nephew?"

"I think he's fed up. He did the afternoon shift. Now he's nowhere to be found."

"Did you look in the window seat?"

Chief Harper's eyes widened. "Do you mean...?"

"Well, that's where the other body was. You better look in the window seat."

"I can't do that. Edith's hysterical as it is. I start looking in window seats, she's going to think something happened to Charlotte."

"If she's been gone this long, something probably did happen to her."

"Come on, Cora. I need your help."

Cora heaved a sigh. "Fine. Go out there and hold her off."

"Aren't you coming?"

"Mind if I get dressed first?"

Cora watched Harper go down the walk. She took her time collecting the poodle to make sure the chief actually left, then hurried back to the bedroom.

Barney was gone.

"Barney?"

The toy poodle was sniffing under the bed.

Barney poked his head out. "Is he gone?"

"What the hell are you doing?"

"You said get under the bed."

"I was joking."

"Oh."

Barney crawled out from under the bed.

Cora threw off her robe, began pulling on clothes.

"What are you doing?" Barney said.

"I gotta go out to the Guilford house. Stay there. I'll be right back."

"But—"

"Don't worry. Buddy will keep you company. Right, Buddy?"

Cora pulled on a sweater and slacks, hopped in her car, and tore out to the Guilford house. The front door was open. Cora went in, found Chief Harper in the kitchen trying to comfort Edith. His face lit up like a man who's been thrown a lifeline.

"See," Harper said. "Cora's come to help. It's going to be all right. I'm sure nothing's happened to your sister."

"Nonsense," Cora said. "If she's been gone that long, something probably *has* happened to her."

Edith stopped wailing, looked at Cora in astonishment.

"So, let's find her. Did you look in the window seat?"

Edith gasped.

"She's *not* in the window seat," Harper said icily.

"Well, let's rule it out. That's the first place I'd look. The second would be the grave in the cellar. The third would be the attic. You do have an attic, don't you?"

Edith blinked. Nodded.

"Well, first things first." Cora headed for the living room with Edith and the chief trailing along behind.

Cora marched up to the window seat, flung it open, took a look, and scowled.

The body of Charlotte Guilford lay in the window seat.

There was a crossword puzzle on her chest.

ACROSS

1 Credits listing
5 Dubious sighting
8 Jai alai basket
13 First name in scat
14 "Stat!"
15 Summertime allergen
16 Start of a message
18 Buckeye Stater
19 Metallic marble
20 Time to revel
21 ___ -med
22 Pin count
23 Predicate part
25 Left over
29 More of the message
34 Chair fixer
35 Hobby farm dweller
36 Plantation gear
37 Same-old-same-olds
38 Not well-thought-out
40 Swarm member
41 Nobelist Wiesel
42 Prado display
43 Move like a 51-Down
44 Still more of the message
47 Patches up
48 Many August births

49 "___ nuts?"
51 IRS hiree
54 Circus Maximus greeting
55 Ill-bred
60 Do poetry, say
62 End of the message
63 Letter signoff
64 Mrs. McKinley
65 Heidi's milieu
66 Portended
67 "Roll ___ bones!"
68 Hall fare

DOWN

1 Disney collectibles
2 Oceans
3 Purplish fruit
4 Heist haul
5 Set free, in a way
6 Stir up, as a revolt
7 Be in the hole
8 Hold together
9 Samuel's mentor
10 Zero-star fare
11 Hotfoot it
12 First name among diarists
15 Destitution

17 Take in, say
20 Long jump, e.g.
24 VIP
25 Cheat out of money
26 Abdul with six #1 hits
27 Thumbs-down group
28 Freezer bag verb
30 Can't avoid
31 Yorba ___
32 Taken as a whole
33 Running mate of Adlai
38 Home to Dartmouth College
39 Cropped up
43 Capital-letter producer
45 Had room for
46 Hero's welcome
50 Bawdyhouse figure
51 Critter with eyestalks
52 Cozumel cash
53 Didn't merely pass
56 Brewski topper
57 Twiddling one's thumbs
58 Takes a sample of
59 Infamous Spandau inmate
61 "___ been had!"
62 Kept under wraps

THIRTY-NINE

"HOW MANY LETTERS?" Sherry said. "Oh, there's a good baby girl."

"What?" Cora said.

"I'm talking to Jennifer."

"Could you concentrate? I'm in rather deep doo-doo."

"Sorry to hear it. We just had a diaper change, and we feel fine. Don't we, Jennifer?"

"I'm thrilled. It's five letters. Third letter n."

"What was the clue again?"

"Are you paying any attention? It's 'Chair fixer.'"

Finding Charlotte Guilford's body had shredded Chief Harper's last vestige of civility. He had bagged the puzzle, and ordered Cora to solve it on the spot. In desperation, she had holed herself up in the Guilford study, and she and Sherry were attempting to solve it on the phone. Which might have been easier had Jennifer been napping.

"It's caner," Sherry said.

Cora copied the answer onto the rough sketch of the puzzle grid she had drawn on a piece of paper. Since the puzzle was in a plastic evidence bag, she couldn't write on it. She had offered to run out and Xerox the puzzle, which would have given her a chance to rush home and let Sherry solve it, but Chief Harper was having none of it.

"Okay, then. 15 across. 'Summertime allergen.'"

"How many letters?"

"Six."

Chief Harper burst into the room, saw Cora on the phone. "What the hell are you doing? I told you to solve the puzzle."

"Sorry, Chief," Cora said, tap-dancing nimbly. "I had to call Sherry to tip off Aaron there'd been a murder. I gotta live in your town, but I gotta live in their house."

"Hang up, I got problems."

"Call you back," Cora said, and slammed down the phone. "What's the matter now?"

"I can't find Barney. His wife says he's not home, and he's not answering his pager."

That was not surprising. Barney had turned the ring off on his cell phone when they got into bed.

Cora exhaled in exasperation. Everything was coming down on her head. "What's that got to do with me?"

"I'm desperate. I need your advice." Harper lowered his voice. "Should I look for him at Becky's?"

"Not unless you want your head taken off. And like being sued for slander."

"How is that slander? Just asking if someone's there?"

"You're splitting hairs with a lawyer? Don't do it, Chief." Cora heaved herself out of the chair. "I've got this."

"What?"

"Becky's my friend. Let me handle it. Then you're not the bad guy."

Harper exhaled in relief. "Thanks, Cora." He ducked back out.

Cora grabbed the puzzle, shoved it into her purse. She hurried out, hopped in her car, sped back to her house. On the way a car that looked very much like Aaron's flew by in the other direction. Cora kept going, rocketed up the driveway, ran inside, flung open the bedroom door.

Barney Nathan was lying in bed with the dog on his lap. Both jumped up. Buddy fell to the floor, yelped indignantly.

"My God, you scared me to death!" Barney said.

"Get used to it," Cora snapped. "Get up, get dressed, sneak out to my car, get in the backseat, and keep your head down."

"What?"

"Charlotte Guilford's dead, Harper's trying to find you. I gotta get you to the Country Kitchen to pick up your car. Hop to it. I'll keep Sherry busy."

"Oh, my God!"

"And don't let the dog out!"

Cora raced through the breezeway that connected the old house to the new extension, raced through the living room, pounded up the stairs. Why did they put them at the end of the house? It would have been more convenient if they had been near the middle. But then they would have been closer to her. Better where they were.

Cora clattered down the hall into the bedroom.

Sherry was sitting up in bed. She put her finger to her lips. "Shhh!"

"Can't you put her down?" Cora said.

"What the hell is going on?"

"Chief Harper caught us playing phone tag. I tap-danced my way out of it, told him I was calling you to tip off Aaron."

"I did. He just left."

"I think I passed him on the road. I was going too fast to tell."

"How did you get away?"

"I snuck out. That was easy. I gotta get back before he misses me. Can you do the damn puzzle?"

"It's not easy one-handed."

"Sherry."

"Give me a magazine."

There was a copy of *People* on the bedside table. Cora handed it over.

"People. People who read *People*," Cora began.

"Don't sing," Sherry said. She balanced the magazine on her thigh.

Cora slapped the grid she'd drawn down on it, and handed her the puzzle and a pencil.

"This is a drag," Sherry said. "Can't we just run off a copy?"

"Then Harper would know I left. Here, I'll hold the puzzle for you."

Sherry looked at the crossword. "Oh, that's what you were trying to tell me." She held the grid to the magazine with her wrist, scribbled in the answers.

"Can I help?" Cora said.

"Yeah. Hold the grid on the magazine."

"Can I do anything else?"

"Yeah. Shut up."

"Jennifer, I hope you didn't hear your mother say that."

Sherry whizzed through the puzzle.

Cora grabbed it, headed for the door.

"Aren't you going to look at it?"

"Yeah, I guess I should."

The crossword grid contains the following filled answers:

Row 1: CAST | UFO | CESTA
Row 2: ELLA | NOW | POLLEN
Row 3: LOOKATME | OHIOAN
Row 4: STEELIE | EVE | PRE
Row 5: TEN | VERB
Row 6: SPARE | THEREILIE
Row 7: CANER | ANT | GINS
Row 8: RUTS | HASTY | GNAT
Row 9: ELIE | ART | SIDLE
Row 10: WASASNOOP | P | HEALS
Row 11: LEOS | AMI
Row 12: CPA | AVE | RAFFISH
Row 13: RECITE | HADTODIE
Row 14: ASEVER | IDA | ALPS
Row 15: BODED | DEM | MESS

She held it up, read, "Look at me. There I lie. Was a snoop. Had to die."

"What does that mean?" Sherry said.

"I haven't the faintest idea."

Cora plunged the puzzle into her drawstring purse, ran out the door. She thundered down the stairs, went out the door at the far end of the house, and raced across the lawn and hopped into the car.

"Barney. Are you there?"

From the floor of the backseat, a small voice said, "Yes."

"Keep your head down until we're out of the driveway."

Cora started the car, tore down the driveway.

As she turned on the road Barney said, "Can I get up now?"

"Yeah. Just duck down if you see headlights."

Barney got up, sat on the backseat. "What the hell is going on?"

"I'm taking you to the Country Kitchen. Go in, have a drink, turn on your cell phone. You'll have a missed call from Chief Harper, telling you to get out to the Guilford house. Or just telling you to call him. Whatever he says, do it."

"Why do I order a drink?"

"Because that's where you were, drinking at the Country Kitchen."

"Do I have to say that?"

"You don't *have* to say that, just in case someone asks. Come on, Barney, use your head. If he *happens* to ask, you were at the Country Kitchen, you turned on your phone, you got the message."

Cora screeched into the Country Kitchen parking lot, skidded to a stop in the shadows at the far end away from the restaurant.

"What if there's no message?"

"It's an emergency, meathead! You're a nice man, now get out of my car."

Barney went out the back door.

Cora gunned the motor and peeled out. She left enough rubber to make a spare tire, and took off down the road.

FORTY

DAN FINLEY WAS snapping pictures of the crime scene. Chief Harper tore himself away and met Cora at the door.

"Well? Was he there?"

"Was who where, Chief?"

Harper kept his voice down, difficult considering his mounting anger. "Barney Nathan. Was he at Becky's?"

"That's the wrong question to ask, Chief. I'm not going to answer that question. All you really want to know is, was I able to contact the doctor?"

"Were you able to contact the doctor?" Chief Harper said it through clenched teeth. His jaw never moved.

"He should be calling in any minute now, Chief. In the meantime, take a look at this."

Cora whipped out the crossword, shoved it in front of his face.

"Wait a minute. You solved the puzzle? I thought you went to get Barney."

"I'm an amazing multitasker, Chief. It would appear we have an actual message from the killer."

"You're kidding."

"Take a look."

"Look at me. There I lie. Was a snoop. Had to die." Harper snorted. "That's not from the killer. That's from the victim."

"Somehow I doubt that, Chief. The killer may have written it from the victim's point of view, but it's surely from the killer."

"It doesn't tell us a damn thing."

"Actually, it does. Charlotte was a snoop who got killed for poking her head in the murder."

"Maybe. I don't know what it does for us."

"Where's Edith?"

"Having hysterics in the drawing room. Her nephew and his girlfriend are taking care of her."

"You think that's a good idea, Chief? Letting her alone with the suspects?"

"Now they're suspects?"

"Well, you already suspect Alan. The girl gets credit just for proximity. Where were they when we found the body?"

"Over at her place. They heard Edith screaming and came over to see what happened."

"See? Proximity."

Barney Nathan came bustling in. The poor man was terribly self-conscious. He had tied his bow tie, as if to give every appearance of respectability. He couldn't bring himself to look at Cora.

"Barney," Chief Harper said. "Where the hell were you?"

"I was out having a drink. Didn't notice my cell phone. What have we got here?"

"Body in the window seat."

"Again?"

"This time it's one of the sisters."

"Poisoned?"

"You tell me."

"Right."

An agonized wail from the other room reminded him. "Before you do, you wanna give Edith something to damp her down? The woman's getting on my nerves."

"Good idea."

Barney went out to see to Edith.

"All right," Harper said. "You found him for me. That's on the credit side of the ledger. On the debit side of the ledger, you found Charlotte Guilford dead."

"Hey, don't shoot the messenger. She was dead, no matter who found her."

"Yeah, but it happened to be you. And you suggested the possibility before you even got here."

"Not a big leap of logic, Chief. I'm sorry you didn't make it. Though I'm sure you *did* make it, you were just trying to wish it away."

"Ain't that the truth. But the fact is, you walked in here and within minutes you were pointing at Charlotte's body."

"Once again, not that hard to do."

"It makes me wonder if you knew it was there."

Cora referred to the chief as an ignoramus with an amazingly wide variety of sexual practices, only some of which could be considered consensual.

"Cora!"

"I did not know Charlotte was dead. I did not know she was in the window seat. I had never seen her in there before. I did not plant the puzzle on the body or even see a puzzle on the body. I did not add to, subtract from, or in any other way contaminate the crime scene. I am innocent as the driven snow. Though I'm not entirely sure what that means. Does anyone actually *drive* snow?"

Barney Nathan came back from the study toting his doctor's bag. "That should hold her for a while," he said. He still didn't look at Cora. He knelt down by the window seat, leaned over, and examined the corpse. "Well, no smell of almonds. Probably not cyanide."

"How about arsenic?"

"No thanks, I've eaten," Cora said.

Harper scowled, but Barney ignored the interruption. "From the bruising on the neck, I'd say she was strangled."

"That's what I thought," Harper said. "Any idea when?"

"Five or six hours sound about right?"

"Yeah, that'd do it."

"Okay, let's get her to the morgue."

"Soon as Dan's done," Harper said. "You got enough pictures of the corpse?"

"Yeah, fine," Dan said.

Barney went out.

Harper watched him go, said, "Boy, I'm sure glad *I* didn't find him."

"What do you mean?"

"The cold shoulder he's giving you. The guy didn't like you before, but this really ices it. Thanks for doing it. I don't need the medical examiner mad at me right now."

Two EMS boys came in with a gurney. Cora wasn't sure, but she thought they were the same ones as before. They loaded up the body, carted it away.

Alan and Arlene came in from the study.

"How's your aunt?" Harper said.

"She's all doped up. It's for the best, but she's gonna have a rude awakening. You know the TV crew's already here."

"Dan," Chief Harper said, accusingly.

"Hey, don't look at me. You said don't call 'em, I didn't call 'em."

"Well, someone did."

"I think it's dreadful," Arlene said. "You know what they've been saying? They're saying this is all just a movie. That someone's acting out *Arsenic and Old Lace* for real."

"Yeah," Harper said. "What do you think of that?"

"I think it's really stupid. Have you seen the movie?"

"No."

"Well, it's not like the movie at all. In the movie you think someone kills one of the aunts?"

"They don't?"

"It's a comedy. How is that funny? You bump off an old lady."

"They kill a lot of old men," Cora said.

"They're *extras*. *Bit* players. No one gives a damn about them. The aunts are killing them. That's what's funny. Little old ladies who murder. Who are so sweet, and innocent, and open about it. They're absolutely darling. You couldn't kill them."

"Don't tell me," Harper said. "Tell them that."

"Huh?"

"Rick Reed. The TV reporter. When he interviews you, you might point out that this is not like the movie at all. I'd like to nip that theory in the bud."

"I'm not doing an interview."

"Not a formal interview. Just if he asks you."

"I'm not talking to reporters." Arlene shuddered. "It's ghoulish. Every time some kid gets killed you see the mother on TV saying what a good kid he was. How could she bear to be on TV? Even in this terrible tragedy, they can't say no to the cameras."

"It's okay," Alan said. "You don't have to talk to them."

"Are you going to talk to them?"

"I have to talk to them. She's my aunt."

"See what I mean?" Arlene said. "The relatives feel they have to be on TV."

"If you don't want me to, I won't. But I'd like to spare poor Edith."

"Of course. I hadn't thought of that. I'm not thinking

clearly. It's all so awful. You have to tell them it's not like the movie. Your aunts aren't poisoning people. And Charlotte didn't accidentally poison herself. Was she poisoned, by the way?"

Chief Harper shook his head. "No."

"How?" Alan said.

"It would appear she was strangled."

Arlene made a face, hid her head in Alan's chest. She gathered herself, said, "Not *at all* like the movie. It's so stupid. If it was like the movie, Alan would have a criminal brother who looks like Boris Karloff. And a crazy brother who thinks he's Teddy Roosevelt and runs up the stairs shouting, 'Charge!'"

"Which I certainly don't," Alan said.

"No fingerprints, Chief," Dan called from the window seat.

Harper snorted in disgust. He didn't expect any, but even so.

"You have any leads?" Alan said.

"I just got here."

"Yes, but it must be the same person. Who committed all the crimes. Aren't there any leads at all?"

"There's a crossword puzzle. Cora solved it. It indicates Charlotte got killed for snooping around."

"That's ridiculous. What could she have possibly found?"

"I don't know. But I intend to find out. When's the last time you saw her?"

Alan thought for a moment. "This morning. I'd come over to shave."

"I beg your pardon?"

Alan flushed. "I was at Arlene's. I'd left my electric razor in my suitcase. I ran into Charlotte on my way out."

"Did she say anything?"

"Not really."

"What do you mean, not really?"

"Well, nothing helpful. Just chitchat."

"About what?"

"About breakfast. You know old ladies. They always ask about the silliest things." Alan blinked. Looked at Cora. Flushed. Looked away.

Cora pretended not to notice. "Having met Charlotte, I know just what you mean. Ditsy, scatterbrained, and you're never quite sure what she's talking about."

"Exactly," Alan said, happy to be off the hook. "Yes, she was. Very nice, but sometimes hard to follow."

"So, what did she say about breakfast?"

"She asked me if I liked my pancakes."

"You told her you had pancakes?"

"No. See, that's what I mean. She just decided that, out of the blue. Probably that's what *she* had for breakfast."

"But you didn't?"

"No, I had bacon and eggs."

"Did you tell her that?"

"Sure."

"Did you talk about anything *besides* breakfast?" Chief Harper put in.

"I can't remember."

"Could you try?"

"Is it that important?"

"I don't know what's important. But, aside from Edith, you could be the last person to see her alive. What time was this?"

"I don't know. Ten thirty. Eleven."

Harper turned to Arlene. "How about you? When was the last time you saw Charlotte?"

"Well, it wasn't today. Let me see. Was it yesterday? Alan, help me out here. When's the last time we saw Charlotte?"

"You saw her with Alan?"

"I wouldn't have been over here without Alan."

"But you might have been here looking for him?"

"That's possible. I don't recall."

"Well, search your recollection. If you come up with anything, let me know."

Dan Finley came back from outside. "Someone's gotta talk to the TV people."

"Aw, hell," Harper said. "Cora?"

"Don't look at me. I'm peripheral as all hell. Alan?"

Alan grinned. "Looks like I've got no one to pass the buck to. I'll do the best I can, but they're gonna want to talk to someone official."

"And there's a guy outside trying to get in," Dan said.

"Who's that?" Harper said.

"Some guy. Claims he's a relative."

"Of the decedent?"

"Yeah."

"Get him in here. Maybe he knows something."

"I don't see how."

"Dan."

"Sorry. I'll go get him."

Harper turned to Alan. "You got any relatives you haven't told us about?"

"Not to speak of. Of course, if you're talking distant relatives, everyone has some. But if you're talking about people involved with the family, there's no one."

Dan came back with a gaunt man in a button-down shirt and slacks. He couldn't have been more than forty, but his long face, sunken eyes, and ashen complexion made him look older. Indeed, he looked like some apparition dredged up from hell to cast a pall over an already somber scene.

Alan's mouth fell open. "Sebastian?" he murmured.

The apparition grinned. "Hello, kid brother."

FORTY-ONE

"YOUR NAME'S SEBASTIAN GUILFORD?"

"That's right."

"You are Alan's brother?"

"Half brother. Same father, different mothers. Daddy was a rolling stone."

"You're his older brother?"

"That's right." Sebastian loosened his shirt collar. "Could I have a glass of wine?"

"I wouldn't advise it."

Chief Harper was questioning Sebastian Guilford in the study. Edith had been taken upstairs and put to bed, and Alan and Arlene had been banished to her house. Only Cora remained. She sat in the corner, tried to look inconspicuous.

"The wine was poisoned?"

"That's right."

"Did Charlotte drink it?"

"No, she was strangled."

"Good God! That's awful!"

"Whereas poisoning is rather sweet," Cora said.

Sebastian pointed his finger. "Who's she?"

"Cora Felton. She often assists on these cases. She's very good at detecting guilt."

"Detect away. I happen to be innocent."

"We'll be the judge of that. Where were you at one o'clock this afternoon?"

"Is that when she was killed?"

"It's in the ballpark."

"Yeah, well, I wasn't. About that time I was in the airport."

"Where?"

"Seattle."

"You flew in from Seattle?"

"In a manner of speaking. Seattle to Dallas. Dallas to Atlanta. Atlanta to Bradley." He shook his head. "Big mistake. Yeah, the airport's closer, but three planes to get there? I could have flown nonstop to JFK."

"So, what are you doing here?"

"Are you kidding? My aunt's been killed."

"Yeah, but you didn't know that."

"What?"

"When you left. She'd just been killed. The body wasn't found for hours."

"Then why'd you send for me?"

"What?"

"I got an e-mail. From the police department. Saying my aunts were involved in a murder, and I should come at once."

"The police department?"

"That's right."

"I didn't send you an e-mail."

"Well, someone did."

"Do you have it with you?"

"No, it's an e-mail."

"You don't have a printout, or a laptop, or an iPad, or an iPhone, or whatever-the-hell people use these days?" Cora said.

"No. It's on my computer at home. I didn't figure I needed to bring it with me. What the hell is going on here?"

"That's what I'd like to know," Chief Harper said. He bellowed, "Dan!"

A few moments later Dan Finley stuck his head in the door. "Yeah, Chief?"

"This guy says he got an e-mail from the police department. You know anything about it?"

"No. Was it a form letter?"

"It was a letter telling him there'd been a murder."

"Gee, Chief, I can't imagine. I didn't send it, and I'm sure Sam didn't. Are you sure it was from the police department?"

"It said it was from the police department. I don't remember the address, because I didn't answer it."

"What was the heading?" Dan said.

"Let me see. 'Guilford aunt murdered.'"

"*Murdered* or *murder*?" Cora said.

Sebastian's eyes narrowed. "Why do you ask me that?"

"It makes a huge difference. *Murdered* is specific. It means only one thing. *Murder* is open to interpretations."

"I don't remember. I thought it was *murdered*. It could have been *murder*. But when I read it, I thought it was my aunt."

"So you hopped on a plane and came here?" Cora said.

"Yes."

"Why didn't you call first?"

"I didn't have the number."

"Come again?" Chief Harper said.

"What can I tell you? I don't have it. It's been years since I've seen them. Or my baby brother, for that matter."

"You couldn't call information?" Cora said.

"It's unlisted."

"They run an *unlisted* bed-and-breakfast?" Harper said, incredulously.

"I'm sure it's listed. But not under their names. And I don't know what they call it."

"So you dropped everything and flew here from Seattle?"

"Of course I did. My aunts and I are not close, but a murder is a murder."

"Do you have any experience with murder?"

Sebastian's eyes narrowed. "What's that supposed to mean?"

"Outside of the fact it's your aunt. You're not a police officer, are you?"

"No."

"What do you do?"

"I'm an investment broker."

"What does that mean?"

"I handle other people's money."

Chief Harper's manner was not reassuring. He reacted to that announcement as if Sebastian had just admitted to scamming elderly widows out of their social security.

Seeing Sebastian was about to clam up, Cora butted in. "You can easily prove you had nothing to do with this. Do you happen to have your plane ticket?"

"No."

"Or a copy of your itinerary?"

"No. I have no idea when I'm going back. I got a one-way ticket."

"And you don't have it?"

"I threw it away on the plane. Why do I need it? I got a carry-on. I didn't check any baggage. Once I'm on the plane, it's just a useless piece of paper."

"You had to change planes."

"Yes, I did. On the last one, I threw it out. You know why? Because I didn't expect anyone to care." Sebastian looked at Chief Harper. "My aunt's been murdered, and the best you can do is suspect me? That's not very encouraging."

"No one suspects you. We'd like to eliminate you as a possibility. You show up here, unannounced, with a story that doesn't hold water. You get all huffy when we point out where it doesn't."

"What do you mean, it doesn't hold water?"

"You claim the police sent for you, but they didn't, and you have no evidence that they did. You claim you just flew in from Seattle, but you got no evidence of that. Where's your suitcase, by the way?"

"In my car." He snapped his fingers. "There you go. My car. I rented it at the airport. Doesn't that prove anything?"

"It proves you rented a car," Cora said.

"Oh, come on."

"You killed your aunt, drove up to the airport, put your car in the long-term parking lot, and rented a car."

"And then I drive all the way back and deliver myself into the arms of the police, who never suspected me anyway. You're saying that's my plan?"

"I'm not saying it's a *good* plan."

"What about motive?" Harper said. "Do you profit from your aunt's death?"

"No."

"You're sure about that? Suppose they both should die? Would you inherit this house?"

"I certainly hope not. I wouldn't know what to do with it."

"You could always sell it."

"In this market? I'm not so sure they own it free and clear. There may be a bit of a mortgage."

"I see you've given this some thought."

"Not really. But when you ask the question, that's my immediate reaction."

"So you don't expect to profit from their death?"

"No, I don't."

"You think Alan might? I mean, he's here, he's been ingratiating himself with them. Any chance they'd give the place to him and bypass you?"

"I suppose it's possible. Frankly, I could care less."

"But your brother might have a motive."

"Alan might? Take a look at him. Can you imagine him killing anybody?"

"All right. You tell me. Can you think of anybody who'd want to hurt your aunt?"

Sebastian nodded. "Her sister, of course."

FORTY-TWO

CHIEF HARPER GAWKED in astonishment. "Edith Guilford?"

"That's right."

"Sweet little Edith Guilford?"

"She's little, but she's not so sweet. Not when you live with her. Why do you think I left? You think this was a dandy home? My God, those two women are enough to drive you nuts. Nice as can be, in front of other people. Alone? At each other all the time."

"Interesting," Cora said.

"Interesting?" Chief Harper said. "That's not interesting. That's absolutely incredible. I've known the Guilfords all my life."

"Are you related to them? Not so nice in front of family. Vicious, vindictive, at each other's throats."

"Your brother doesn't seem to think so."

"Alan?" Sebastian laughed. "Alan may act that way. He's got a lot of Guilford in him. You should hear him when he's alone."

"If he feels that way, why would he live there?"

"You have to ask? Free rent."

"Nonsense. He has an apartment in the city."

"Which will also turn out to be free rent. Some girl he lives with."

Harper frowned.

"There is one, isn't there?" Sebastian said. "See? Some things never change. Anyway, the way the sisters felt about each other, it was just a matter of time."

"Well, that makes no sense. If Edith did this, she didn't just kill her sister. She killed four other people."

"So?"

"Why would she do that?"

Sebastian shrugged. "Isn't that your department?"

"It's your theory."

"Yes, it is. You don't have to like it."

"But how can you think that, in the face of what's happened?"

Sebastian chuckled, shook his head. "You expect me to defend it? I'm really not obligated to. But, okay, I'll take a crack at it. She did it to cover up the crime."

"The other people were killed first."

"Okay, she did it for practice."

"Now you're just being facetious."

"Well, it's a stupid idea, you asking me for reasons. I was in Seattle this morning. You expect me to fly in here, solve your crime."

"I don't expect anything of the sort. You volunteered the suggestion. I'm trying to determine if it has any basis, or if you're just a kook I can ignore."

Sebastian smiled. "Fair enough." He considered. "How about if she just killed her sister, you'd suspect her at once. So she kills some other people first, so when she kills her sister you don't suspect her at all."

Harper frowned.

"On the other hand, I'd look at baby brother. Particularly if he's manipulated them into leaving everything to him."

"He'd only inherit if he killed them both."

"Maybe Edith's dying. Maybe he found out. He's got to kill Charlotte before Edith dies, because Edith would be easier to manipulate, particularly if she's weakened. Whereas Charlotte would be more apt to dig in her heels.

Oh, sure, she plays the weak and ditsy role, but trust me, she isn't like that at all. Wasn't. Hard to believe she's gone. That type of woman tends to live forever."

Harper turned to Cora. "You buying any of this?"

"I'm keeping an open mind."

"That isn't what I wanted to hear."

"Okay, I'm keeping a closed mind."

"Cora."

"Let me ask a few questions here. When was the last time you saw your aunt?"

"I don't know. Must be twenty, twenty-five years."

"Same as your brother?"

"That's right."

"He must have been pretty young when you left."

"He was old enough to know better. He *did* know better. He just didn't have the guts."

"You mean to leave?"

"I mean to do anything but go along. Passive, that's what he was. Passive aggressive."

"Have you kept track of your aunts in any way? I mean, how would you know they're still alive?"

"I assume if they died I'd hear from their solicitor."

"How do you know they have one?"

"I don't. You're asking me for assumptions."

"If you don't like your aunts, why did you come?"

"Are you kidding me?" Sebastian grinned. "It's a murder."

FORTY-THREE

EDITH GUILFORD WAS still woozy from the sedative Barney Nathan had given her.

"Why are you waking me up?"

"We need to ask you some questions," Chief Harper said.

"I'm too tired."

"I know. I have to ask you nonetheless."

"I don't see why."

"Do you know your sister's dead?"

"You woke me up to ask me that? I thought you had something new."

"How did you feel about your sister?"

"We were very close."

"Didn't you ever fight?"

"About what? Sometimes we argued about what TV channel to watch."

"I thought you didn't have TV," Cora said.

"The guests don't have TV. We do."

"You said you hadn't seen the report of the murders because you don't have TV."

"I meant we hadn't watched."

"But that's not what you said. You said you hadn't watched *because* you didn't have one."

"Did I say that? I don't remember saying that. Maybe it was Charlotte. She made mistakes sometimes."

"Like what?"

Edith didn't answer.

"Like what?"

She shrugged. "Sometimes."

Cora took a breath. "When Charlotte was missing, why didn't you look in the window seat?"

Edith's face contorted. "What a horrible idea. Why would I look in the window seat? I wouldn't want Charlotte to be in the window seat. That's just stupid. I wanted her to be somewhere I could find her."

"But you thought something might have happened to her," Chief Harper said.

"Why do you say that?"

"Because you called me."

"To find her. Not to look for her body."

Edith dissolved into sobs.

Cora, watching carefully, couldn't tell if she was faking. She wasn't acting naturally, but then she'd been drugged.

"Snap out of it," Cora said. "Your sister's dead, and we've gotta find out who killed her. You want to help us, don't you?"

"Yes," Edith blubbered. "I guess so."

"Who was closer to your nephew, you or Charlotte?"

"I don't know."

"Your nephew Alan. You don't know who was closer?"

"No."

"Who did he like better?"

Edith looked at Cora, then at Chief Harper. "Why is she doing this?"

"I'm trying to sort out the relationships," Cora said. "Because it's the only way to figure out what happened here. I want to find out who killed your sister, so I'm asking personal questions. I know they're difficult. So you don't know who Alan liked better?"

"No."

"How about Sebastian?"

Edith looked like she'd been slapped in the face. Her mouth fell open. Her eyes shifted. It took her a few moments to pull herself together. When she did, she seemed more focused than before. She waved her finger. "You mustn't believe a word he says."

"Why?"

"He lies."

"About what?"

"Everything. Every word out of his mouth is a lie. He's always been that way, ever since he was a little boy."

"You never mentioned you had another nephew," Harper said.

"Why should I? He's an embarrassment. Better forgotten. You spoke to him on the phone?"

"No."

"No? Who did? I should warn them. This is very bad. Who did he speak to?"

"Actually he spoke to both of us," Cora said.

"Oh?" Edith's eyes widened in alarm. "Oh! You mean he's here?"

"Yes, he is."

Her face hardened, her jaw snapped shut in a firm line. "He did it! I might have known. Back to kill us, after all these years."

"I don't think so," Harper said. "Apparently he was in Seattle at the time of the crime."

"Can he prove it? I suppose he mocked up some phony evidence to make it look like he was in Seattle, but, trust me, he wasn't. Oh, my God! You have to protect me from him. It's a wonder he didn't kill us both."

"Sebastian seems to feel his baby brother was to blame for a lot of the things he got blamed for."

"Of course he does. He's always tried to put it off on Alan. He's here. Where is he?"

"Right outside."

"Don't let him in! Don't let him get to me! Arrest him! Put him in jail!"

"I can't arrest him."

"Why not? You're the police. That's what you do. Arrest people."

"He hasn't done anything."

"That's what you think. If he's here, he's done something. And he's been here from the beginning, and he's killed all those people, and I should have known it but it's been so long I just didn't think of it and I had no idea he was around."

Edith sprang up and began to pace the room. In spite of the drugs she'd been given, she was pretty steady on her feet. "It's too much! It's too much! After all these years, he's back, devil himself, to kill my sister! I hate him, I hate him! It's been so long I thought he was dead. I *hoped* he was dead! Oh, forgive me, I wish he were dead!"

Harper lowered his voice, said out of the side of his mouth, "She going to need another sedative. You think Barney's home?"

"I wouldn't count on it."

FORTY-FOUR

SHERRY WAS UP with the baby when Cora got home. She was walking the floor of her bedroom, joggling Jennifer on her shoulder.

"Colic," Sherry said. "Just a little colicky, she'll quiet down soon."

Jennifer's crying was getting on Cora's nerves, but she wanted to talk to her niece. She waited it out until the baby stopped blubbering. Sherry nodded, smiled, took Jennifer into her room, and put her down in the crib.

Sherry came back into the bedroom. "So? Tell me all about it."

"Aaron hasn't called?"

"He's busy with the story. You want to tell me what he's writing? You didn't give an interview to Rick Reed."

"Yes, I did."

"I don't think 'No comment' counts as an interview."

"I actually said more than that. There was an awful lot he couldn't use on the air."

"So what's up?"

Cora gave Sherry a rundown of the evening's events.

"My God," Sherry said. "The criminal brother. Just like in the movie. Does he look like Boris Karloff?"

"Yes and no. He's tall and gaunt, with a lean, ashen face."

"Okay, how *doesn't* he resemble Boris Karloff?"

"He's not being pursued by a horde of angry villagers."

"Cora."

"And he doesn't have a plastic surgeon sidekick who talks like Peter Lorre."

"And he thinks his aunt did it?"

"Either that or brother Alan."

"That nice young man? He wouldn't hurt a fly."

"Where did you meet that nice young man?"

"I can't remember."

"Oh, my God. Is your marriage over so soon? The baby's not even walking and already the seven-year itch."

"What in the world are you talking about?"

"You don't remember where you met Alan?"

"He was pointed out to me somewhere as the nephew. I really can't remember."

"Of course not."

"And what reasons did Boris Karloff give for Edith killing her sister?"

"They didn't like each other."

"No, really."

"Yeah, really. According to him, the whole family's batty."

"Like in the movie. Oh, my goodness. How did Rick Reed ever miss this guy?"

"I don't think he knows about him."

"Dan Finley didn't tip him off?"

"I think Chief Harper read him the riot act."

"Rick Reed?"

"Dan Finley."

"Even so, I'm surprised Rick didn't pounce on him the minute he came out the door."

"He never got the chance. The chief let him out the side way."

"So Rick doesn't have the story. Does Aaron know about this?"

"Sherry."

"Well, it would be a scoop."

"Yeah, it would. And the chief would know exactly where it came from. I'd be in more trouble than I am now."

"Are you in trouble now?"

"Not really."

"You're not making any sense."

"I know. This whole case doesn't make any sense. And then this guy Sebastian shows up."

"Who?"

"Boris Karloff. And he rolls out all these theories why the sister did it or the nephew did it."

"Because they're nuts?"

"Basically. But why kill all these other people? To cover up the crime. But it hasn't happened yet. Like for practice. What about to camouflage the crime so it wouldn't stand out?"

"Does that make sense?"

"I don't know. It's a generic reason. It could apply to anyone at all. But in this particular case, I don't know these people. I certainly don't know them the way he describes them."

"So, what's your theory?"

"I don't have one. That's the whole problem. I can't get a grip on anything. I'm wondering if you'd take another look at the puzzle."

"What do you mean, take another look at the puzzle? You think I solved it wrong?"

"No, I'm sure you solved it right. I just don't understand the message. It tells us Charlotte's in the window seat. We know Charlotte's in the window seat. It says Charlotte was nosy. We could have guessed that, too."

Sherry considered. "Does it tell you she was *killed* because she was nosy?"

"That's implied."

"Yeah, but it's not necessarily true. To start off, there are two possibilities. The killer put that implication in the puzzle deliberately. Or the killer put that implication in the puzzle accidently."

"How could it be accidental?"

Sherry smiled. "Hey. You don't construct crossword puzzles. They're not easy. You're writing a short little poem, it's gotta be symmetrical, the first and last line having the same number of letters, the same with the middle two. And it's gotta rhyme. You got very few words to convey the idea."

"You're saying the killer could have said she was snoopy just because it satisfied the meter?"

"Why not? What could it hurt? Unless your theory is the killer is trying to help you figure this out and convict him. In which case, he would be scrupulously careful not to give you a false lead. Assuming getting caught is not the killer's intention, implying the woman got killed for being snoopy doesn't hurt him in the least."

"You keep saying *him*."

"Well, I'm not going to say *him or her* every time. I'd go batty. Anyway, say the killer put the implication in the puzzle deliberately. He either put the implication in the puzzle because it's true, or he put the implication in the puzzle because it's false. If he did it because it's true, it's because he's playing a game with you. Because he's trying to taunt you. Or because it's an elaborate double-bluff, telling you what's actually true in the hope you'll think it's false.

"If he did it because it's false, it's because he's trying to mislead you."

"Oh, my God," Cora said.

"What?"

"You know what you're doing? You're being me. You're thinking like me. And do you know why? Because *I'm* not thinking like me. Because I'm totally buffaloed by this case, and I'm not thinking at all, so you're stepping up and doing it for me. Because I've become addled and stupid and can't do it myself."

"Oh, I don't believe that."

"Well, don't panic. It's not irreversible. I'm just momentarily fuddled."

"Knowing that, you can now think clearly?"

Cora sighed. "I'm afraid so."

FORTY-FIVE

"WE HAVE TO break up."

"What?"

"Sorry, Barney, but you're cramping my style."

"Huh?"

"I can't think. I can't function. I'm like a ditsy teenager with a high school crush." At his expression, she said, "No, no, don't panic, that's not what I mean. It's just been a long time since I've been in any relationship. I've forgotten what it takes. I mean mentally. Emotionally. The fact is, it's clouding my thinking."

Barney blinked at Cora, sat on the edge of the bed. "You picked me up at the Country Kitchen, smuggled me into your house so your niece wouldn't know I'm here, to tell me you're breaking up with me because this is just a schoolgirl crush? Why couldn't you have slipped me a note in study hall?"

Cora smiled. "Why, Barney Nathan. Good for you. It's nice to see the feisty side of you. I mean, when you're not defending some autopsy."

"I'm glad you like it. I'm still baffled. I have no idea what you're talking about."

Cora shrugged. "I used to be such a playgirl. Ever since I've come to Bakerhaven my social life has dwindled. For one thing, I quit drinking. If you're not hanging out in singles bars, you're not going to get much action. Not that there are singles bars in Bakerhaven, but you catch my drift. Anyway, I sublimated my primal urges into something else."

"Crossword puzzles."

"I was going to say crime solving, but it's the same idea. And I got good at it. I honed my mental agility, reached the point where I could approach a problem logically, and do my best to reason it out."

"While decimating a medical examiner or two."

"It was never personal, Barney. Always business. Not that it makes a lot of difference. I doubt if the guys who got shot in *The Godfather* cared if it was personal or business."

"What's this got to do with us breaking up?"

"I'm trying to explain where I'm coming from. Which I'm not exactly sure of myself. Since I've been here I've had one serious relationship, and it ended badly. Very badly. I mean, on a scale of one to ten, a dead groom is gonna cost you a lot of points.

"And I pulled myself together and I solved that crime. And I haven't had a serious relationship since. Not that my ex-husband Melvin hasn't tried."

"Is that the one who got arrested?"

"You'll have to be more specific." At his expression, she said, "Yes, he's the one you know who got arrested. Anyway, without the distraction of a man, I've been sharp and focused and aware and good at what I'm doing. And now I'm not. My senses are dulled. It's worse than alcohol."

"Can't you work through it?"

"I couldn't work through alcohol. I had to quit drinking."

"You're saying I make you stupid."

"That's an oversimplification."

"This is all because you don't know what happened to Charlotte Guilford."

"No, this is all because I don't even *suspect* what happened to Charlotte Guilford." Cora sighed, shook her head. "How are things with your wife?"

"Huh?"

"You know. The woman you married. How are things with her?"

"What do you think?"

"I don't know. That's why I'm asking."

"You *do* know. She thinks I'm having an affair with Becky Baldwin."

"Yeah, but things were bad before that."

"Not this bad."

"How bad is this bad?"

"She hadn't thrown me out of the house."

"She has now? She still hasn't, or you'd be in a motel and we wouldn't be doing all this sneaking around."

"I suppose."

"Men," Cora said. "Just like with the damn baseball cards. You can't throw anything away. You can complain all you want, but you can't let go of your wife. You're not getting along, life together is living hell, but you're still not out of the house because she hasn't thrown you out yet. I suppose you can argue you like the house. How long have you been married?"

"Twenty-three years."

"There you go. You fool around before?"

"Of course not."

"Did she?"

"Really!"

"See, you're still not over her. I can always tell. Which is what's making me stupid. The amount of mental energy I'm spending on this damn relationship."

"You know she slapped Becky Baldwin?"

"I was there."

"What was that like?"

"Better than if it was me."

"She was really angry?"

"In a cold, methodical way. Kind of scary. Trust me, I've been there. On both sides. Thank you, Joni Mitchell."

"Huh?"

"Oh, you're younger than I am." Cora sighed, shook her head. "'Both Sides Now.' Google the lyrics."

They sat awhile in silence.

Barney got up from the bed.

Cora got up, too.

He took her in his arms.

"Well, I guess this is good-bye," Barney said.

Cora smiled, patted him on the cheek. "Let's not be hasty," she said, unbuttoning his shirt.

FORTY-SIX

CORA DROPPED BARNEY off at the Country Kitchen and drove over to the *Bakerhaven Gazette*. Downstairs the presses were silent. Printers stood around waiting to start the job.

Cora found Aaron in his cubical working on the story.

"They're retooling the front page," Aaron said. "Not for me. The editor's whipping it up from what I gave him. Which wasn't much. I'm doing the expanded coverage on page four. Which is a rehash of the same things, since he's just quoting me."

"You happen to see a thin man in the crowd who looked like a walking cadaver?"

Aaron's eyes widened. "Are you telling me…?"

"Alan Guilford's older brother flew in from Seattle to join in the fun."

"What's his story?"

"He thinks her sister did it."

"What!?"

"Or his baby brother. Not big on family, I gather. Still, his first choice is Auntie Edith."

"Who knows about this?"

"Chief Harper, Dan Finley, and Sebastian Guilford."

"That's his name?"

"You got it."

"And Rick Reed doesn't."

"Bingo, right on the button."

"You telling me this off the record?"

"Did I say that? I don't recall saying that. Must have slipped my mind."

Aaron snatched up the phone, pressed the intercom for his editor. "Hold the front page! I'll be right there!" He slammed down the phone, checked with Cora. "Sebastian Guilford?"

"That's right."

Aaron ran out the door.

FORTY-SEVEN

CHIEF HARPER WAS tipped back in his chair with a cup of coffee and a California bun from Cushman's Bake Shop. The *Bakerhaven Gazette* was open on his desk. The headline read: CHARLOTTE GUILFORD MURDERED. The right-hand column dealt with the facts of the murder. The sub-headline read: NEPHEW ACCUSES AUNT. The left-hand column, an exclusive by reporter Aaron Grant, dealt with Sebastian Guilford's accusation.

"What's up?" Cora said.

Harper took a bite of bun, washed it down with coffee. "Nothing much. Seen the morning paper?"

"I glanced at it."

"It appears that Aaron Grant found out about Sebastian Guilford."

"I read that," Cora said.

"I wonder how Aaron Grant got *that* story."

"Do you really?"

"No, I have a pretty good idea."

"And yet you're not leaping up and ripping my throat out."

"What's the point? I knew you were going to give him the story. You knew you were going to give him the story. The only one who didn't know you were going to give him the story was Dan Finley, who was very careful not to give it to Rick Reed."

"Why'd you care about that?"

"You don't want to see Rick Reed scooped by Aaron?"

"No, but I can't imagine you manipulating the witness just to make it happen."

Harper smiled. "You got me. I certainly wouldn't. On the other hand, there's a big difference between some nut job on TV screaming about how his aunt's a killer and reading about it in the morning paper in an article peppered with the word *alleged*. And it's not just that the guy alleges that his aunt is the killer. The guy is *alleged* to have alleged that his aunt's the killer. Aaron never talked to the guy himself, he only talked to you. Which buys me time before Henry Firth starts pressuring me to arrest the aunt."

"Ratface wouldn't do that."

"Wanna bet? And don't call him Ratface. There's five bodies kicking around. The prosecutor's so eager to charge someone, he'll take anything he can get."

"Can I quote you on that, Chief? The prosecutor doesn't care who's innocent or guilty as long as he can make a case?"

"You do and we *will* have trouble," Harper said. He took a bite of his California bun, chewed it around. "You know Barney's wife slapped Becky Baldwin?"

"I was there."

"How was it?"

"It was beautiful. She swung from the hip, got her weight behind it. It was pretty loud. I gotta tell you, Becky was shocked."

"How'd Becky take it?"

"Not well. She couldn't place the woman. Asked who it was. Mrs. Cushman had to fill her in."

"Do you buy that?"

"What? That she didn't know who it was? Half the people in this town I know by sight but I don't know who they are."

"Yeah, but you're not sleeping with their husbands."

Cora gave him a look.

Chief Harper blushed bright red.

"You got anything on the crime," Cora said, "or would you rather just gossip?"

"You know as much as I do."

"I certainly hope not. I haven't had Dan Finley making phone calls for me. What's he found out?"

"Basically nothing."

"You identify the lodger yet?"

"No."

"Well, that doesn't add up. It's been over forty-eight hours. He should have been reported missing. Unless he's foreign, in which case you would expect him to have a passport."

"No one of his description has been reported missing. At least within the given time frame."

"What about outside the given time frame?"

"Nobody's been reported missing at all."

"That makes no sense."

"Tell me about it. A perfectly ordinary man killed for no apparent reason. And when you go to check him out, he's a total mystery. A complete nobody. The man who wasn't there."

"A movie title. That should mean something. It's a shame to think it doesn't."

"What about your movie?"

"What about it?"

"You said this crazy nephew was just like one of the people in it."

"What about it?"

"How do you account for that?"

"I don't account for it. Just chalk it up as another bizarre circumstance."

"Yeah, but there's been so many."

There was a knock on the door. Alan Guilford and Becky Baldwin came in.

"I see you brought reinforcements," Harper said.

"Arlene thought I should have a lawyer."

Cora cocked her head. "Arlene suggested you bring Becky Baldwin?"

"Yeah. Why?"

"Doesn't quite compute." Cora waved it away. "Never mind. What's up?"

"What do you mean, what's up? You asked me to come in here."

"*I* asked you to come in here. I'm the chief of police. Cora only *appears* to be running things."

"That's just it," Alan said. "You asked for me *again*. It's getting to be a habit. Makes it look like I'm your chief suspect. Arlene felt I should protect myself."

"That's really not the case," Harper said. "I wanted to talk to you about your brother."

Alan rolled his eyes. "Ah, my dear, sweet brother. Just shows up and moves right in."

"What?"

"How do you like that? Accuse your aunt of murder, and move into her house."

"Wait a minute. Are you saying Edith invited him to stay?"

"What do you mean invited? He just moved in."

"How can he do that?"

"Why not? He has his key."

"Sebastian has keys to the house?" Cora said.

"Of course he does."

"I'll be damned."

"Did you run into him last night?" Harper asked.

"I avoided him last night. I stayed at Arlene's. I'll tell

you one thing, I'm not going to sleep in the same house with that man."

"You're afraid of him?"

"I'm worried about him, that's for sure. You know what he used to do when he was a kid? He used to steal things, blame it on me."

"Wait a second," Becky said. "My client is not making any accusations against his brother. He is merely pointing out that he did not have an easy childhood, and that his brother's sudden appearance is a totally unexpected occurrence that he is attempting to adjust to."

Alan looked pained. "See, that's what I don't understand. You and Arlene both seem to feel I need to watch my tongue. I am not in any trouble and I'm not going to get in any trouble. Nothing I can say will hurt me. And I certainly trust these people not to twist my words around. May I speak plainly without fear of being quoted in some legal action taken by my brother?"

"Absolutely," Cora said. "Anything you say may be used in evidence against you if they arrest you for murder. But in terms of a civil suit for defamation of character, our lips are sealed."

"Is that right, Chief Harper?" Becky said.

"Well, I wouldn't go that far."

"Stop it, Chief," Cora said. "We're all friends here. Even if the kid did bring a mouthpiece. Becky, I know you want to earn your money, but we got five killings to sift through. Can we kind of speed it up?"

"We can speed it up if you're not going to treat us as adversaries. To begin with, I'd like to clear my client of this crime. Do we have a time of death yet?"

"Don't you know?" Harper said.

Becky frowned. "How would I know that?"

"You're confusing her with Perry Mason, Chief. She

doesn't have Paul Drake and a flock of detectives. She's got me when she can afford to hire me, which hasn't happened lately, and that's about it. So go ahead and tell her. What's the time of death?"

"It would appear she was killed yesterday afternoon somewhere around one o'clock."

"Aw, hell," Alan said.

"What's the matter?" Cora said.

"I got an alibi from two o'clock on. I was with Arlene."

"Where were you at one?"

"I went out to the mall."

"Did you buy anything? Do you have a receipt?"

"Now here," Becky Baldwin said, "I would like to speak to my client before he speaks to you. Not that he has anything to hide. But these are matters I have not yet discussed with him, and I'd just like to know what his answers are before he makes them."

"That's certainly fair," Cora said.

Harper turned on her. "*You're* deciding which of my questions the witness should answer?"

"I really don't see what I'm a witness to," Alan said. "I didn't see anything. I didn't hear anything. I wasn't there."

"You're still the last person to see Charlotte alive."

"Really? Counting Edith?"

"Edith saw her earlier. Charlotte said she was going shopping. As far as Edith knew, she went. Did you happen to see her in the mall?"

"Here again," Becky said, "I would like to confer with my client."

"Oh, nonsense," Alan said. "There's nothing to discuss. I went to the mall. I did not see Charlotte there. The last time I saw Charlotte was when I had a conversation with her earlier that morning."

"To get back to *my* questions," Harper said, "I want to know about your brother. I would like to know, without some paranoid concern that you are going to be sued for slander."

Becky started to complain.

Cora jumped in. "I'm sure the chief means no offense. He's just a trifle stressed by the fact the mortality rate in this town is beginning to resemble that of a PlayStation videogame."

"Can he talk off the record?" Becky said.

"Of course he can," Cora told her.

"Is that right?" Becky asked Chief Harper.

"With her assurance, why do you need mine? Fine. Talk off the record. Just talk."

Alan looked to Becky, who nodded okay.

"My brother was the type of kid who pulled the wings off of flies. Cruel, mean, vindictive, sly, sneaky, cunning. He never got caught. At least, not in the beginning. A newspaper would disappear. A page of it, folded into a paper airplane, would be found in my pants drawer. Sebastian would bring me a present. I'd open it up, it would be Aunt Charlotte's ring. I'd get caught putting it back. One time he held me down and poured pudding down my throat. Butterscotch pudding. Five or six times, I don't know how many, until I got an incredible tummy ache. Then he went to our aunts and told them I ate all the pudding. It was hard to deny it. I was throwing up pudding in the bathroom."

"And eventually he got caught?"

"He got more and more daring, the more he got away with. One afternoon when they were out he took the car for a joyride, smashed it into a tree. I'm sure he would have pinned that on me, too, if there'd been any way, but he got picked up on the scene. He also broke his arm.

After that they took his stories with a grain of salt. When they cracked down on him, he left."

"And his accusations against you?"

"Are lies, plain and simple."

"What about his accusations against Edith?"

"Absolutely disgraceful and utterly absurd. Edith wouldn't harm a fly. But if he's really pushing it, I would start looking at him for the crime. It's just what he always did. Do something bad and blame someone else."

"And you didn't see him in town before he showed up at your aunts' last night?"

"No. It was an absolute shock."

"You recognized him at once?"

"He hasn't changed. Even as a kid he looked deathly ill. That's how he'd get away with things. Look frail and helpless, poor little boy."

"And yet he was strong enough to hold you down?" Cora said.

A flash of anger crossed Alan's face, but was quickly suppressed. "He was older. Six years older. Made a huge difference."

"And you hadn't seen him from the time he left home until last night?"

"That's right."

"Could he have been around here for a while without you seeing him?"

Alan's eyes narrowed. "What are you getting at? If I didn't run into him, sure. If I saw him, I'd know. You don't forget that face."

"I really think we're done here," Becky said.

"One more thing," Harper said. "The last time you saw Charlotte. Yesterday morning. You came over to shave and she asked you about breakfast. Have you given that any thought? Anything come to mind?"

Alan looked at Becky.

"That's sort of a touchy subject," Becky said, "what with you claiming Alan was the last one to see his aunt alive."

"Arlene didn't like it," Alan explained. "She thought it was antagonistic. Like saying I had the most opportunity."

"You're the one who brought it up," Cora said.

"I just want to know about the conversation. In case I could pick up a clue."

"Afraid I can't help you," Alan said. "I told you everything I remember."

"Tell us something you don't remember," Cora said.

Alan looked confused.

Becky rolled her eyes, put her arm around her client, and steered him out the door.

"Do you have to antagonize everybody?" Harper said.

"A lawyer and a client? Come on, Chief. They're already hostile."

Harper sighed. "Well, we didn't get anything."

"Yeah, we did. Alan Guilford doesn't want to talk about his meeting with Charlotte."

"That's because he was the last person to see her alive."

"That's what he says. But it's not necessarily true. He has his lawyer primed to intervene. And he trots out his girlfriend as an excuse. That's particularly telling."

"Why?"

"It's an irrelevant detail. He's explaining without being asked. It's defensive as hell. Under normal circumstances, a guy doesn't volunteer the fact his girlfriend doesn't want him to do something."

"Is that so?"

"Didn't you ever date anyone?"

"Not in this lifetime."

They were interrupted by loud, angry voices and a cackle of laughter.

"What the hell is that?" Cora said.

"I don't know, but it can't be good."

Cora followed the chief outside where all hell had broken loose. Alan Guilford was attempting to kill his demonically grinning brother, who kept taunting him and dancing out of range. Becky Baldwin had gotten between them and was trying to restrain Alan. Rick Reed and the Channel 8 news team were filming gleefully.

"The jig's up, little brother," Sebastian cried. "I wasn't in time to save Charlotte, but you'll never get Edith now that I'm here."

FORTY-EIGHT

"BECKY'S GOT SOME nice moves," Aaron said.

"I thought you promised Sherry not to compare her with your old girlfriends," Cora said. "It's not fair to a new mom. At least not while she's still nursing."

"I was referring to the way she ducked under her client's right hook. Very impressive, considering she was holding him back from his brother at the time."

"It was a nice move," Sherry said. "Strong and agile. Marvelous qualities in a woman. It's a wonder she's still single."

"Oooh!" Cora said. "Look at the claws on mama cat. If I were you, I'd ease up on praising the lady lawyer, Aaron."

"Well, they keep showing it," Aaron said.

They did indeed. The shot of Becky ducking the roundhouse right was not only being replayed on Channel 8, it had also made the network news and had gone viral on YouTube. Over a million people had seen Alan Guilford swing wildly at his brother.

Cora, Sherry, and Aaron were having dinner in the living room in front of the TV, just like in the good old days. Cora wasn't seeing Barney Nathan that night. The doctor was the speaker at some dinner function in Danbury. Cora wondered if he took his wife.

Jennifer was in one of those low, plastic highchairs on wheels, more like a cart with a tray. She was motoring happily around the room, leaving a trail of Cheerios and chicken. Buddy was vacuuming them up, and being a good dog and not grabbing food off her plate.

Jennifer piloted the highchair into the wall, looked offended when it didn't go any farther.

"She got a license to drive that thing?" Cora said.

Jennifer pushed off the wall, headed toward the TV, where Rick Reed was waxing eloquent. She picked up a piece of apple, hurled it at the screen.

"Is that an editorial comment?" Cora said.

"If it is, she's got good taste," Aaron said.

Rick kept on talking, oblivious to the fact a baby was critiquing his performance. "Today, another bizarre twist in the *Arsenic and Old Lace* murders. The prodigal nephew returning and picking a fight with his stay-at-home brother, just like in the movie starring Cary Grant. We caught up with local boy Alan Guilford, just this afternoon."

The picture cut to a shot of Rick Reed shoving a microphone in Alan's face as he came out the front door of his house.

"No comment," Alan said.

"His brother Sebastian Guilford was not so reticent."

The picture cut to a shot of Sebastian's mocking face. "Someone killed my aunt, and no one seems to have the slightest idea who did it. That's the problem with living in a small town. You have to put up with small-town people. That's why I moved out long ago."

"Are you blaming the police department for not catching the killer of your aunt?"

"No. I'm applauding and giving them a medal. All I can say is, if I had to look for a killer, I wouldn't look that far from home."

"Are you referring to anyone in particular?"

"Obviously not. If I were, I'm sure they'd be arrested on my say-so."

"You're being sarcastic?"

"I'm being facetious. It's a subtle difference. Ask that puzzle person to explain it for you."

The picture cut back to a shot of Rick Reed. "I'd be happy to ask Cora Felton, but she hasn't seen fit to come on camera. This is Rick Reed, Channel Eight News."

"Wanna give Rick an interview?" Aaron said.

"So I can lecture him on semantics? Not in this lifetime." Cora stood up and clapped her hands. "Okay, I've got the night off, maybe I can do something here."

"What do you mean, you got the night off?" Sherry said.

Cora tap-danced fast. "Nobody's killed anybody. Chief Harper's not asking me to do anything. Hell, it's like a vacation."

"What'd you have in mind?" Aaron said.

"Solving the crime would be nice. But I'm happy just taking a shot at it. I haven't been myself lately, Nancy Drew–wise. It's time for that to change."

"You have a new philosophy of life?" Aaron said.

"Yeah." She grinned. "Let Cora be Cora."

FORTY-NINE

CORA PUT ON cotton pants, a knit sweater, and running shoes. She was so psyched to be going into action she didn't even bother to consider if they matched. They didn't. The pants were green, the pullover was blue, the running shoes were purple. No matter. She wasn't going to a fashion show.

Cora dug in her drawstring purse, pulled out her gun. She flipped the cylinder open, checked that it was full. It was. She dumped the bullets out to make sure there was no expended cartridge. Of course, there wasn't. Cora always reloaded the gun after she fired it. Her ex-husband Melvin had taught her well.

Cora put the bullets back in the gun, flipped the cylinder closed. She wondered if she had something lighter to carry it in. The hell with it. She was comfortable with the drawstring purse. She had her cigarettes in it. If she left them behind, she'd be a nervous wreck.

Cora got in the car, drove out to the Guilford house. She smoked along the way, trying to calm her jangled nerves. Which shouldn't have been jangled. She had nothing riding on the outcome of this one. No one was threatening her family. She had nothing to fear. Nothing to lose.

Except her sanity. The idea that she couldn't think straight because she had a man. That would be devastating. A crushing blow from which she might not recover.

Cora slowed down a few blocks from the turn, looked for a place to put out the cigarette. She'd stopped using the car ashtray when the baby was born. Sherry had made her stop using it, insisting that Jennifer ride in a smoke-free car. She wasn't supposed to smoke in it, let alone use the ashtray. She'd kept the windows open on the way.

Cora stopped the car, got out, and stomped on the cigarette. Hoped the tobacco wouldn't get caught up in the sneaker's tread. She'd have to inspect her feet before she went back in the house. Something else to worry about. Or was she just reaching for things to worry about, so she wouldn't worry about the biggie?

Cora slammed the car door, turned onto the Guilfords's street. She didn't stop, however. She drove right by and kept going, didn't slow down until she had turned the corner onto the next block.

The Channel 8 news team was camped out in front of the house, interviewing the neighbors. There was no way she could get into the house unseen. Rick Reed would pounce on her the minute she got out of the car.

Cora drove down the side street. The house she was passing would be Arlene's. It bordered on the Guilford property, which was how Arlene heard the noise she sent Alan to check out, only to get arrested as a prowler by Sam Brogan.

When was that? The first or the second murder? The second. The drunk in the window seat. And the crossword puzzle in the bushes. Was it even related to the crime? Did it have to mean anything?

It did, of course. The answer was *Arsenic and Old Lace*. Which is how they all got in this mess.

No it wasn't. It came with the second murder, not with the first. If that puzzle was what it was all about, why wasn't it found on the first body?

Cora parked in the shadows of the side street, away from any house. She approached Arlene's house from the side, keeping low in the bushes, feeling her way along for any strand of barbed wire. Could there be one? No, then Alan couldn't have gone back and forth. There had to be easy access between the houses.

A light in Arlene's house was on. Through the window Cora could see what appeared to be a living room. There was no one there. If Arlene and Alan were home, they would be upstairs. There was a light on in one of the bedrooms.

Cora slipped around the back of the house. In the dark she could make out the outlines of a picnic table, a grill, what appeared to be a water fountain but turned out to be a bird feeder, and a large doghouse. There did not seem to be a dog. Unless he was inside, and unaware of prowlers.

Cora went farther, encountered the fence. It was too flimsy to climb, not flimsy enough to push down. Not that Cora would have done such a thing, still that was how she thought of it.

Cora followed the fence to the right, came to a dead end at the edge of the property. She retraced her steps, followed along to the left and found the hole. Or rather the gap. A space wide enough for a person to slip through.

A thin person. Not a person who had put on a few pounds lately. Damn it, must she be reminded of that at every turn?

Cora wriggled her way through, making sure the drawstring purse didn't snag. Ahead of her was the Guilford house. It was more lit up than Arlene's, but then there were more people staying there. The boarder had checked out, after supplying Chief Harper with his name and address and IDs of all descriptions, locking the barn door after the horse had been killed in the back of a bus, but Sebastian and Edith were staying there. And Alan still had a room there, when he wasn't staying at Arlene's, which he wasn't necessarily doing. From experience Cora knew girlfriends and fiancées did not always wish to suffer the presence of even the most ardent suitors until after the knot was tied. If so, Cora wondered what room he was in. It occurred to her she could knock on the door and ask. She realized she was getting giddy.

Bright lights reminded her of the presence of the TV crews. There was no chance of sneaking in the front door. There was a kitchen door right off the back porch, but it was locked. Cora could see the skeleton key sticking out of the lock on the inside. In an emergency, she could have gotten in just by breaking the pane of glass in the door, but this was not an emergency, she told herself, this was merely indulging a whim.

Cora came down off the back porch, worked her way around the side of the house. A light from a downstairs window formed a long rectangle on the lawn. Bushes in front of the window mottled the light spill, so it resembled the surface of the moon. She crept closer, peered in the window.

A fireplace on the opposite wall gave Cora her bearings. It was the living room. This was the window the drunk had climbed in. It had been unlocked at the time. Surely it would be locked now.

Cora scanned the room. It was empty, at least the part she could see. There might have been someone sitting in the corner just out of her line of vision, but why anyone would sit there she couldn't imagine. They'd be away from everything, up against the wall.

Not that it mattered, with the window locked anyway.

Cora put her fingers under the bottom and pushed.

The window shot up.

Cora, expecting to encounter resistance, nearly fell over the sill. She righted herself, shrank back into the shadows. The window slamming open was loud. Surely someone would come.

No one did.

The room was exactly as before. The door to the foyer was still shut.

Cora took a breath, flung her drawstring purse over the sill. She took ahold of the sill, and climbed in. Instead of landing on the floor, she found herself perched on the window seat. She climbed down, looked around.

Everything was quiet. There was no one there.

On the far side of the room, next to the fireplace, was a portable bar. There was a carafe of wine on it. It was half full. On the lower tray were half a dozen wineglasses.

The bottle of wine intrigued her. She hadn't expected to see a bottle of wine in the house. But there it was, a glass decanter, right there on the tray as if to be ready for afternoon tea. Cora wondered if it was elderberry.

Cora took the stopper out of the bottle, tried to see if she could smell bitter almonds. She didn't think so, but she wasn't tasting the wine just to make sure.

She put the stopper back in the bottle, looked around the room, and went to the door. She put her ear to the keyhole, heard nothing. She opened the door a crack and peered out. There was no one in the foyer. The hallway to the kitchen was dark. But there was a light shining in from the pantry. If she remembered correctly, that was where the door to the cellar was. Could someone be down in the cellar? For what conceivable reason?

Cora tiptoed down the hall.

The creak of a door startled her. Cora froze. Had it come from the pantry? It was hard to tell.

A door shut. It was definitely from the pantry. The cellar door. And steps coming her way.

Cora tiptoed quickly back down the hall, went in, shut the door, and listened at the keyhole.

Footsteps. Coming in her direction.

Cora ran for the window. She was almost there when the door started to open. There was no time to climb out.

Cora raised the lid of the window seat, hopped inside, closed the lid.

FIFTY

CORA LAY IN the dark, holding her breath and counting footsteps. Cold, deliberate, menacing. It couldn't be Edith, it had to be Sebastian. She wouldn't have thought such a gaunt man would have such a heavy tread. Had he seen her? Was he coming straight for the window seat?

Cora fumbled in her purse for her gun.

The footsteps stopped. Cora could imagine Sebastian looking around. How could he miss the open window? He'd see it, it would lead him to her, and what would she do? Shoot him? You could get away with shooting an intruder, but the police frowned on it when an intruder shot an occupant.

The steps resumed, approached the window.

"Ah, look who's here!"

The voice came from the direction of the door. A male voice. One Cora thought she knew.

"What are you doing here, little brother?"

"What do you mean, what am I doing here?" Alan must have been right next to the window, but had turned back toward the door. "I live here."

"Well, yes and no. I thought you were staying with the fair Arlene."

"Keep her out of this."

"Oh, but she's so much in this, isn't she? They all are. Aren't they, little brother? Lucky for you. It's your only skill."

Alan's voice was nasty, taunting. "And don't you

wish you had it? It's so much harder having to live by your wits."

"You got a little short-suited in that department, didn't you, brother?"

"I'm smart enough to stay out of trouble. Which is something you never learned."

"Till now. Why'd you have to start killing people? You got a nice, rich girlfriend. I thought you had it made."

"Sure you did," Alan said. He took a few steps toward his brother, away from the window. "That's why you had to screw it up. What tipped you off? You got spies on the East Coast now? I know you're not living here. It's not safe for you anymore. Unless you had plastic surgery, like the guy in the movie."

"What movie?"

"You know what movie. Don't play dumb. *Arsenic and Old Lace.*"

"Oh, that movie."

"Yeah, that movie. Happen to ring a bell?"

"Sure it does. It's what you patterned your crime around. You never were an original thinker. Always had to copy someone else. What I don't understand is why you killed Charlotte. Your aunts are your only buffer against the outside world."

"Would you keep your voice down," Alan warned.

"What, you afraid Edith will hear? Don't worry. Doctor gave her some pills to sleep. He said one every four hours. I gave her three."

"So, what's your game, big brother? Why are you here?"

"Are you kidding me? My baby brother's got himself in the soup. I wanted to see how bad."

"So you could help, of course," Alan said sarcastically.

"Okay, so I like to gloat. But you gotta admit, it is

pretty funny. Here you are, perfect setup. Rich, young heiress falls into your lap, right next door. Gorgeous, gullible, taken in by the Guilford charm, what could possibly go wrong? So what happens? You suddenly snap and go on a killing spree."

Cora couldn't bear it anymore. Risk or no risk, she raised the lid a crack and peered out.

Alan Guilford and his brother were circling each other like predatory cats, slowly, purposefully, move and counter, each face a picture of contempt, Sebastian's gloat matched by Alan's sneer.

"You're too pleased, big brother," Alan said. "Too happy about how perfect it is. I detect a sense of pride. As if you can't stop congratulating yourself on how clever you are to have pulled it off."

"You get all that?"

"I certainly do."

"Well, that's wonderful. I must applaud your powers of perception. Tell me, little brother, how did I do all this? How did I set it up? How did I carry it out? What was my sense of purpose? What did I hope to obtain? Just as a matter of curiosity, what the hell do you think happened here?" Sebastian grinned. "Stupid question. You know perfectly well. You engineered it all."

"That's a good bluff, Sebastian, pretending to think I did it, as if you hadn't done it yourself."

"Right back at you, bro. But stop and think for a minute. Does this look like one of my scams? It's an awful lot of effort for no tangible reward. What do I hope to get out of all this? Aside from seeing you fall on your keister. Which is a wonderful sight, but I wouldn't kill five people to see it."

"I don't know why you did it, I just know you did."

"See, now there's where you make your mistake. Your

dogged insistence that I'm guilty. Like pretending to believe it's me will prove it isn't you. It's only having the opposite effect."

"Who's pretending?"

Sebastian grinned. "Why are we kidding each other? We know who did it. The question is, are we going to help each other, or are we going to bring each other down?"

"What do you have in mind?"

"I want in. On the fortunes of the fair Arlene. Why should you be the only one reaping the benefits?"

"What benefits? We're engaged, not married."

"Might be a good time to seal the deal."

"Sure. Perfect time. My aunt's dead, wanna get married?"

"I would phrase it differently, but that's the general idea."

"So this was your plan all along. Blackmail. You come here, threaten to take me down unless I let you in on the play."

"Oh, baby brother, I am so *proud* of you. Calling it a play, like the grifter I taught you to be. You have really outdone yourself with this one. How much is she worth, anyway?"

"I have no idea."

"Well, I do. Seventeen point two million. That is the approximate worth of the estate she came into when Granddaddy died. And with no closer relatives, who should it go to but his favorite grandchild? Who was promoted to that position by the death of her parents in a car accident, and has been living on a fixed income and not much else, until the death of Granddaddy made her the catch she is today."

"How do you know all this?"

"It's my business to know. Don't tell me I know more than you do."

"You act like I engineered this. The girl happens to live next door."

"Yes, in that fancy house. I bet you check it out every time misfortune brings you back here. For years it's no go, and then, jackpot! The lovely Arlene, formerly a cocktail waitress from the Upper West Side, about to lose her apartment because the girl she was living with flunked out of Columbia, is suddenly an heiress, and moves into the country house right next to baby bro. How'm I doing so far?"

"You're cruising for a fat lip."

"See, that's not what I wanted to hear. That's the type of talk makes me think maybe I should be talking directly to Arlene."

"Well, you can try. You think I haven't warned her about my psychotic brother who might drop in?"

"I'm sure you did. But when I start piling on the details she'll take note. Like the last apartment you paid rent on. Oh, wait, there isn't one. Your last fixed address was the apartment of an "actress" who moved back to Minnesota when Daddy found out she was using her allowance to keep a man."

"Is that the best you've got? Arlene will laugh in your face."

"Maybe, maybe not. The way I see it—" Sebastian broke off and his voice became sharp. "What the hell!"

"What?"

"The window's open!"

Cora held her breath, eased the lid of the window seat down.

She could hear the footsteps of the brothers starting for the window seat. She didn't wait for them to get there. She flung open the seat, stood up, and leveled her gun.

FIFTY-ONE

"WHAT THE HELL are you doing?" Alan said. "Put down that gun."

Cora shook her head. "Two young men against one old lady. This evens the odds."

"I don't like having guns pulled on me," Sebastian said quietly. "I get angry."

"Well now, if you boys would sit down over there, I could maintain a distance where I wouldn't have to aim."

"How long have you been in the window seat?" Alan demanded.

"As long as we've been in the room, moron," Sebastian said.

"Everything he said was a pack of lies," Alan said. "Is it my fault if some maniac goes around spewing garbage about me?"

Cora motioned with the gun. The brothers sat down by the sideboard.

Sebastian smiled, picked up the decanter. "Might I interest you in a glass of sherry?"

"Sorry, I don't drink poison."

"That's a shame. Little brother, it would appear we have an intruder in our house. Since Aunt Edith is incapacitated, it's up to us to deal with it. What do you think, should we call the police?"

"Please do," Cora said. "You'll save me a trip to the station. While you're at it, you want to ask your fiancée to come over?"

Alan put up his hand. "Now look, let's not do anything hasty."

"Caution is my middle name. I stopped using it when I was married to Melvin, because Cora Caution Crabtree was just too much alliteration."

Alan looked at her in anger and disgust. "What?"

"Sorry," Cora said. "I know that was a real stretch. I'm just so happy to have my mojo back." She sat down, cradled the revolver in her lap. "So, no one's calling the cops. At least, not yet. No one's waking your aunt, who's had three sleeping pills—see, I could hear everything. What I want to know is which one of you would like to help me catch a killer."

"I would." They said it in unison and glared at each other.

"That's what I like to hear. Cooperative murder suspects. Okay, to start off, I have good news. One of you is innocent. That's not to say one of you is guilty. One of you might be guilty. Then again you might not. But one of you is innocent. Which is so much better than if you were working in collusion. Then you'd be hard to trap." Cora grinned. "Bet you wish you were, now. Anyway, what we need is a brilliant plan. Since we don't have one, we have to improvise. Here's what I propose. The TV cameras are out there, just hoping for a crumb. Let's give 'em one."

"What do you mean?" Sebastian said.

"I'd like you guys to go out there and give TV interviews." Cora looked at her watch. "Perfect time to do it. They'll be able to get you on the eleven o'clock news."

"I don't want to give a TV interview," Alan said.

"Why not?"

"Arlene wouldn't like it."

"Oh, then I guess we'll have to scrap the whole idea,"

Cora said mockingly. "You can tell her you didn't want to do it, but there was this crazy lady with a gun."

"What do you want us to say?" Sebastian asked.

"Give them your theories of the case. That's what they're going to ask you."

"I don't *have* a theory of the case," Alan said.

"That's all right, we'll make 'em up. Let's see. Your theory of the case is your brother did it to get his hands on your aunts' money. He's the older brother, he's the one who would inherit. So your aunts were the intended victims, everyone else was just collateral damage. You're outraged, of course. He's killed one of your aunts, now he's living with the other. It's not safe. He's already admitted to giving her an overdose of sleeping pills. What if he gave her more?"

"Hey, that's right," Alan said.

"Oh, sure, baby brother. Pretend like you're buying it."

"Don't worry, I'm not going to do it."

"What's my theory of the case?" Sebastian said. "Do I think Alan did it?"

"Of course you do. You're convinced of it. That's why you're here. You've been trying to warn people, but they won't listen. That's why you moved into the house. It's the only reason Edith is still alive."

"Oh, sure," Alan said. "And why am I trying to kill my aunts if Sebastian's the one who inherits?"

"You're not. That's just a smoke screen. You're trying to kill Arlene."

"What!?"

"Of course you are. She's an heiress. She just came into a small fortune, plus that big house across the way." Cora explained to Sebastian. "His plan all along was to kill her and get his hands on the money. The other murders were camouflage. So when he kills Arlene no one will think twice."

"Arlene's just my girlfriend. If I killed her, I wouldn't inherit a dime."

"That's right," Sebastian said.

"Yeah, but they're secretly married. I don't know what reason he gave Arlene for keeping it secret, but the real one is so he won't be suspected at the time of the crime. So Arlene's murder will get put down as just another of the *Arsenic and Old Lace* murders. Once that's firmly established the relationship will come out."

"Are you really married?" Sebastian said.

"Hey, this is just her wild theory. Don't tell me you're buying into it."

"Yeah, but I like it. Particularly if you're spreading that outrageous story about me."

"Yeah, but I'm not going to do that."

"Suit yourself," Cora said. "But then your brother's theory will be the only one they've got."

"Are you giving an interview?" Alan said.

Sebastian grinned. "Try and stop me."

"There you are," Cora said. "It's probably better if you both do it, but suit yourselves."

The brothers looked at each other.

Sebastian smirked.

Alan's face purpled. "This is outrageous!"

Cora shrugged. "Yes, it is. Once you start killing people it's never nice. So. You know your lines. Get out there and give 'em hell."

"Now?" Alan said.

"No time like the present. And consider this. If you advance your theory first, Sebastian's will look like retaliation. On the other hand, if he goes first…"

Alan scowled. "What are *you* going to say?"

"Me?" Cora said. "I'm not going to say anything."

"They're going to ask you questions."

"No, they're not."

"Why not?"

Cora smiled. "Because I was never here," she said, and hopped out the window.

FIFTY-TWO

CORA CHECKED HER WATCH. It was ten minutes to ten. She leaned against the condiments counter, sipped her latte, made room for a woman adding cream and sugar. Cushman's Bake Shop was crowded that time of morning. There was a line for coffee and muffins.

Barney Nathan pushed his way through the door, spotted Cora, came over. "All right, what's so important?"

"Keep your voice down, Barney. We don't want to cause a scene."

"Well, why'd you want to meet me here?"

"You look tense, Barney. Have a latte."

"Cora."

"I know it's caffeine, but it's comfort food."

"Please. I have patients waiting."

"They'll wait. They're patient. That's where the name comes from."

"Why'd you want to meet here?"

"Because people are creatures of habit."

"Huh?"

"Sorry, I don't mean to be flip. I'm just so happy I got my groove back."

"What are you talking about?"

"How was dinner?"

Barney made a face.

"That bad, huh? You take your wife?"

"It was a formal dinner. Charity event. I was the speaker. Been scheduled for months."

"So you did. How did that go?"

"It was excruciating. She was polite. Frosty, reserved, and polite. I couldn't look at her. The speech was a disaster. I couldn't focus, kept losing my train of thought."

"Welcome to the Monkey House."

"Huh?"

"It's a Kurt Vonnegut short story. It seemed appropriate somehow."

"I've really gotta get back."

"Not just yet. I need you, Barney."

"Why?"

"As a buffer."

Becky Baldwin came in, got in line. She looked around, spotted Cora. Her eyes widened. She strode up to her. "All right, what the hell do you think you're doing?" she demanded.

Cora took a step back, managed to maneuver Barney in between her and Becky. "Hi, Becky. What's up?"

"Don't hi Becky me. Why don't you answer your phone?"

"Oh, were you trying to get me?"

"You know damn well I was trying to get you. What's the big idea?"

Cora glanced around the coffee shop. Everyone was looking at them. "Why don't we take this outside?"

Without waiting for an answer, Cora pushed by Becky and went out the front door.

Becky came out and confronted her in the street.

"Don't you want to get a coffee, Becky? It'll perk you right up."

"Damn it, Cora, this isn't funny. My client's very upset."

"Oh, really? *He* gave an interview and *he's* upset? He's a big boy. He can make his own decisions."

"He says you pulled a gun."

"In the interview?"

"Don't be dumb."

Barney Nathan came out the door, saw the two women arguing in the street. He hesitated, not knowing what to do.

"Hold on, Barney," Cora said. "I'll be right there." She turned back to Becky Baldwin. "What's wrong with what your client said?"

"It's not what he said, it's what his brother said about him."

"Sebastian? He's not your client, is he?"

"Of course not."

"Then I don't see how you can be upset about what I told him."

"Don't play dumb with me. Alan told me the whole thing. You concocted the whole scheme. He accuses his brother of trying to poison his aunts, and Sebastian accuses Alan of trying to poison Arlene."

"What's wrong with that?"

"Arlene is furious."

"That's understandable. No one likes to be poisoned."

"No one's poisoning her. It's a total fabrication. Something you made up out of whole cloth. And he's feeding it to the media. What are you trying to do, break his engagement?"

"Of course not. Alan's much too young for me. You, on the other hand, are just the right age."

Becky's eyes blazed. "*I'm* not breaking up his marriage. *You're* breaking up his marriage."

Becky had raised her voice. A woman coming out of Cushman's Bake Shop turned her head to look, then quickly averted her eyes.

Cora suppressed a smile. "Come on, Becky. If your client's got a nutso girlfriend it's hardly anybody's fault."

"It is if you keep pissing her off until she makes her boyfriend fire me."

"That's not going to happen."

"How do you know?"

"Clearly Arlene doesn't want publicity. Firing you would just make more. Plus she'd lose her leverage on keeping him in line."

"You miss the point. Alan's got no money. She does. Her money's paying me."

"Then I certainly hope no one's trying to kill her. It would be a shame to get killed and wind up paying for it."

"The whole idea they're secretly married is a lot of hooey."

"I'm sorry to hear it."

"Really?"

"If they were married, their money'd be community property. You could get your retainer out of him."

"I already have a retainer. I've been retained to do a job. You're making that job incredibly difficult."

"You're retained to defend Alan Guilford from a murder rap. What's so hard about that?"

"You keep throwing monkey wrenches into the works. Getting him to accuse his brother. Getting his brother to accuse him. You're stirring up a hornet's nest and creating a bunch of bad publicity, which is just exactly what Alan doesn't want."

"Wow. Monkey wrenches and hornet's nests. I must really have you flustered."

"Oh!" Becky Baldwin stomped her foot in frustration just as two women came out of Cushman's Bake Shop.

Cora turned her back on Becky. "See, Barney, I told you I'd need help."

"Huh?"

"Walk me to my car."

"Why?"

"It's okay, Barney," Cora said. She smiled. "Someday you'll understand."

FIFTY-THREE

"I HEAR BECKY bawled you out in front of half the town."

"Where'd you hear that?"

"My wife told me. But everyone seems to know."

"Just what does everyone seem to know?"

Harper looked embarrassed. "Understand, this is not coming from me. This is just what I heard."

"Yes?"

"It was over Barney Nathan."

"Really?" Cora said. "Well, that's a fine state of affairs. Here I am, minding my own business, having a cup of coffee. A woman yells at me, which is something over which I have no control, and the next thing you know everyone is spreading malicious gossip."

"Believe me, I'm not spreading anything."

"Then how'd you hear it?"

"I told you. My wife told me. I haven't told anyone."

"You told me."

Harper opened his mouth, closed it again.

"What's new with the case?" Cora said.

"Aside from the nephews hurling outrageous accusations at each other on TV? A lot of negatives. The husband and wife of the philandering couple who got killed have ironclad alibis. At the time they were seen by dozens of coworkers, couldn't possibly have done it."

"They were a long shot anyway."

"Nephew Sebastian is another story. He's an unscrupulous conman, and he's pretty good at it, because his rap sheet is rather short. You just know there's more to it than that. The guy's got four convictions spread out over twenty years; those weren't just the isolated instances when he decided to go bad."

"That's a rather uncharitable assessment of the gentleman's character."

"Indeed. Anyway, I'd be willing to peg him for this crime, if he didn't happen to be in Seattle when the killings started."

"Are you sure?"

"Relatively sure. I can't find anyone who can verify his presence, but there's some pretty strong circumstantial evidence. Someone flew from Seattle to Bradley on the day in question using a ticket purchased in the name of Sebastian Guilford. With airport security these days, it's difficult to fly with someone else's ID."

"It can be done."

"Granted. There's also the e-mail."

"What e-mail?"

"The one from the police, telling him his aunt was killed. The one we didn't send."

"Who did?"

"I don't know, but I know where it was sent from."

"Where's that?"

"The Bakerhaven Public Library."

"How'd you figure that out?"

"I had a computer nerd check out every public computer in town."

"Really?"

"No, but that's what I'm saying I did, so I don't get the boys in Seattle in trouble."

"The Seattle police broke into Sebastian's apartment and looked at his computer?"

"See, that's *exactly* what I don't want people thinking. Luckily the computer nerd story is holding up."

"There really was an e-mail?"

"Yeah, there was. Doesn't mean he got it. Doesn't prove who sent it. Frankly, I'd like to drag him down to the library, see if anyone recalls him hangin' around."

"You think he sent it himself?"

"Well, if he needed an excuse to be here. Or needed to prove he was there."

"Can't they tell if an e-mail's been opened?"

"Sure. All that proves is someone checked his e-mail. It couldn't be that hard to arrange. Speaking of arranging things, how'd you get the two brothers to accuse each other?"

"What makes you think that was me?"

"Are you kidding me? The Alan's-trying-to-kill-Arlene theory is straight out of your playbook. And Sebastian didn't have it before."

"You don't think much of that theory?"

"What, Alan's trying to kill Arlene so he kills five other people? You think maybe he's practicing up for when he actually is married to her? And no, I cannot find any record of a marriage between Alan Guilford and Arlene Winnington."

"Too bad. It's a nice theory."

"Not that I'm washing him out as a suspect. He was the last person to see Charlotte alive."

"A statement he volunteered."

"Yes. Which he immediately tried to bolster by making up a story even *he* doubted. Charlotte asked him how he liked his pancakes, only he didn't have pancakes, he had scrambled eggs and toast. Instead of bolstering his story, it casts doubt on it."

"That's the thing. It's such a stupid lie, it almost has to be true."

"Too bad we can't ask Charlotte."

"Yeah." Cora shrugged. "That's the problem with murder victims. They're dead."

FIFTY-FOUR

"HI, BECKY. GLAD you're here. I need a favor."

Becky Baldwin looked up from her desk, blinked. "You want me to do *you* a favor?"

"Quick study. I always liked that about you. Call your client, get him in here. Him and his girlfriend. Get 'em both."

"And just why should I do that?"

"It's a favor. I'll owe you one."

"You don't think you owe me one already?"

"Why?"

"For making trouble for my client. For making trouble for me."

Cora waved it away. "You think I did that deliberately? I'd never interfere with your relationship with your client. Hell, I sent him to you in the first place. I got Chief Harper to scare him into hiring you. Come on, kid. We may have our differences, but we're all in this together."

"And just why do I want my client to come in here?"

"Because I asked you to."

"No. What reason do I give *him*?"

"Oh. You want to fill him in on the case."

"What do I want to tell him about the case?"

"That's up to you."

"Cora."

"You just heard from me. I'm calling a meeting tonight at the Guilford house to discuss the crime. I want everyone there."

"What if they won't go?"

"Then my accusation will go uncontested. They can deny it, but not before it's made the front page of the morning paper and the eleven o'clock news lead."

"You're going to make an accusation?"

"I certainly hope so."

"You're not sure?"

"Well, I don't know who to accuse."

"What?"

"Don't tell 'em that part, will you?"

"What are you doing, running a bluff? Telling everyone you know who did it, and waiting to see who tries to kill you."

"Hey, that's a much better plan than mine. Except for the trying-to-kill-me bit. I hate it when that happens."

FIFTY-FIVE

CORA HOPPED IN her car, sped out to the Guilford house. A car passed her going the other way with two people in it who looked like Alan and Arlene. She hoped it was.

Cora drove by the Guilford house around the block, parked in front of Arlene's. There was no car in the drive, a good sign. Cora got out, went up the walk, banged on the front door. There was no answer.

Cora came down off the porch, went around the house to the back door. It was locked. So was the kitchen window. A window farther down might have been open, but the ground fell away there and Cora couldn't reach it. She looked around for something to climb on. The picnic bench looked promising, except it was long and clumsy. It was better than nothing. Cora lugged it over, placed it under the window. Due to the length of the bench and the slope of the land, it was on a slant. Cora climbed up. It was like standing on a slide. She caught her balance, reached up, and grabbed the windowsill. She pulled up with one hand, wedged her other hand under the window, and jiggled. It moved. Unfortunately, that was as far as she could push it.

Cora hopped down, looked around for something else. There was nothing higher except for the picnic table itself, and she wasn't up to moving it without help. She took the other bench, lugged it over, placed it on top of the first one. She stepped back and surveyed her work.

She had created a leaning tower of benches. The sort of thing one might climb on if it were the only way to escape a raging fire.

Cora put her foot on the bottom bench, tried to pull herself up to the second. Of course the bench itself was in the way. If she kept her foot on the bottom bench, she'd fall backward before she could reach the second. And if she tried to reach the second, her foot would slide off the first.

Cora took the top bench down, moved the bottom bench about six inches out from the wall. She lifted the other bench on top, pushed it up against the wall. This created a more precarious slide than the one she'd been attempting to scale. She put her foot on the bottom bench, pushed up, swung her knee over the second. The top bench lurched away from the wall, teetered for a moment on two legs. Cora flung her arm out, groped for the sill. She caught it with her fingertips, clawed her fingernails into the wood, and pulled. The bench shuddered, nearly collapsed in on itself, then swung back against the wall. Cora pulled herself onto the bench and stood up. She took hold of the window and pushed.

If the window had been locked, Cora would have broken the glass, but it slid up easily. She exhaled the breath she'd been holding, reached in, got a grip. With a little hop off the top bench, Cora heaved herself over the sill.

Cora was prepared to roll over onto the floor, but she never reached it. Instead she flopped unceremoniously into what proved to be a laundry sink. She climbed out, looked around.

She was in what must have been a maid's room. It had a single bed, an end table, and a black-and-white TV.

The door was closed. It had a keyhole. If it was locked, Cora was going to flip out. It wasn't. It led to the back hallway. Cora went out, set off in the direction she assumed the kitchen would be. She found herself in a dining room with glass breakfronts full of china, and an oak table that could have seated twelve, though there were only eight chairs around it now.

At one end of the dining room was a swinging door. Cora pushed her way into what proved to be the pantry. A door off the pantry led to the cellar, just like in the Guilford house. Only this cellar had a light switch right inside the door. Cora snapped on the lights, hurried down the stairs.

There were no graves in Arlene's basement; it had a cement floor. There was a lot of junk, none of it likely to be hers: trunks; suitcases; an old bicycle; an air conditioner; a battered dresser, complete with a broken mirror.

In one corner were stacks of newspapers, mostly the *Bakerhaven Gazette,* but some from out of town. Cora checked the dates. None were more recent than last year.

One pile appeared to have been pawed through.

Cora looked at her watch. She was taking too long. She had to get out. She hurried up the stairs, went into the kitchen.

It was a large country kitchen with an eight-burner stove, a wall of refrigeration units, a butcher block table, and a whole wall of cupboards and cabinets. Cora wasn't quite sure of the distinction between a cabinet and a cupboard, but there were a lot of places to look. She began opening doors.

Only one refrigerator had anything in it. Milk, eggs, mayonnaise, cold cuts. It didn't look like Arlene did much cooking.

The cabinets were as bare as the refrigerator. A few cookies, some crackers, some cans of soup.

There was no pancake mix. Cora hadn't expected there would be.

In the next cupboard, Cora found what she was looking for.

A bottle of maple syrup.

FIFTY-SIX

"Hi, Chief. Got a minute?"

"Why? What's up?"

Cora reached in her purse, took out the bottle of maple syrup. "Can I get this tested for fingerprints?"

"Where did you get that?"

"That's not important. Unless the fingerprints are. In which case, I won't mind saying."

"All right. Whose fingerprints are on it?"

"I really can't say."

"Cora."

"Because I don't know. I can tell you whose fingerprints I'd *like* to be on it."

"Yeah? Who's that?"

"Charlotte Guilford."

"You're hoping to find the fingerprints of the victim?"

"Yeah."

"Why?"

"So I'll have something to talk about tonight."

"What's happening tonight?"

"I'm assembling the suspects at the Guilford house. You should probably be there."

"Why are you assembling the suspects at the Guilford house?"

"To tell 'em who the killer is."

"Who's the killer?"

"I have no idea."

"Cora."

"But I'll know more after you trace these prints."

"But only if they're Charlotte Guilford's."

"No, I'll know more no matter whose they are. It would be *nice* if they were Charlotte Guilford's. But I'll take anything I can get. Just trace any fingerprints you find."

"What if there aren't any?"

"Then I'm going to look mighty foolish. I may even have to resort to Becky's idea."

"What's Becky's idea?"

"See who tries to kill me."

FIFTY-SEVEN

SHERRY WAS FEEDING Jennifer in a highchair. Or rather Jennifer was feeding Jennifer in a highchair. Jennifer had taken control of the spoon lately, and the resultant chaos was dramatic. Every now and then some food actually got in her mouth.

"You should issue people raincoats to watch her eat," Cora said.

"That would take some of the fun out of it," Sherry said.

"You find this fun?"

"Buddy does. He's getting half her dinner."

"Mostly in his fur. I think she's aiming for him. If so, she's pretty good."

"So what's up tonight? Aaron called, said he wouldn't be home. When I asked him why, he said to ask you."

"I'm throwing a little shindig at the Guilford house. Jennifer's a little young or I'd invite you."

"Aaron said you had something in mind. But he didn't know what it was."

"That's because I don't know, either."

"Are you serious?"

"Only partly. I've got hunches. Not enough to prove anything. Just enough to hang myself."

Jennifer hit Cora in the face with a spoonful of glop.

"Is that egg?" Cora said, wiping off her cheek with a well-stained dish towel. "It would be fitting. That's what I'm going to have tonight. Egg on my face."

"Are you nervous?"

"Why? The worst that can happen is I make a fool of myself, get sued for slander, and someone tries to kill me. I've had worse dates than that."

The phone rang.

"Don't get up," Cora told Sherry. "I've got it."

Cora went in the kitchen, answered the phone. "Hello?"

"Cora. Chief Harper."

"Well?"

"We got it."

"And?"

"It's Charlotte Guilford's fingerprints, all right."

"Jackpot! Anyone else's?"

"Yeah, but it's not what you wanted."

"What do you mean?"

"It's none of your suspects."

"Oh?"

"It's not Edith Guilford. It's not Sebastian Guilford. It's not Alan Guilford. It's not Arlene Winnington."

"You have all their fingerprints?"

"Sure. We printed Edith when we were trying to see who touched the carafe. Alan gave us his prints. Sebastian didn't, but he has a record. Arlene also refused, but she has a record, too."

"Really?"

"Pot bust. Pled no contest, paid a fine. Some public defender trying out his training wheels."

"You really have a cynical side, Chief."

"Well, it would be nice if something in this damn case panned out. This print will probably turn out to be the grocery clerk in the Stop and Shop, who sold Charlotte the bottle of maple syrup."

"You could be right. Anyway, when you show up at the Guilfords' tonight, you might want to bring Henry Firth."

"Why?"

"In case you're wrong."

FIFTY-EIGHT

CORA FELTON, DRESSED in her finest "Miss Marple" out-fit—a white blouse, tweed skirt, and matching jacket—stood in front of the hearth and surveyed the gathering in the Guilfords' spacious living room.

Edith Guilford sat in a straight-back armchair with a shawl around her shoulders, looking like a cross between the family matriarch and a frail old woman the slightest breeze might blow away.

Barney Nathan sat beside her, his medical bag open, ready, willing, and able to administer a sedative should the occasion arise.

Edith's nephew Sebastian sat solicitously by, managing to simultaneously project a warm concern for her and an insolent disdain for everyone else.

Alan Guilford sat on the couch, flanked by Becky and Arlene. Cora figured if he managed to get a word in edgewise, it would be a minor miracle.

Chief Harper sat across the room with Henry Firth, who was obviously extremely unhappy to be there, and looked as if he might bolt at any moment.

Aaron Grant sat in the very back of the room and tried to fade into the woodwork.

Cora walked out and placed a small end table in the center of the room. Heads turned. Conversations stopped. By the time she was finished, everyone in the room was watching her.

Cora surveyed her work, found it to her approval.

Without a word she turned, walked back to the fireplace, and resumed her position.

There was an uneasy silence.

"What's that for?" Sebastian said.

Cora raised one finger. "Ahhh! I was wondering who would be the one to ask me that. It turned out to be you. Interesting." She nodded knowingly. "I need it for my presentation. We'll get to it in a while." She shrugged. "I suppose I could put my purse on it, but when you've got a gun in your purse, you hate to leave it lying around."

Cora smiled at the gathered assembly. "Before we begin, would anyone like a glass of elderberry wine?"

There was a stunned silence. She continued, "Probably not. But it's as good a place to start as any. Someone poisoned the Guilford sisters' wine. A lodger drank it and died. A prowler drank it and died. Two other lodgers also died. And finally Charlotte Guilford. Since then the killings have ceased. Did everyone notice that? Since the murder of Charlotte Guilford there have been no attempts on anyone else's life. The question is, why?

"There is an obvious answer, which we must examine. In a case like this, the most obvious answer is often true. That answer, of course, is that Charlotte Guilford was the intended victim all along. That with her death, the crime is complete.

"Is there anything to support this theory? Well, Charlotte is not a lodger or an intruder, she is an owner of the house. As such, she is important. And with her death the killings apparently stop.

"Is there any reason to doubt that theory? Any contradictory facts? There is nothing readily apparent. And yet, there are tiny seeds of doubt.

"What are they?

"For that, we must go back to the beginning and examine these crimes. First up is the lodger who drinks the wine served at tea and expires on the floor. A perfectly ordinary man, who to all appearances wouldn't harm a fly. Who is he and why was he killed? Amazingly, both questions are equally hard to answer. The man had no identification on him whatsoever. Attempts to trace him have been futile. His fingerprints are not on file, apparently he has never been arrested for a crime. He would appear to be exactly what he seems. An elderly man who just happened to get poisoned.

"Why has he no identification on him? The obvious answer is, the killer took it. Without going into why the killer might do that, not to mention how, the problem is, that answer's just not good enough. He not only has no identification on him, but there is no other way he can be traced. He does not have a car. He appears to have taken a cab from the Danbury bus station, but even that is not certain. It is possible he came to Danbury on a bus from New York, in which case he could have flown into La-Guardia, JFK, or Newark on any airline from any city in the United States. Or abroad, for that matter. Wherever he came from he left no trail, and the name he checked in under is most likely not his own.

"Could a killer arrange all that? Certainly not after the crime. The killer might be able to lift the guy's wallet, but to erase every trace of his life? It could only be done by the man himself.

"So, all evidence to the contrary, this simple, ordinary man is not who he seems.

"Which is too bad. Because a man like that is much more likely to be the killer than the victim."

Cora paused, looked around the room. "Confused? How do you think I felt? I thought I'd lost it. I thought my brain was going soft.

"As if that weren't bad enough, there was a sudoku on the body. Why? What for? What did it mean? Clearly someone was trying to involve me in the crime, but for what reason? I solved the sudoku, but it didn't shed any light on anything. Nor did the crossword puzzle left under the doormat."

Cora smiled, held up one finger in the air. "The next murder did. The murder of Ned Crumley, the town drunk. I hate to speak ill of the dead, but that's how people knew him. The town drunk climbs in the window, drinks poisoned wine, passes out in the window seat, and dies. What the hell is that all about? It's like the first murder, but it's not. There's no attempt to hide the victim's identity, and if there had been it wouldn't have done any good. The drunk is local, he's known. So, is he just a poor man who broke in to steal wine and picked the bottle that killed him? He could be. Except he isn't. And how do we know he isn't? He has a sudoku on him. Just like the first one. Proof positive the two killings are connected.

"But that's not all.

"Alan Guilford is found prowling in the bushes."

Becky and Arlene both jumped up to speak.

Cora waved them down. "Your objection to the word *prowling* is sustained. The point is, he hears noises, sees the lights, comes over to investigate, and Sam Brogan apprehends him.

"Something else happens at that time. Something important. Sam Brogan, making that arrest, finds a newspaper lying in the bushes. A Hartford newspaper from 2005. It is folded open to the crossword puzzle page. Staring up from the paper is my smiling face. It is a Puzzle Lady column, just in case I don't get the hint from the two sudoku puzzles. The paper was left by the killer, and is meant to involve me.

"One interesting thing about the puzzle. It has been solved and then erased. That's unusual, it should mean something. The puzzle, when solved, is made up of Cary Grant movies, the answer in the middle is *Arsenic and Old Lace*.

"This is where the crime goes off the rails. Everyone knows *Arsenic and Old Lace*. Well, except the chief. And the parallels are striking. Two sisters run a boardinghouse, a lodger is poisoned, with elderberry wine, no less. The sisters have a nephew, the nephew is engaged to the girl next door. Not to mention the body in the window seat.

"How is this possible? It can't be, but it is. And just in case there's any question about it, a grave is dug in the cellar.

"What happens next? Two people are strangled in the back of a school bus. Whoa. Time out. Flag on the play. This is not in the script. This is as far from *Arsenic and Old Lace* as you can get.

"Clearly, this is not in the killer's plans. The couple were an annoyance, an intrusion; two characters who wandered in from another movie. They are simply removed from the game.

"Is there any chance that they are the main focus all along, that their murder is what this is all about?

"No, there is not. In that case their killing would be staged to look like the other murders. So as to disguise the motive. That is if they were killed by the betrayed husband and/or wife. But the killer didn't do that. The only attempt to link the crimes is a sudoku. But it seems like an afterthought.

"Now we come to the real crime, the main crime, the central crime. The murder of Charlotte Guilford. The killing is made as much as possible to look like the others.

The body is put in the window seat. A crossword puzzle is found on the body. The crossword puzzle indicates that she was a snoop, that she was killed because she couldn't keep her nose out of the killer's business. This concept is *not* out of the movie. There are no snoops in *Arsenic and Old Lace*. So one wonders why the crossword is there.

"It is obvious the killer is trying to throw us off the trail. To make us think Charlotte Guilford was killed for something she found out. In support of the theory that the murder of Charlotte Guilford is the central murder is the fact that the killer is trying to make it look as if it isn't.

"What happens next is particularly revealing. Sebastian Guilford shows up in town. This is straight out of the movie. The older brother with the criminal past showing up to plague our young hero." Cora gestured to Alan.

"Only he doesn't just show up. He is summoned. He receives a message, presumably from the police, informing him of his aunt's murder and asking him to come. However, the police have no record of any such message.

"Why does this happen? What is the purpose of Sebastian being here?

"Is he the killer?

"Once Sebastian is here—or I should say, once we are *aware* Sebastian is here...yes, yes, your outrage is duly noted, Sebastian—the crimes stop." Cora smiled. "See how you can twist everything around? Once Charlotte is dead, the crimes stop. Once Sebastian is here, the crimes stop. Once I switch to decaf lattes, the crimes stop. While the obvious explanation is often true, things do not necessarily mean what they seem.

"From this point on, theories abound. For some inexplicable reason Sebastian and Alan go on TV and accuse each other of the crimes for the most outlandishly contrived reasons. To inherit his aunts' estate. To get his hands on Arlene's money. Really!

"How do you sort it out? Well, you start looking through the clues, trying to find something that sticks out, something that doesn't dovetail. The odd event. Do we have one in this case?

"Actually, we do.

"Charlotte Guilford asked Alan Guilford how he liked his pancakes. And he did not, in fact, eat pancakes. Why did she do that? Was that merely senility, or something more sinister? It is, in any case, the odd event.

"Or is it?

"Think about it. We have only Alan Guilford's word it ever happened at all."

This time Becky Baldwin beat Arlene to her feet.

Cora put up her hand. "You can object all you want, but that happens to be the case. There is nothing to substantiate Alan Guilford's claim. Nothing to prove that is what Charlotte said when Alan met her that morning. Indeed, there is nothing to prove that Alan ever met Charlotte that morning at all.

"In a case like this, where no such proof exists, what would one necessarily expect to happen? That someone will attempt to manufacture some. To plant some evidence to bolster their story. This is where so many murderers slip up. In gilding the lily. In trying to cover up their crime."

Cora paused, surveyed the room.

"I have found just such a clue."

Cora let that sink in. "The only question is, is it real or is it planted?

"You be the judge."

Cora reached in her drawstring purse. "I will show it to you now."

She pulled out the crossword puzzle. "This is the crossword puzzle found on Charlotte's body." She held it up, paused for a moment. "The clue is not in here."

She reached into her purse again, pulled out the puzzle in the newspaper. "And here is the crossword puzzle with the answer *Arsenic and Old Lace*." She looked around the room. "The clue is not in here, either.

"This is the clue."

Cora pulled out a bottle of maple syrup, set it on the table, walked away.

She turned back, pointed a finger. "Edith Guilford looks positively baffled. So do Alan and Sebastian.

"But Arlene looks like she's seen a ghost. I wonder why. Let's check the fingerprints on the bottle, Chief, and maybe we'll find out."

With a howl of rage, Arlene sprang from her seat, and hurled herself at Cora Felton in a blind fury.

Chief Harper leapt to his feet, but he wasn't close enough to intervene.

Barney Nathan was. The little doctor jumped up, took a flying leap, and tackled Arlene before she could strike his woman down.

FIFTY-NINE

BECKY CAME BACK from the holding cells, joined the party in Chief Harper's office.

"She doesn't want me as her lawyer."

"What a surprise," Cora said.

"She's not talking, either. She's hiring some attorney from New York."

"That's a shame," Henry Firth said.

"You were hoping for a confession?" Cora said.

"Without it we have very little evidence. Aside from your opinion that the woman turned white when confronted with maple syrup. She also found you irritating enough to take a swing at. Under that criteria…" The prosecutor shrugged.

"Thanks a lot," Cora said. "You'll get your evidence. The chief's tracing her fingerprints now. It doesn't matter who she turns out to be, if she isn't Arlene, she's dead meat."

"I still have to present a case to the jury."

"No problem. Now that we know what happened, we'll be able to identify the first victim. After we know who he is, everything else will fall into place."

"How do you know that?"

"Well, I know who he must be. He's either a lawyer or accountant or trustee of Arlene's parents' estate."

"Traveling incognito with no identification?" Henry said sarcastically.

"Exactly."

"You want to tell me how that works?"

"Sure thing. Arlene's parents die and she inherits umpty million dollars. Huge lifestyle change for a girl who's been sharing an apartment with a Columbia student in New York City. It's also a huge lifestyle change for her roommate. Arlene, as a result of her windfall, will be moving out and leaving her with a rent she cannot afford. If Arlene had made provisions for her roommate, things would have been okay. Or, not to be uncharitable, perhaps Arlene *did* make provisions for her roommate, but it wasn't enough. The roommate is insanely jealous of Arlene. The roommate doesn't move out, she murders Arlene and takes her place."

"Oh, come on," Henry Firth said.

"You asked the question. This will all come out when the IDs are made. I'm telling you what I think. Unless you don't want to hear it."

"We want to hear it," Chief Harper said. "You say she took her place as if there was nothing to it. How could she pull it off? Surely Arlene's friends would know the difference."

"Yeah, but she immediately cuts ties. Moves out of New York to a house in Connecticut. As for the rest of it, all it takes is a little old-fashioned forgery. The estate is on the West Coast. Most communication is conducted by e-mail. Anyway, it works. The girl inherits the money, moves to the house in Bakerhaven.

"Initially it's kind of boring, because she's keeping her head down. She watches a lot of TV. Does crossword puzzles. Which she doesn't even have to go out to buy. Arlene's relatives were hoarders. There's a mother lode of old newspapers stored in the basement."

"How do you know that?" Henry Firth said.

"Lucky guess. Anyway, life is pretty boring until she

meets a handsome young man who happens to live right next door. Now things are popping very nicely indeed. All things considered, it couldn't be better.

"Then disaster strikes. A letter or e-mail or phone call arrives. From the attorney, accountant, trustee, or whatever. He's coming east and wants to pay his respects.

"She's trapped. There's no place to hide. The man, whoever he is, will take one look and know she's not Arlene. So she comes up with her plan. She contacts the man, tells him about Alan. Says he's someone she met since her inheritance, and she's afraid he might be after her money. She asks the attorney if he would mind coming incognito, and checking into his aunts' bed-and-breakfast under an assumed name, so he can meet Alan casually without Alan knowing who he is, and get a sense of the young man's intentions."

"He didn't just come incognito. He had no identification. And no rental car."

"She must have talked him out of it somehow. If Alan really is a con man, he'll be suspicious of everyone and might break into the car to look at the name on the rental agreement. Or something equally ridiculous. And the guy doesn't question it because he's having fun playing secret agent.

"So, she ascertains he likes wine, suggests he have some with the aunts—she knows they don't drink it themselves—and see what they say about their nephew. All she has to do is poison the wine bottle and wait for nature to take its course."

Henry Firth was still skeptical. "And what's the whole *Arsenic and Old Lace* bit?"

"That's a smokescreen dreamed up by Arlene—I'm going to call her Arlene, until we know who she turns out to be. She can't just kill the solicitor. Eventually someone will figure out who he is and realize why he was killed. Arlene's just seen *Arsenic and Old Lace* on Turner Classic Movies. At the time it registered with her she'd just done a crossword puzzle with *Arsenic and Old Lace* in the theme. And it occurs to her how many parallels there are between the Guilford sisters and the aunts in the movie. Both have old creaky houses, both have basements and window seats, both take in lodgers. And in both cases the young man of the house is engaged to the girl next door.

"Is that enough to suggest the connection? Not really. The solicitor is killed and no one notices.

"Arlene was prepared for this contingency. With the crossword puzzle that said *Arsenic and Old Lace*. Ideally, she'd have liked to have had it in the solicitor's pocket. But there was no way to swing it. It was hard enough just getting him to carry the sudoku. She probably sent it to him in the mail, told him to carry it in his pocket to test Alan."

"Test Alan?" Henry Firth said. "Oh, come on."

"Hey, I'm making this up in lieu of a confession. Anyway, she finds a way to get him to carry a sudoku. But she needs a crossword puzzle. Remember how we got it? She brought it in the door. Said she found it under the doormat. Well, that works with a computer printout, but a newspaper dated 2005? Besides, she doesn't want to be the one to introduce the concept of *Arsenic and Old Lace*. But to suggest the killer is leaving crossword puzzle clues? That's just great. Because we'll be sure to pay attention to the next one. Particularly when it comes in an old paper. Which, luckily, she didn't throw away. The only problem is it's been solved. You can't give the Puzzle Lady a solved puzzle. She has to erase it. And she needs a delivery system. She gets the town drunk, probably plies him with liquor, and persuades him to break into the Guilford house, hide in the window seat for a while, then come out and do goodness knows what—it doesn't matter, he's never going to do it. She gives him a bottle of wine to keep him happy while he's waiting. The wine is poisoned. Which is perfect. A body in the window seat with a crossword puzzle on him that says *Arsenic and Old Lace.*

"Only two things go wrong. The guy makes so much noise breaking in, he wakes up the sisters and they call the police. If he was still alive when they found him, the jig would have been up. He also drops the newspaper in the bushes, so we found the body but not the clue.

"But all is not lost. When Arlene sends Alan to make sure everything is going smoothly she lucks out. In arresting him in the bushes, Sam Brogan finds the newspaper where the drunk dropped it." Cora frowned. "Actually, I think Sam found the puzzle before he arrested Alan. Which is why we didn't associate the newspaper with him. When solved, it says *Arsenic and Old Lace,* and we're off to the races. I make the connection, want to know if the poison was in elderberry wine. When the poison turns out to be actually three poisons mixed in the same proportions as in the movie, it's clear the killer is copying *Arsenic and Old Lace.* Perfect plan.

"Only the chief clamps the lid on and keeps it out of the media. Bad luck for Arlene. She doesn't know if her plan is working.

"So she has to keep going. She doesn't want to kill anybody else, but she has to copy the movie. So she digs the grave. Which we immediately find. If we hadn't, I'm sure something would have suggested we look there. Perhaps another puzzle clue. We can never have too many of those. Anyway, she digs the grave. And she might have gotten away with it, if not for the maple syrup."

"What's the big deal about the maple syrup?"

"That was the key to the whole thing. Alan Guilford was the last person to see Charlotte alive. He claims he went over there to shave, he ran into her, she asked him about breakfast. Specifically, she asked him how he liked his pancakes. Well, assuming she's not just a dotty old lady, why would she do that? The cellar door's off the pantry, and someone dug a hole in the basement. If Charlotte ran into Alan as he was coming up from the basement after digging the grave, he might say he just popped over to borrow some maple syrup for breakfast. In that case he would have to get a bottle—Charlotte might even hand it to him—and take it with him when he left. Then it would be perfectly natural for her to ask him later how he liked his pancakes. Is there anything wrong with that?"

Henry Firth thought it over. "No, that works."

"No, it doesn't," Cora said. "For one simple reason. Alan brought it up. We wouldn't know Charlotte asked him about pancakes for breakfast if he hadn't mentioned it. And if he'd dug the grave and covered it up by pretending he was borrowing maple syrup, he certainly wouldn't have.

"But if Arlene dug the grave and borrowed the maple syrup, it works just fine. Charlotte could ask Alan about it, he could be baffled, and he could tell us about it, which he did. Which means he's either totally innocent, or the stupidest accomplice in the annals of crime.

"If Alan's the accomplice, Arlene has no problem. She just tells him to go along with the pancake story. Tell Charlotte they were delicious. She will then proceed to forget all about them, and there will be no need to kill her. It's only the idea that Charlotte will be claiming a breakfast that Alan is denying that makes her dangerous."

"What makes her think Charlotte would do that?"

"Alan tells her. He comes back from shaving and says Charlotte's really losing it, she has some crazy idea he had pancakes for breakfast. When Arlene hears that, Charlotte's gotta go. She doesn't want to bump off the old biddy, but by now she's in too deep. She's already bumped off the cheating couple, who saw her do something suspicious—or maybe not—by now Arlene's paranoia must be so high she might just *think* they saw something suspicious. She bangs them over the head, sticks 'em in her car, and drops 'em in the bus in the back of the high school."

"How did she know it was there?" Henry Firth objected.

"A little bird told her," Cora said. "Are you going to say this about everything? The answer is how the hell should I know? I'm giving you the broad brushstrokes of what you are likely to find out once the facts are in. If you prefer to sit back and wait for those facts, suit yourself. Personally, I think I solved the case. But if you don't wanna buy it, feel free.

"The point is she drops 'em on the bus. I don't know if she started digging graves in the cellar for them and then got interrupted, or whether the one thing has nothing to do with the other. But it's a good bet she didn't put 'em in the window seat because two bodies wouldn't fit.

"Anyway, she sticks 'em on the bus, adorns 'em with a sudoku to tie 'em to the other crimes, because she's still trying to sell that idea, and heaves a big sigh of relief. And the next thing she knows, Charlotte Guilford is making a big fuss about the stupid bottle of maple syrup."

"Granted, this is conjecture," Henry Firth said, "but that's all it is. You can't prove any of it."

"No, but *you* can, now that I've given you a hint. A lot of things point to it. Arlene claims she couldn't do crossword puzzles. Remember that, Chief? You were there. So was Becky Baldwin and a lot of other witnesses. It was when she brought us the crossword puzzle she said she found under the doormat. Why did she claim she couldn't do puzzles? To distance herself from the puzzle. In point of fact she copied it from one of mine she'd found in an old newspaper. She'd printed it out in the library, most likely on the same computer she sent the e-mail to Sebastian that brought him here.

"That's another thing, Chief. You recall Arlene scoffing at the idea this was like the movie, saying if it was, Alan would have a criminal brother who looks like Boris Karloff. That's because she knew Sebastian was coming and she wanted to make sure we made the connection."

"That's right," Harper said.

"You're buying into this?" Henry Firth demanded.

Chief Harper looked at him. With his face scrunched up, the prosecutor looked more like a rat than ever. The chief had a narrow escape from a giggle.

"Why don't we wait for the ID?"

SIXTY

JENNIFER TOOK TWO steps and plunked down on her bottom. She looked around startled, then giggled.

Sherry, Aaron, and Cora applauded.

"That's a small step for a baby, a giant leap for great-aunthood," Cora said.

Buddy came trotting up to see what was going on.

Jennifer squealed in delight, and started crawling off after the dog.

"Smart kid," Cora said. "Walkin's for show, but crawlin's for dough."

"I thought you were keeping her away from the dog," Aaron said.

"They made friends," Sherry said.

Buddy turned around, waited for the baby to catch up.

Jennifer sat up, reached for the dog. He scooted away again. Jennifer squealed in glee, set off after him.

"There you are," Cora said. "A built-in babysitter."

The phone rang. Cora reluctantly got up, went in the kitchen to answer.

It was Chief Harper.

"You win all the way around."

"Oh?"

"The man is Michael Bennett of the law firm of Crowl, Crawford, and Bennett, solicitors for the late Fredrick and Ethel Winnington. He was never reported missing because he left on vacation and told the firm he'd be unreachable."

"And the girl?"

"She hasn't cracked yet, but it doesn't matter. She's been positively ID'd as Rachel Simpson, ex-roommate of Arlene Winnington. As a result Arlene's assets have been frozen, and Rachel's high-priced attorneys are going to discover they aren't getting paid. So maybe Becky Baldwin will get the case after all. Small consolation after her debacle with the doc."

"What?"

"Here I am, talking out of school again. But for your information, it's all over town. Barney's estranged from his wife all right, but it would appear Becky Baldwin has been beaten out by another woman." Harper's tone was teasing. "Of course you wouldn't know anything about that."

"Good thing you don't like to gossip, Chief. My reputation wouldn't be worth a plugged nickel."

Cora got off the phone and called Barney Nathan.

"I thought you weren't going to call me in the office," Barney said.

"Sorry, Barney, but we wrapped up the case and I'd like to celebrate. How'd you like to go out to dinner?"

"I thought you didn't want to be seen with me in public."

"That was then, this is now. I'm not a home-wrecker anymore. Just ask anyone in town."

"What are you talking about?"

"I didn't break up your marriage." Cora smiled happily at the thought. "I stole you away from Becky Baldwin."

* * * * *